"Listen well, Merlin,

for the evil approaches and you must be armed against it.

"Two duties have you—one to bring the full power back into the Great Beacon . . .

"Your second order is to provide such a leader for this land as to bring all its present quarrels to naught, and establish a time of peace in which we can come again, meeting with man and working together.

"These are what you must do, and Nimue will prevent you if she can. Be warned, Merlin, for you are our hope and the time grows short wherein this may be accomplished. Fail and the Dark shall encompass utterly your world and man shall be left to brutish life without the sun of knowledge!"

D1570921

Andre
Norton

MERLIN'S MIRROR

DAW Books, Inc.
Donald A. Wollheim, Publisher
1633 Broadway, New York, N.Y. 10019

FIRST PRINTING, JUNE 1975

9 10 11 12 13 14

PRINTED IN THE U.S.A.

1.

The beacon still called from deep within the rough-walled fastness of the cave. Its message was fainter now. Each planet year had put more strain upon this mechanism, though its creators had attempted to make it everlasting. They believed they had foreseen every eventuality. They had—except the weakness within their own rule and the nature of the world from which the beacon called. Time had been swallowed, was gone, and still the beacon kept to its task, while outside the cave nations had risen and decayed, men themselves had changed and changed again. Everything the makers of the beacon had known was erased during those years, destroyed by the very action of nature. Seas swept in upon the land, then retired, the force of their waves taking whole cities and countries. Mountains reared up, so that the shattered remains of once-proud ports were lifted into the thin air of great heights. Deserts crept in over green fields. A moon fell from the sky and another took its place.

Still the beacon called and called, summoning those who had vanished and left behind only legends, strange, time-distorted tales. And now there was another period of chaotic darkness in the affairs of men. An empire had crashed under its own unwieldy weight and the strain of years. Barbarians ravaged, picking its carcass like vultures. Fire and sword, death and the living death of slavery marched across the land. And yet the beacon called.

Its heart-fires were dim now. From time to time the call faltered, as a man in mortal danger might gasp for breath between shouts for aid.

Then that call, so faint now, was finally heard far out in space. A strange arrow of metal caught the impulse, and deep in this ship's heart installations which had been silent and unresponding for centuries were activated. The arrow

5

altered course, using the beam of the call as a line to draw itself down.

There was no living thing aboard that ship. It had been devised with desperate hope by entities close to the extinction of all they held important, more important than their own lives. They had sent six such arrows of life into the void, their only desire being that at least one of the searchers might find a goal their records said existed. Then they were overrun by their enemies.

Relay after relay clicked into life without a quiver of fault as the arrow sped toward earth. It represented the fruits of a thousand years of experimentation, the highest triumph of a race which had once traveled the starlanes with the ease of men walking familiar paths on brown earth. Made for one duty alone, it was now about to go into the action for which it was programmed.

It smoothly shifted into orbit about the planet and prepared to descend in answer to the beacon call. As it flashed across the sky men below watched its passage with primitive awe. The knowledge which had once been theirs was long since buried in myth.

Some cringed in skin tents as their shamans beat drums and howled strange guttural chants. Others stared wide-eyed and spoke of shooting stars which could be omens of good or evil. It neared the mountain where the cave of the beacon was hidden, then it broke apart.

The husk which had carried the so-precious cargo through space opened and from it issued other objects. They did not plunge instantly into the sea which was now fast coming under the arrow; they spun away rather, as if with volition of their own, winging for a mountainside.

They hovered for an instant or two in the air before drifting easily to the ground. And if anyone in those heights witnessed this, he did not speak of it again. These particles were protected by a distortion of the fields of visibility. The makers had taken all precautions they could foresee to protect their project.

Once on earth the jumble of objects produced appendages of their own and crawled steadily, with a mindless need to unite with the failing power of the beacon. They made their way into the cave.

In some places it was necessary to enlarge the passageway and that, too, had been foreplanned. But at length they were all sheltered in the depths about the beacon, where they proceeded to go to work. Some of them cut bases in the rock, settling themselves in with cable roots from which they could never be torn. Others rose from the surface of the cave, hovering back and forth like great mindless insects, except that they trailed coils of communicating wire from one based installation to the next.

Within a space of time which they had no reason to measure the net was complete; they were ready to begin the work for which they had been programmed. If this world had not been receptive there would have been no beacon. Therefore, in the memory banks of the largest of the based machines lay information that a systematic sampling would bring into use.

One of the hovering fliers swung to the entrance of the cave, sped outside. There was no moon that night; clouds hung heavy in the sky. The flying thing was not much larger than an eagle, and its distort had gone into action when it had emerged in the open. Now it began to scout in ever-widening circles, the photoeye it carried sending a stream of reports back to the cave.

There was a dusting of snow on the heights and the winds were sharp and cold, though the flying thing noted temperature only as another fact to be transmitted.

The fire in the center of the clan house was high. From the balcony which circled the sleeping family rooms, Brigitta could look down at the men gathered below on benches. The mingled smell of stable, cow byre, woodsmoke, food and drink was as thick as the smoke. Yet there was a solid, secure feeling when the clan house was closed at night against the outer dark, when the hum of voices flowed from chamber to chamber on the upper floor.

Brigitta shivered and drew her cloak closer about her shoulders. This was Samain, the time between one year and the next. Now the doors between this world and the Dark could open, and demons could caper through or crawl malevolently to attack man. There was safety here by the cheer of fire, in the voices she could hear, the snort of one of the horses stabled in the outermost circle of stalls below. She picked up the tankard she had set on the bench beside her and sipped at the barley ale it contained, making a little face at its bitter taste but relishing the warmth within her when she swallowed.

There were other women on the balcony benches, but

none shared hers. Brigitta was the chief's daughter and so took honor here. When the flames flickered they caught the gold bracelet on her arm, the wide plaque necklace of amber and bronze lying on her breast. Her red-brown hair flowed free, nearly touching the floor behind her as she sat, its color contrasting pleasantly with the strong blue of her cloak, the embroidered length of the saffron yellow robe beneath.

She was arrayed for a feast, yet this was no true feast. She bitterly resented the news which had drawn the men to council and left the women to watch and yawn, gossip a little. It was even stale gossip, for they had been together for so long now that there was nothing new to say about each other or events.

Brigitta moved restlessly. War—war with the Winged Hats—that was all a man could think about. There was little betrothing or marrying nowadays. And she was growing older with every moon. Yet her father had not singled out any lord for her. There was gossip behind hands about that also, as well she knew. If they had not already, in time they would give her some flaw of tongue or mind which would turn possible suitors from the door.

War. Brigitta gritted her teeth and the look with which she regarded the company below had little kindness in it. Man thought of fighting first and always. What did it matter if the invaders crept along valleys miles away? What difference should it make to the people of Nyren, safe in their upland fortress? And now this babbling about the evils wrought by the High King. She drank again.

So he had put aside his wife to wed the daughter of the Saxon overlord. . . . Brigitta wondered what the new queen looked like. Vortigen was old; he had grown sons who would be quick to raise sword for their shamed mother. A messenger had brought the news that they were summoning near and far kin to that very effort now. But the Saxons would form a shield wall for the new queen, too. It was all war! She could not remember back to a time when there was not the clang of weapons about the clan house. She need only raise her head a little to see the line of weather-cleaned skulls set along the roof eaves above, the spoils of wars and past raids.

She did not think that Nyren would have much sympathy for the High King. Ten days ago another messenger had ridden in to be received with a far warmer welcome: a lean, dark man with cleanly shaved face, wearing the breastplate and helmet of the Emperor's men. The Emperor was long gone, though it was said that emperors still ruled overseas. But the Imperial Eagles had been lost from this land since her father was young.

It seemed that at least one leader still believed in the Emperor. The dark man had come from him to ask Nyren's men for his war banner, just as the messenger who had spoiled the feast tonight. That one had had a strange, tongue-twisting name, after the style of the Romans. Brigitta said it aloud now, proud that she knew enough of the old speech to say it properly.

"Ambrosius Aurelianus." She added the equally strange title he held, for he did not claim any kingdom, *Dux Britanniae*. Lugaid had said it meant Leader of Britain in the other tongue. It was a lot for a man to claim when half the land was filled with Vortigen's new kin, the Winged Hats from overseas.

Her father had been schooled at Aquae Sulis in the old days when the Emperor Maximus had ruled not only Britain, but half the lands overseas. He remembered how it was when there was peace and one only had to fear the Scotti raids or trouble along the border. So he was one who had inclined to the Roman, one of those Vortigen had hunted out of the cities because the High King feared their influence.

Thus Nyren had returned to the clanship of his fathers, had drawn around him those of kin blood. Perhaps he had only been waiting ... Brigitta sipped her ale again. Her father was one who kept his own counsel, even among the kin.

She studied him now where he sat in the high seat of the clan house. Though he wore the dress of the hills it was in more somber colors than that of the men around him. His tunic of fine linen had been worked by her own hands with a pattern copied from an old vase, a wreathing of leaves in threads of gilt and green. His trousers were of dark red, his cloak of the same shade. Only the wide torque of gold about his throat, the two brand-bracelets on his wrists and the seal ring on his forefinger, equaled in splendor the ornaments of his fellows.

Yet he held authority among them, and no man entering the clan house and setting eyes on Nyren need ask who was chief in this place. Brigitta felt the swell of pride as she watched him now, displaying not a flicker of emotion as he listened with surface courtesy to the words of the High King's messenger, who was leaning forward, plainly ill at ease as he tried to impress this small chief, as the High King might rate Nyren.

But the influence of the lord of this clan reached beyond the walls of his kin house and many among the hills listened closely to any words of his. For his wisdom was great and he was a wily and successful raider and war leader. He might have called himself king, after the fashion of others hereabouts, but he did not choose to do so.

Brigitta stirred again impatiently. She wished that her father might speedily send the High King's man about his business, that they might feast at their ease with no troubling from the world outside on this night.

She could catch the roar of the wind above the sounds of the court hall below. There was a storm, and a storm on this night was unlucky. It might well carry the hosts of the Dark to wreak their evil will on men.

Now she looked for Lugaid where he sat near her father. He had the old knowledge and he had set up the spirit protections about them this night. Though his unshaved beard was white, his lean body was not stooped, nor did he have the signs of age about him. His white robe was bright in the firelight and one thin hand stroked his beard absentmindedly as he, too, listened to Vortigen's man.

The Romans had striven to stamp out the old knowledge and while they were in power men such as Lugaid had moved secretly, keeping to their own silences. Now they were honored once more among the kin and their words were listened to. Brigitta doubted that Lugaid would favor the High King, for he and his kind held the ancient mysteries of this land and they liked the Winged Hats no better than they had the Romans.

The ale was strong and made her a little dizzy. She shoved the tankard aside, her eyes now drowsily watching the play of the flames on the great hearth below. In and out they danced, swifter, more gracefully, wilder than any maid could weave her way across the grass on Beltaine Eve. In and out. . . . Now the wind was roaring so loud she could hardly catch more than an echo of the murmur from below.

It was dull anyway. This feast which had promised so much in the way of excitement had been spoiled by the stupid affairs of war. Brigitta yawned widely. She was both bored and disappointed. Distant kin had come riding in yesterday, and she had had a wan hope that among them her father would find a suitor he approved.

She tried now to search out those strangers below, find one face which was to her own liking. But they were only a blur of flesh, reddened by the flame play; the gaudy colors of their plaid and checkered clothing bewildered her. Though there were both young men and seasoned warriors, none had caught her attention when they arrived. Of course she would have gone dutifully to the one her father named.

That he did not name any was her present grievance. They would march to war, all those possible suitors, and many would die, so there would be far fewer to choose among. It was a sad waste. She shook her head, muddled by the ale she had drunk, the half-hypnotizing play of the flames. Suddenly she could stand it no longer.

She rose from her bench and went back into her chamber. The opposite door of her room opened out on the parapet of the wall, their outer defense. It was tightly closed, yet through it the whistle of the wind came even closer. A lamp burned very dimly in the far corner. She shrugged out of her robe and, in her chemise, her cloak still about her, she burrowed into the covers of the bed against the wall. She shivered, not so much from the chill of the stone against which that bed was set as from the menace of the wind and the tales she had heard of what might ride its gusts this night of all nights. But she was also sleepy and her eyes soon closed as the lamp sputtered out.

Below, in the warmth of the fire, Lugaid's hand was suddenly stilled. His head turned so that he no longer regarded Nyren or the man so eloquent in his plea for the support of the hill chief and his people. It was as if the priest of the Old Ones were listening to something else.

His eyes were wide, startled. Yet there was no sentry horn sounding, or if there was, only his ears caught it. His hand moved from his beard to the emblem embroidered on the breast of his robe, the spiral of gold, as if he hardly knew what he did or why his fingers traced the lines of that spiral from outer edge to inner heart. He might have been half-consciously seeking some answer of vast importance.

Now his eyes lifted to the balcony on which the women sat, and he deliberately looked from face to half-seen face until he came to a gap in their number. Sighting that, he gave a small gasp. Then he glanced hastily right and left. He might have feared that his involuntary sound had betrayed him in some manner, but the rest of the company was intent on Nyren and the uninvited guest. Lugaid drew back a little, his eyes closed, a look of deep concentration on his bearded face.

Planet time meant nothing to the installations. The flying things reported, memory banks sorted, classified, worked to feed information to the more sophisticated final judge of the project. A decision was made, twice tested. Then the most delicate and complicated portion of the space-carried equipment was prepared.

Once more one of the fliers spiraled out. It made a wider swing, its distort on full. The farthest reach of that swing carried it across another spur of rock reaching skyward. The beacon which had summoned the installation out of space and time had died. Only now, deep within other rocks beneath, another signal woke to life. Undetected by the flier, it began to pulsate, its wavelength sweeping higher and higher as its energy built and roared to full power.

Outward into the high heavens sped a new beam, climbing starward. It would take a long time, perhaps years for that warning to be caught by those who patrolled there. But it could not be quenched. Ancient battles might begin, lesser in force now than of old, because both adversaries were depleted to a thousandth, a millionth of the power they once possessed. Time and exhaustion had not, however, wearied their resolve. They were as implacable as ever. Though now they must face each other with new and lesser strength, yet they would do it.

The flier wheeled, coasted through a fierce wind, fluttered along within its grasp as a leaf might. Yet it was not powerless; it had a task it must do and nothing man or nature could devise in this time could prevent it from accomplishing that act.

Brigitta slept heavily, yet it seemed to her that in truth she waked. The wooden wall of the kin house was no longer about her. She stood instead on a path she knew well, the one which led to the spring of prophecy where the goddess might bless with eternal good fortune someone who flung an offering. Nor was this the dread night of Samain with its dark, veiled hunters waiting to ensnare mankind. About her now was the green freshness of first spring, of Beltaine when the fires would burn high and maids and men would leap over their flames hand and hand, united in worship of those forces which increased rather than diminished the tribes.

There was a golden light about her that did not come from the sun overhead. It made a spear point which reached to her sandaled feet, though the source remained hidden by bushes just leafing with the spring. The glow leaped up from that triangle of light into her heart, so she laughed joyfully and began to run through the brilliance, a great excitement filling her. Never had she felt so free, so alive, so entirely happy as in this moment.

Then she saw him as he moved out of the green and stood waiting for her. This, her heart knew at once, was the face she had so long searched for among the visitors to the clan house, or in those few times when she had traveled abroad. This was the one meant by the Great Mother to give her full happiness.

He was all light, clothed with radiance and warmth. She reached him and that warmth and light encased them both in a private place which was theirs alone. No one else in the world might ever find or share it. She was a part of him and he was a part of her, and so they became one in a way Brigitta could find no words to explain.

The world about them was golden, and it sang as if all the true-toned birds in the woodlands raised their sweetest notes at once to blend. She was lost in the warmth, the song and in him until there was no Brigitta left, only another one who was fulfilled as a field sown with grain is fulfilled, ready to bring forth an abundant harvest.

In the clan house Lugaid edged back into the shadows. His body swayed slightly to right and left; his features were mask-like, without expression. He might have been concentrating with his whole being on something he heard, or sensed or imagined. But with that concentration was a growing bewilderment. It was as if a man who each day passed some long-ruined temple of a faceless, forgotten god, suddenly heard from within that desolate sanctuary a summons to a worship old beyond the memory of any man.

Then bewilderment became exultation. The mask of Lugaid's face broke and he was like one who, after years of aridity from serving a lost cause, had been proved the victor in truth. His hands folded over the spiral on his breast, he whispered words in a tongue not of the tower town which held him, nor of the Roman state which had been torn into nothing, but a language far older than either. In these latter days the words were largely meaningless even to those very few who still learned them as part of a discredited ancient belief.

Above, Brigitta smiled, crooned, stretched her arms to embrace him who stood in her dreams. And over the chief's hold the flying thing began a slow downward flight. Swooping through the roof opening, it unerringly found the inner door of the chamber in which the girl lay.

Within the cave the installations hummed to a high pitch and then began to sink again, almost drowsily, as though some beast had used its powers to the uttermost and must now rest to recoup its strength. But in that other distant crag there was no ceasing of outward flow. The beam signal strengthened, searched out farther and farther, a finger crooking into space to draw down aid in the old, old war.

Lugaid's eyes were open, fixed on the door of Brigitta's chamber. He could only guess a small portion of what had happened there this night, and of that he would say nothing until he was sure. But he drew a deep breath of wonder that such a thing could happen in these troubled days. The gods had long since withdrawn, yet it would seem that they still lived. He must go as soon as possible to the Place of Power. Surely there he would find some answer, some assurance that this thing had meaning for his people.

He heard the drone of voices about him and knew impatience. They occupied themselves only with the things of this earth, with death. Yet this night he was sure the things of the sky had touched here and brought life, not death. Truly this was the hour that legend promised, when the Sky Lords would come again!

2.

It was thickly hot within the upper chamber. Brigitta, between the waves of pain, longed to lay her swollen body in the stream which ran from the Fortunate Spring. She was dimly aware that most of the people in the fort village had been gone before sunup, out into the fields to celebrate the Feast of Lughnasa when the harvest fell to the sickle. Julia, who had been her mother's nurse, sat patiently beside her, dipping a cloth into a basin of tepid water, using that to wipe the dripping salt-sweat from the girl's face. There was a brazier in the far corner and from that came the scent of burning herbs, strong enough to make Brigitta cough and gasp when some trick of the breeze blew it in her direction. They had opened all the doors within the house, untied all knots, done what they might to make this birth an easy one. But, Brigitta thought dully, it was not easy. How could it be easy for a mortal woman to bear the son of a god?

The past months—how strangely they had eyed her. It was only Lugaid's prophecy which had kept the kin from laying black shame on her and so on the House of Nyren. There had been times when she would have willingly taken her own sharp dagger and cut from her living body this thing some strange force had bred in her. It was very hard now to remember the golden happiness of her dream, though Lugaid had assured her that it had actually been no dream, but that one of the Sky Sons had come to claim her.

Now she knew nothing but the pain, and between the onset of that, the fear that the next would be worse and worse. Yet she set her teeth and would not cry out. If one bore a god's son one did not wail him into the world.

Her body heaved again and Julia was quick beside her. Then Lugaid somehow was there also, his dark eyes hold-

16

ing hers. And from that meeting of their gaze came a strangeness which removed her from the pain, sent her spinning far out among sparks of light which might be stars. . . .

"A son." Julia placed the baby on the fair piece of linen ready to receive it.

"A son." Lugaid nodded as if he had had no doubts from the first that this would be so. "His name is Myrddin."

Julia looked at him with hostility. "It is the father who names the son."

"His name is Myrddin." The Druid dipped a finger into the bowl of water and touched the baby's breast. "His father would have it so."

Julia hunched a shoulder. "You talk of Sky Lords," she sniffed. "I am not denying that you saved my lady from shame with such, when there were those who believed. But there is not one even under this roof who believed wholly, or will ever do so. They will say 'son of no man' and talk tattle afar."

"Not long." Lugaid shook his head. "This will be the first of his kind and through him the old days will return. Those tales of the past are not only the words of bards meant to amuse. Within them lies a core of truth. Look to the babe, and your mistress." He glanced at Brigitta with less interest, as if, having served her purpose, she was of lesser account now.

Julia made a sound close to a snort. She bustled about caring for the child, who did not cry, but lay looking about him. In those few moments after his entrance into the world, he seemed far more aware of his surroundings than any infant should rightfully be. And the nurse, noting that odd awareness, made a certain sign before she gathered him up. Brigitta slept heavily.

It would seem that in Myrddin's early childhood Julia had the right measurement of the feeling within the kin house. He was indeed "son of no man," but since the chief accepted—outwardly at any rate—Lugaid's assurance that his daughter had been impregnated by a Sky Lord, the boy was not openly shamed. Neither did he find any ready acceptance among those of his own generation, however.

In the first place he was oddly slow to learn. The women of the house looked on his backwardness as a fit-

ting answer to the mystery of his conception. Nor was he
forward in walking either. Had it not been for the fierce
championship of Julia he might have been neglected, allowed to fade away into early death. For within six
months of his birth Brigitta had been given in marriage to
a widowed clan leader old enough to have fathered her.
She left Nyren's fortress and her son behind.

She had made no protest over his separation for, from
the hour of his birth, after she had awakened from the
swoon into which she was always sure Lugaid had sent
her, she had had no feeling of tenderness toward the baby.
Rather the Druid appeared to have taken her place, with
Julia to supply those comforts of physical existence
Myrddin needed most at his age. And it was Julia who became most fiercely maternal when comments about the
child's slowness were voiced aloud. It was to Lugaid that
Julia appealed when her own faith in Myrddin's intelligence wavered.

"Leave him be." Lugaid had taken the child on his
knee, was locking eyes with eyes. "He lives by another
time, this one. You shall see. When he talks it will be
clearly and with purpose; when he walks it will be
straightaway walking, not crawling about after the manner
of the animals. His heritage is not ours, so we cannot
judge him by the actions of those wholly of this world."

Julia sat quiet for a moment, glancing from Druid to
child and back again.

"I have thought sometimes," she confessed, "that the
tale you told was to save my young lady from shame. But
that is not so. What you say you believe. Why?"

Now he looked from the child to her. "Why, woman?
Because on the night he was conceived I felt the coming
of the Power which was to bring him into being. We have
lost so much." He shook his head regretfully. "So very
much of the knowledge which made men great enough to
challenge the stars themselves. We gabble odd tags of legend and are not sure which is truth, which the embroidery
of some later man. But there is enough remaining that he
who is trained can sense the Power when it is at work.

"This 'son of no man' shall be great enough to make
and unmake kings. Yet I believe that was not what
he was sent to do. No, he is an opener of gates. And
when he comes to his full strength he will speak the High
Language and we shall see the beginning of a new world."

The passion in his voice awed Julia and she took the child back from Lugaid's hold, regarding the boy strangely. For she knew that the Druid believed what he had said. And from that moment she watched for any sign of coming greatness in Myrddin, not knowing how that might first manifest itself.

Myrddin walked when he was four and, as Lugaid had said, he stepped out strongly from the first moment he found his feet, not wavering or crawling as was normal. A month later he spoke, and his words were as well pronounced as those of a grown man.

But he made no attempt to join the other children at their games. Nor did he ever show interest in sword play, or hang about listening to the lounging warriors telling their battle tales. Instead he tailed Lugaid whenever the Druid was in sight. And it became accepted that Myrddin would become a bard, or one of those learned in the law and the descent of houses. Nyren agreed to this on one of the rare intervals when he was at home.

For the chief had made his choice. He and his men rode with Ambrosius, harrying both the High King who had betrayed them and the Saxons he had brought in as allies and who were now nearly his masters. The war band was often gone from the mountain-hidden kin house, leaving only a token force of defenders, with women and slaves to work their few fields and herd the sheep which were their small wealth.

In Myrddin's fifth year, when he was pressed into aid as a shepherd, the clan being nearly bereft of men, he found the cave. He had gone higher among the lichen-tinted rocks of the uplands than he had ever ventured before, mainly because the older lads had left him to scramble up the roughest way. But as he rounded one pinnacle he forgot the sheep he sought and those waiting below.

Like a sleepwalker he veered to the right where there was a small opening, hardly large enough for his small, wiry body to wedge into. The fall of rock which had half sealed the cave had occurred not too long ago, but it was an effective screen and Myrddin might not have discovered the crevice at all if that sudden compulsion had not taken charge of his mind, drawn his body toward it.

He wriggled through the hole to find himself in a much larger passage whose outer limits were dim, because the only light came from the crack through which he had squirmed. No sense of fear touched him; he was filled instead with a strange and growing excitement, as if something wonderful lay just beyond, meant only for him.

So he marched on into the dark unafraid, only impatient to find what he knew must lie there. But, as he drew away from the entrance, he was surprised to discover that there was a pale sort of radiance around him, stretching three or four of his short strides ahead, as if he were wearing a giant cloak of light. Nor did that discovery seem in the least strange. Something deep in his mind welcomed it as a nearly forgotten bit of knowledge.

He knew the tale about him, that his father was of the Sky People. And from Lugaid he had learned more, that far, far back in time men had often come from the sky and the women of earth had borne sons and daughters to them. Those sons and daughters had had certain gifts and knowledge which men had never had and which had been forgotten when the Sky People came no more and their blood thinned through earth interbreeding. Few men believed in them anymore, and Lugaid had cautioned Myrddin that this was a story which he must keep to himself, until by his deeds he could indeed prove his heritage. Lugaid also said that unless the boy could learn by himself what the Old Ones knew he would be helpless, for nowhere on earth was there now any teacher of more than vague shadows of this forgotten lore.

There remained a part of Myrddin that was of Brigitta's giving and that shrank within him, lonely and lost, unable to make contact with those about him. He thought a lot about what would happen to him if he could never discover what he must know. For here even Lugaid failed him, saying that those who might once have taught him were long dead, and only small fragments, probably much distorted, remained in the trained memories of such as the Druid himself. But the priest promised that when the time was ripe, he would give what he could to this one who was truly like a fosterling of his own.

The grayish light which accompanied the boy grew stronger. Now he believed that it was given off by the walls, rather than gathered around his own person. And, when he rubbed an investigating finger along the stone, he discovered something else: a vibration within the rock. Quickly he put his ear flat against that wall to listen, but it was a feeling rather than a sound, a beat like from a creature's own heart.

All the tales of monsters lairing within caves swirled into his mind then and he hesitated. But the excited feeling drew him and he went on. So he came through an opening into a larger area where a light winked into flaring brilliance. Myrddin shrank back, his hands over his eyes, blinded by that glare. The vibration was a steady hum which he could hear now as well as feel.

"There is no need of fear."

Myrddin was suddenly aware that a voice spoke, had been speaking while he crouched, eyes covered, struck dumb for the first time in his life by real terror.

He strove to fight his fear, though he did not yet drop his hands to see who spoke. But the very fact that he heard lessened his first terror, for surely no firedrake nor ghoul would use the tongue of man!

"There is no need of fear," the same words repeated.

The boy drew a deep breath and, summoning the full force of his courage, he dropped his hands.

There was so much to be seen, and the objects were so alien to all his experience, that wonder overcame the last of his fear. For here was no scaled monster, no evil creature. Instead, under the light stood burnished squares and cylinders for which his native language had no names. There was also a kind of life which he could sense, though it was not the life of fleshed creatures, but of another species altogether.

The cavern seemed very large to him, and it was very full of the objects. Some flashed small colored lights along the surfaces facing him. Others were blank, yet they all possessed that alien life.

Myrddin still could not see who had spoken to him and he was too cautious to venture far into the crowded chamber. Now he moistened his lips with tongue tip and answered with all the boldness he could summon, his voice sounding shrill in that chamber.

"I am not afraid!" Which was in part a lie, but in part only, for the fascination of this place was far outweighing, with every moment he lingered, his first wariness.

He expected to see someone step into view around the bulk of those huge square or round pillars. But, as the moments passed, no one came. Again he spoke, now a little displeased that there had been no real answer.

"I am Myrddin, of the clan of Nyren." He took two more steps into the rock-walled place. "Who are you?"

The lights spun in broken patterns, the things about him never ceased their humming. But no voice replied to his demand.

Now he saw that facing him, near the far end of the aisle formed by the ranks of the blocks and cylinders, there was a kind of shimmer uniting two of the blocks and forming a glistening wall. As his eyes centered on that, the shimmer died away and he could see some sort of form, one no bigger than himself, in it.

Determined to meet the stranger, Myrddin moved forward quickly, paying no heed now to the blocks flanking his way, intent only on what grew ever stronger in the mirror-like surface. He had never seen his own reflection so bright and sharply clear, for the mirrors of the clan house were either of polished bronze in a size so small one held them in the hand, reflecting perhaps only one's face, or the distorting surface of a well polished shield. But this was entirely different and he had to stretch forth his hand, see the reflected boy do likewise, before he was convinced that it was only a mirror. The novelty of seeing the whole of himself interested him at first.

His dark hair, so neatly parted and combed by Julia that morning, was now in a tangled dark mass about his shoulders, with bits of stick and leaf caught in it, left when he had battered his way through the bushes. His small face was very brown and he had dark brows which met in a bar across his nose. Beneath them his eyes were startling green.

The tunic which Julia had enlivened with a chaining of red thread about neck and cuffs was torn and mud-bespattered, and his long breeches of green and white checked woolen stuff were tucked into ankle-high laced boots. Down the breast of his tunic dangled his one ornament, the claw of an eagle fastened to a red cord, and there was a streak of dried mud on his chin, a briar scratch on his cheek. Though his clothing was warm and of good quality of cloth, Julia's own weaving, he did not go as splendid as a chief's grandson might. In fact only the good knife sheathed at his leather thong of a belt suggested that he was more than huntsman or spearman's son.

Myrrdin raised his hands now, brushing back his tumble of hair. This, he decided, was a place where one should come with some pride. Perhaps whoever had spoken thought him, at second glance, to be a person of such little account that there was no need to answer—

"You are"—startling him once more, that voice rang out without warning—"awaited, Merlin."

Merlin? They—he—it who stayed here wanted someone called Merlin. Myrddin's fear woke up again. What would happen when they—he—it found there was a mistake? Again he drew a deep breath and faced the mirror stoutly, mainly because somehow seeing himself on its surface gave him a small measure of confidence.

"You, you are wrong," he forced his voice out loudly. "I am Myrddin of the House of Nyren."

Stiffly he awaited some reprisal. He fully expected to be hurled out on the mountainside again, at the least. And somehow he longed deeply to remain where he was, to learn what this place might be and most of all who spoke to him, calling him by that strange name.

"You are Merlin," the voice replied firmly. "You are he for whom all has been prepared. Rest your body, son, and see what you are and learn."

From one of the squares—that to his right—there swung out a solid bar. Myrddin felt it gingerly. It was wide enough to accommodate his small bottom and seemed solid enough to support his weight. Also, he thought there was no use arguing with the voice. It was far too authoritative in its statement.

Warily he seated himself on the bar facing the mirror. Oddly enough, though its surface appeared so solid, it seemed to yield a little under his slight weight, accommodating itself to form the most comfortable seat he had ever known. The reflection of Myrddin in the mirror flashed into nothingness. Before he had time to feel any alarm at this seeming erasure of himself there was another image there. And Myrddin's education began.

At first there was an odd inhibition placed on Myrddin so that he could not share his very strange adventure with anyone, even Lugaid, whom of all the clan he thought might understand. But there was no barrier on his thoughts or memories. And sometimes he was so excited by what he had learned from the mirror that back at the clan house he went about in a kind of daze.

Lugaid, who might have suspected a little, was at that

time absent, acting as messenger between Nyren and certain other chiefs and petty kings, trying to hammer into being an alliance which would hold, even among hereditary enemies, until after this season's raids on the Saxon encroachers. For Ambrosius did not often have the forces to take the field boldly against the Winged Hats and Vortigen's traitorous followers; he had, rather, to employ other means of whittling down their strength, mainly swift punitive raids across the unrecognized border lands.

Thus Myrddin was enabled, during the years which followed, to slip away to the cave often and there lose himself for long hours with the mirror. He did not at first grasp much of what he was shown. He was too young, too limited in experience. But the mirror's succession of scenes, while not repetitious in detail, did repeat over and over certain facts until they became as much a part of the boy's memory as incidents of his daily life had always been.

Myrddin tentatively began to put into practice what he learned. He discovered that the information imparted through and by the mirror had practical use. And young as he was, for short times he was able to influence the boys nearly old enough to take weapons in the war bands. He learned early that apparently no one else could see the crevice in the mountainside through which he was able to enter the place of the mirror, though he had no knowledge of distorters in action.

In addition to the fact that he could thus vanish without a trace, he could also implant in the minds of any companions he might have on the hillside during hunts, or herding, the idea that he had been with them throughout the day, even though he had been spending those same hours in the chamber of the mirror.

As eager as he might have been to use this talent for his own end, however, there had been planted with the knowledge of how to use it a kind of safeguard blockage which, when he tried twice to make Julia see what was not there, prevented him from achieving his goal. Thus he learned that his new weapon-tool was not to be used for any light purpose, but mainly to cover his time of schooling.

News trickled in very slowly to the mountain fastness. Lugaid did not return. They learned instead that he had gone on a journey of even greater length to some mysterious Place of Power, inspired by some desire of his own.

And Myrddin took this ill, for he had hoped to share with the Druid some of the wonder of his own discoveries, feeling that he could only communicate them to the one man of Nyren's people who already held some bits and pieces of the ancient knowledge.

Shortly after the message concerning Lugaid, a deeper and more tragic word came with a handful of broken and beaten men, some only keeping in the saddles of their wiry mountain-bred ponies by strong will or their comrades' ropes. For Nyren's force had met with betrayal during a foray and their chieftain and more than half of their people were cut down. The harried survivors made their way home through the heavy mists and torrential rains of late autumn, and they brought such ill tidings with them that all in the clan house cowered, waiting for the blow to strike them down.

When there was no swift pursuit they brightened a little, but the house was a place of mourning and dread. Gwyn the One-Handed, younger brother of Nyren, took command of the house, since Nyren had left no son. Gwyn could not truly be named chief because of his maiming, though he had a clever arrangement of bronze which he could strap to his left wrist to serve him as a mighty war club.

Had Myrddin been older he might have claimed kin right, but this was no time for a child lord, and the men accepted Gwyn by acclamation. This was a season when men garnered in the harvest—what remained in their small fields—looking over their shoulders constantly, spear or sword to hand. And the watchmen in the heights kept vigil near beacons piled ready for the torch.

Myrddin found little chance now to slip away to the mirror cave and sometimes he chafed with impatience, but he did not realize how much of the teaching he had absorbed. One afternoon he was finally able to edge through the slit to face once more that magic mirror. Perhaps it was chance alone, perhaps it was something more, which kept him overlong at his lesson that day. But when he edged out through the slit he found that twilight was already gathering.

Afraid that the outer gate would already be barred, he scrambled down the slopes, dodging in and out among the stone spurs of the mountain's ribs, intent only on reaching the clan house as soon as possible. Thus he went unheeding of certain shadows which slipped from place to place, unheeding until a hand shot out and closed about his ankle. He took a hard fall, which nearly jarred all the breath from his body.

There was a heavy arm across him, pinning him easily to the ground in spite of all his vain struggles. Then a hand twisted painfully in his hair, jerking up his head so that his face could be seen.

"By the Grace of the Three," someone said explosively, "this is the very brat! He's come to our hand as easily as a cockerel follows a trail of grain."

Myrddin had no time to assess his captors. Now over him dropped a cloak which smelled sourly of human and horse sweat mingled. And that was speedily tied about him, making him into as helpless a bundle as any pack trader could fling across a horse. And like such a bundle he was hoisted to lie at a painful angle, bent over a horse which moved at a bone-shaking trot.

3.

At first the boy thought he must have fallen into the hands of a Saxon war band. But why had they not slain him out of hand? Then, as he tried to order his wits, the words he had heard spoken in his own tongue came clearly to mind. He was "the brat" of whom they had plainly been in search. But why was he of any importance to strangers?

Myrddin fought for breath in the stifling folds of the cloak and struggled within himself for courage. Obviously he was of value . . . as a slave? No, there were slaves in plenty. Because he was who he was, the close kin of Nyren? But Gwyn was the lord of the clan. . . .

His head hanging against the horse's flank throbbed from the awkwardness of his position and he began to feel queasy. Besides, it was very hard to hold to any defense against fear.

How long his ordeal lasted Myrddin did not know. He was only half conscious when he was lifted from the horse and thrown without ceremony and with bruising force to the ground.

"Mind yourself!" ordered another voice. "They would have this one living, not dead, remember."

"Devil's brat, ill luck rides with such," growled a second.

Someone clawed off the cloak, but Myrddin was too spent to move. And he had no chance for freedom as hands closed brutally about his thin wrists, wrapping a length of hide into bonds he could not hope to loosen. The man who handled him so roughly was only a dark shape in the night. When his captor gave a last jerk to make sure of the strength of his ties, the boy roused enough to try to see more of the company about him.

Shapes came and went so that he was not sure of the count, and he could hear horses stamping. The night was

27

very cold, with the chill of the ground on which he lay bringing on a fit of shivering he could not control. But his captors were all remarkably quiet and he was no wiser as to the identity of this group, except that he was now sure they were not Saxons.

Another one came riding into the small hollow where they had halted. One of the squatting shadows rose to his feet, went to stand beside the newcomer.

"We have him, lord."

The answer to that was a grunt but the mounted man added: "Ride, then. This is no time to sit idle on your haunches. After all he is of Nyren's blood in part, and clan pride will bring out trackers. Get you going. There will be fresh mounts waiting at the Giant's Tooth."

Having given his orders, the newcomer vanished back into the blackness of the night. Around him Myrddin heard the grumbling of men who were not pleased, but who seemed bound by obedience to a strong commander.

Once more the boy was hoisted up on a horse. Only this time he was fastened in the saddle, a rope beneath the mount's belly linking ankle to ankle, then the cloak was thrown over him. His head ached savagely and he fought against swaying, lest he crash to the ground and be dragged to his death before his captors could rein in his horse.

They rode throughout the night, halting once at a tall finger of rock which might indeed have been the fang pried out of some huge and fearsome mouth, to change to other mounts picketed out to wait for them. Myrddin had long since lapsed into a daze of fear, pain and bewilderment. None of them ever addressed him, or seemed to care about his welfare, except when they had to change him from one horse to a fresh one. His whole body became one sore bruise, so that every step the horse under him took jarred him into a new torment. He set his teeth firmly, determined even in that far-off place into which his consciousness seemed to retreat that he would not give voice to any cry of pain.

They came down out of the hills. Dawn found them trotting along the smoother surface of one of those roads which the Romans had built. Myrddin could see more of the company now. They were men very like those he had always known, only their faces were those of strangers. Of the party of ten, all but two were spearmen such as might serve any clan chief as a levy, and those strung behind.

But the reins of Myrddin's mount were held by one who wore a crimson cloak cunningly worked, if now sadly soiled and frayed, with wide bands of needlework. His hair, the color of polished bronze, swept well below his shoulders in the old way of the tribes. His thick-lipped mouth was bracketed by a heavy moustache and the first stubble of days without touching a razor bristled on his full cheeks.

He was a young man, beefy of shoulder, with bands of worked bronze on his thick arms. A sword of the Roman pattern slapped against his thigh and a small wooden shield with boss and rim of metal was slung between his shoulder blades. His eyes were puffy, as if he had been too long without sleep, and he yawned with jaw-cracking openness from time to time.

Myrddin's companion to his left was in contrast to the other. He was a lean lath of a man, his chest covered by a dented, poorly mended cuirass. A helmet that had lost its crest was jammed well down on his narrow head, for it had been originally fashioned for a much larger man. His weapons were also a sword and a spear with a wickedly barbed point. And he did not ride lumpily, half asleep as did the tribesman, but rather sat stiffly upright in the saddle and kept glancing from side to side, as if he expected some force to burst upon them out of ambush at any moment.

Myrddin was so weary that he weaved back and forth in the saddle, but neither of his captors appeared to take notice of him. Nothing he had learned in his cave retreat told him what to expect now, except that the future these men intended for him held nothing good. And he no longer tried to imagine what that future might be. Nor did he attempt to take any interest for the moment either in his escort or his surroundings. This land, to one born and bred in the mountains, with no personal knowledge of the countryside below, was strange enough.

By noon they no longer traveled a deserted road. Parties of armed clansmen and three bands of Saxons grudgingly gave way to allow them quicker passage. Before them now rose buildings of stone, dressed and set after another fashion than that of a clan house wall.

Myrddin was both hungry and thirsty but he would not

beg from those he rode among. When they stopped at a spring to drink and then water their mounts, however, one of the lesser clansmen filled a small wooden cup and held it to the boy's lips. Myrddin drank thirstily and his wits somewhat recovered. He studied this man who seemed less hardened than his companions.

He was much younger than the rest, a fair down on his chin in patches. And the eyes he raised to Myrddin's were a pale, washed blue; his expression, sullen and heavy.

Myrddin swallowed and swallowed again. His throat felt swollen and sore. When he tried to speak his voice came as a croak.

"My thanks——" he got out before the man in the helmet swung around.

"Hold your tongue, Devil's brat, or we'll clip a wood splint on it." He edged his horse closer, crowding against Myrddin's weary mount. "Aye, your magics we do not need either." He reached over and jerked up the hood of the cloak, dragging that down to form a loose blindfold. "You fool"—he must be speaking now to the clansman who had brought the water—"do you want to be demon-haunted! This one, they say, young as he is, can well call up all ghosts!"

Myrddin heard a gasp, probably from his late benefactor, and was only glad that he had taken those mouthfuls of water before the second leader of the band had interfered. That bounty, small as it had been, had served to rouse him somewhat from the trance of pain and fear in which he had ridden for most of this night. He could hope for no more aid within this party, yet he was beginning to think again. It was as if the shock of his capture after his long visit to the cave had shut off in some strange fashion his ability to reason clearly, until the small gesture of feeling on the part of the hulking boy had roused him out of that daze.

What could he draw to his aid now? The bedazzlement which he had been able to use with the clan boys in order to conceal his visits to the cave? Young as he was, Myrddin's knowledge now far outran his years. And there was something beginning to loom in his mind—no, rather in a part of him which did not truly think, but rather sensed that this adventure was part of the future which he was destined to face.

They had called him "Devil's brat", a name he had

heard before, though it had never been said to his face.
Nyren's blood had certain rights no clansman—or
woman—could deny. But that his father was not one of
the fabled Sky Men, but rather a demon, that was an old
accusation. Was it not true that he had been conceived on
Samain Eve when all manner of evil spirits roamed free?
If he had not found the cave of the mirror, he might even
have accepted that reasoning himself, it fitted so well the
facts which most knew. But the cave was surely of the
vanished Sky People, and he had already learned there
that he had been born to a certain task; he must dedicate
his lifetime to its accomplishment.

Still, he had no enemies he knew about. Gwyn ruled the
clan and he himself would never protest that for he was
pledged to a different life than a battle leader. And it was
already accepted among his kin that he would go to
Lugaid's kind when the time came, to be taught such of
the mysteries as survived.

To what other man could he possibly be a threat? His
mind played with that puzzle as they came into the town
which claimed Vortigen as ruler. For, as they rode, his
captors now talked a little, and the boy speedily discovered that this was their goal. Was he then to be hostage
for his people? But with Nyren gone Myrddin's kin were
not of such account as to make a hostage worth maintain-
ing.

He roused from his thoughts to look around him,
though the hood was drawn down so far on his head that
what he could see was limited mainly to the road underfoot, with here or there an edge of stone wall. Though
half blind, he could listen. At first his ears, in the past only
attuned to the noises of what was a very small clan settle-
ment, were almost deafened. He found it hard to separate
one noise from the other.

At last their lagging mounts came to a stop and the
rope which held Myrddin's feet twitched, fell away. A
heavy hand swept him out of the saddle, shoving him
roughly ahead as his feet nearly buckled under him. So he
entered a confined place of vile smells where the cloak
was whipped away. He could see that he stood in a
stone-walled cubby of a room which had only a length of
pitted stone against one wall for a bench or bed, and only
a slit high in that same wall for a window.

The bonds fell in turn from his wrists, but his arms

were leaden, his hands numb from the hours of their lashing. It was the man in the helm who had cut him free; now he gave the boy a last shove toward the bench.

"You wait on the High King's pleasure," he grunted. And he was gone, slamming the door behind him, immediately plunging Myrddin into a gloom as deep as the twilight in which he had first been taken.

The King. Myrddin shaped those words but did not say them aloud. There was only one king here, though his rule rested mainly on the will of those Saxons he had invited overseas to bolster his armies, first against the raiding Scotti, and then against those of his own blood who might be rivals. Vortigen, Myrddin had been taught from the time he could understand, was a traitor, a nothing man who now listened to the orders of the Winged Hats and cut down his close kin at their pleasure.

And what did Vortigen want of him, Myrddin?

Thinking made his headache worse. He sat on the stone of the bench, rubbing one hand against the other, striving to keep from whimpering as the pain of the returning circulation in his puffed hands was almost more than he could silently bear.

He tried now to call to mind all he had lately heard concerning the High King. The last rumor to reach as far into the mountains as the House of Nyren had been that Vortigen was planning a great fortress tower, one which would rival anything the Romans had built in their day.

But the drifting one-armed trader who had brought the story had also said that there were difficulties in that building, that what was carefully laid stone upon stone on one day was discovered the next morning to be broken away, or set awry enough to be useless. It was said that magic overcame all the efforts of man in constructing the fortress.

Myrddin leaned his head back against the wall. He was so tired that, uncomfortable as he was, sleep pressed upon him until finally he could answer no more to the searching of his thoughts, but rather subsided into a darkness heavier than that of the cell which imprisoned him.

When he woke it was to find a flickering of light about him and for a moment or two he thought he was back in the place of the mirror and those colored squares of radiance which snapped on and off across the squares now faced him. When he opened his eyes fully and pulled himself up on the bench, however, he saw that a pine knot had been thrust into a ring high on the wall. A man stood under that torch, eyes resting directly on Myrddin.

And the boy knew a sudden lift of heart. Such a robe of white he had never seen worn except by Lugaid on high feast days, though this lacked that spiral of gold on the breast which Lugaid's had borne. Yet if he was of the bardic brotherhood, then indeed he could be hailed as friend. And Myrddin knew the words which could claim protection. He was about to repeat the sentence Lugaid had long ago—or so it seemed to the boy—drilled into him, when the other spoke:

"Son of a demon, son of no man living, I order that you use not any devilish wiles. Be warned that there has been laid upon you the greater and the lesser obedience, those bonds of spirit which you cannot break."

As he spoke, his words following a kind of chant, he pointed to Myrddin with a staff, white in part, the rest a rusty red as if it had been dyed with blood.

It was as if the boy's nose was suddenly filled with a vile scent. Myrddin shook his head to try to escape the unseen cloud which surrounded this man who was certainly not of Lugaid's kind. At the same time he realized that all the fear he had felt before was nothing to what he experienced now. For this was not only a threat to his body, but rather also to what he was. And he began to repeat, not the words of greeting which had been on his lips, but rather others which Lugaid had also taught him.

He saw the strange Druid's eyes widen. The staff lashed across the air between them as the other might beat a man down; the wind of its passing touched Myrddin's dust-grimed face. Yet the gesture was only empty menace, as well he realized. And with that realization the boy's control began to regain command over his fear.

"What do you want of me?" Myrddin purposefully did not add any address of courtesy to that demand. This stranger might wear a robe like Lugaid's, but Myrddin's inner sense denied that he was of the breed of Lugaid.

The other had stilled his wand, though its reddened tip pointed straight at the boy as if it were a spear set for the final death thrust.

"You are the one of the foretelling, being born of no father, thus ordained for the High King's purpose. For we who speak with the Powers have learned that never shall his fortress stand until its mortar be slaked with the blood of a youth who has no father kin."

Deep within Myrddin there was a stir, a half memory. There was something—perhaps he had learned it from the mirror and then forgotten. He could not always remember everything he had been shown in the hidden cave once he had left. Instead, some parts of his knowledge seemed to sink so deeply into his mind that they lay hidden there until a chance word, some glimpse of a familiar object brought them to the surface.

This was shown! Not his death, of that he was sure, and his conviction on that point gave him confidence. But he had been brought here, not only by the will of the High King, but for another reason also, one which marched with the tasks he still only dimly suspected lay before him.

If the Druid expected him to cringe, to show fear, then his was the disappointment. For Myrddin, secure in his inner knowledge, faced him chin up and unshaken.

"What Powers do you speak for?" Again he deliberately omitted any title of respect. "Perhaps in these days your voices come not from the Sky Ones, but rather from the desires of men."

The other's breath rasped; his eyes strove to catch and hold Myrddin's in one of those compelling strokes of command such as would make the boy will-less, ready to obey any order laid on him. And Myrddin, summoning all he had learned for the protection of his own secrets, gazed as steadily back.

"What do you know of the Sky Ones?" this stranger asked in a voice which had lost something of its arrogance and now held a note of unease.

"What do you?" Myrddin countered.

"That this is forbidden for any not of the Mysteries to speak of." The stranger's face flushed with anger. "What have you spied upon, demon-bred?"

"Could I be a spy and yet know this?" Deliberately Myrddin spoke the words of recognition Lugaid had taught him so long ago.

But to his surprise the other laughed with harsh relief.

"Those are worthless now. We listen to a new Power. You cannot claim kin, being what you are and already meat for the High King's use. Better you be truly dead so you cannot corrupt any foolish ones with your prattling of forgotten things. Enter." He turned his head a fraction, though not enough to take his eyes from Myrddin, as if he feared that the boy might indeed be more of an equal opponent than he now seemed. "Enter and take him!"

The man wearing the old armor pushed past the Druid, giving him a respectfully wide berth. And Myrddin made no struggle as his hands were once more lashed behind him, as he was pushed toward the door.

The Druid had turned and gone out, but he awaited them bathed in a sunlight which made Myrddin blink, unable as he was to raise a hand to shield his eyes from the glare. More of the guard closed about them, and beyond that row of armed men the boy saw clanspeople and Saxons watching him with a kind of avid greediness which made him sick inside.

The same evil which had flowed like a stench from the Druid hung about this whole company. It was meant to feed on a man's fears, overwhelm his courage, so he would go without struggle to whatever death waited for him.

Yet, much as the boy inwardly shrank from that assault of emotion, he walked firmly, without any wavering, his head up and his control unbreached.

The road they followed climbed a hill toward the piles of stones Vortigen had commanded his fortress be fashioned from. As they went, Myrddin looked from right to left, not now searching the faces of those gathered to see the sacrifice, but rather because he was aware, as if his sight could indeed pierce through the earth, of what lay underground.

They came to a halt before a leveled stone which had been draped with a covering of elaborately embroidered cloaks. And on that improvised throne sat the High King—claiming a title no mountain man would grant him.

Myrddin saw a man he thought close to his grandfather's age, but there was no nobility, no pride, in these features, puffed as they were by too much drink. Vortigen's eyes were never still, but flitted ever from face to face as if he expected treachery with each breath he drew. And his hands played with the hilt of his sword, though by the soft appearance of his body, the swelling paunch about which the belt of that sword had trouble meeting, he was no warrior now.

Behind him stood a woman, graceful, much younger, with the red-gold crown of a queen in a band about her head, resting on hair as yellow as ripe grain. Her robe of red was so overlaid with stitchery of gold that she glittered as hard as any metal figure in the sun. And in spite of her beauty of face there was in her the hardness of worked gold, not the softness of flesh.

There was no timidity nor unease in her, but she looked with boldness where she would, a faint smile carved on her lips, never warming her arrogant eyes. And when those eyes rested on the boy they glinted with what he correctly read as cruel anticipation.

"This is the boy?" Vortigen demanded. "It is proved, he is the son of no man?"

"Lord King," the Druid answered, "it has been so proved, out of the mouth of she who bore him. For one of the Power questioned her and she could not lie. On Samain Night he was conceived through the power of some wandering ghost or demon—"

"Lord King!" Myrddin raised his voice and found that at this moment it was not shrill; rather it sounded assured and steady even in his own ears. "Why have your men of Power lied to you?"

The Druid swung halfway around, his staff moving up. But at that moment Myrddin's deep-planted memory came fully awake. His eyes caught those of the furious priest and held them for a long moment. The flush faded from the man's countenance, his features slackened oddly. He looked dull, drained.

Vortigen watched that transformation with something approaching awe.

"What have you done, demon-born?" He raised his fingers in the sign to ward off bad fortune.

"Nothing, Lord King, except gain for myself a space in which to tell you how ill-served you are."

The King licked his lips. His fingers tightened on the sword hilt, half drawing the blade from its sheath.

"In what manner am I ill-served?"

"In the manner of this tower you would build." Myrddin pointed with his chin toward the piled stones. "Dig beneath and you shall see. For below lies a spring of water which flows to soften the earth, so it cannot hold the weight of the stones you would set on the surface. And within that water you shall find the fate of this land. For there crouches the white dragon from overseas." He glanced beyond the King's shoulder to that upstart Queen, whose gaze was as intent on him now as if she, too, would use her will as a weapon. Faintly he could feel the push of that will. But the force was feeble against what the mirror had built within him.

"Beyond the other edge of the pool is the red dragon of the Old Ones. And these strive ever to win an endless battle. Now the white dragon waxes in strength, and he shall nigh overcome his enemy. But the day lies close, closer than you know, Lord King, when the Red shall prevail. Set your men to spades and let them seek. You shall find it as I have said."

The hand of the golden Queen reached forward as if to touch Vortigen's shoulder. And in that moment Myrddin, carried out of himself, filled with understanding from the mirror, knew her for the enemy. She was more than just the Saxon wench who had seduced the High King, she was—

He frowned, sensing a new menace he did not understand and the nature of which he had not fronted before. Alarmed, he centered his concentration on the High King, instinctively knowing that this was the moment in which his own trained will was at its height.

"Let them dig, Lord King!"

Vortigen, leaning forward on the stone slab so that his shoulder was now well beyond the Queen's reach, nodded heavily and echoed:

"Let them dig."

So they brought spades and cut into the earth, laboring hard and as fast as they might under the King's eyes until there was a swift gush of water from the side of the hill. Then they hurried to lay bare a small cave in which there was a pool.

Myrddin drew on his powers. This was no small clouding of memory so that he would not be seen by his peers, their young minds lying well open to such bewilderments. No, he must create an illusion those here would not forget.

There was a flash of red on one side of the water, a spear of white flame on the other. The tips of those fires inclined toward each other, inclined and wavered. For as long as he might, Myrddin held the illusion and then, drained of energy, allowed the flames to sniff into nothingness. But there was awe on the faces of those about him. Someone hastily cut through his bonds.

The High King turned a blanched, strained face in his direction.

"It is the truth—the truth," he repeated, his voice loud in the silence that had fallen on the hilltop.

"And I will give you another truth." Out of nowhere Myrddin found the words which he knew he must say. "Your day comes to sunset, High King. Know that Ambrosius advances with the evening star!"

4.

~~~~~~

"They speak of you as a prophet, boy."

The commander wore his red cloak flung back to display a breastplate of the old Roman style, one bearing the design of a laurel wreath encircling a god clutching thunderbolts in either hand. He was stocky, with a closed face, as if he never allowed emotion to uncover what he might consider a weakness. He was of the Roman pattern in more than his dress: his weathered, swarthy skin, his hair clipped close to his skull, his jaw shaved clean, though his beard was so heavy that it seemed only momentarily restrained by such measures.

Myrddin sensed this man's strength of purpose like another kind of armor or weapon. This was truly a leader of men. All they had said of Ambrosius Aurelianus was the truth: he was the last of the Romans, with all their virtues and firmness of purpose—and perhaps their faults as well. This was a captain one could follow, but he was not the man Myrddin sought, not one to weld the broken factions of Britain into one nation again. He was too much of a Roman to be anything to the tribesmen but a worthy war chief, looking toward the past and a life which the years of disunion had wiped forever away.

"Lord." The boy chose his words carefully. This was one to whom he could not tell the entire truth, for Ambrosius would not believe it. "Lord, I am of the mountains and I knew this land. I only said what the High King's men should have known, that there can be no firm foundation where a spring eats under the crown of a hill."

"And these dragons—white and red—which our prisoners swear they saw at war?" countered Ambrosius swiftly. "Where did they come from, also out of your spring?"

"Lord, men see what they expect. The water lay as I said, therefore they were prepared to see what else I had

pictured for them. The dragons were in their minds, for
that much was the truth as they knew it. The white
dragon of the Saxons sat in honor in Vortigen's hold and
and the red which is of our land was in defeat."

He met the other's piercing gaze squarely.

"I will not," Ambrosius said with an emphasis which no
one could mistake, "have any practice of sorcery. Such is
both an abomination before the gods and a beguiling of
fools. Remember that, my young prophet! Though a man
may seize any weapon to save his life, he would do well
thereafter not to try it again. I and my men fight openly,
with these." He touched the sword which lay on the table
in front of him. "That magic of the night, the evil of
witchery, is not ours. Let that thrice-damned Saxon witch,
who has so beguiled Vortigen to his undoing, try such
methods."

Myrddin had heard the tale, that it was the Queen who
had produced the poison used in the murder of Vortigen's
eldest son, starting the revolt of the King's own followers
against him.

"Lord," he answered, "I am no sorcerer. And I ask no
more of you than to be allowed to depart to my own
place."

He thought he detected a trace of curiosity in the
other's glance.

"You are of the blood of Nyren, a worthy fighter and a
loyal man. And you are of an age for the taking of arms.
If you wish, I can place you among my troops. Only no
more prophecies or the addling of men by words."

"Lord, you offer me a great honor." Myrddin bowed
his head for a moment to acknowledge the courtesy the
other had extended. "But I am not a man of the sword.
My service to you will lie in other ways."

"What other ways? Do you claim to be a bard with the
power of words? Boy, you lack the long years for the
learning a bard must have. And I am no king to send a
talker rather than a troop against my enemies. I will not
name you coward, for it seems by all accounts that you
stood in mortal danger and came forth unharmed, by the
use of your wits alone. But in this hour it is weapon
against weapon, and the Saxons do not understand the
power of words such as some of our people will listen to."

"Lord, you say sorcery, but there is in me sometimes

the gift of foretelling. Do you also claim that to be wholly evil?"

Ambrosius was quiet for a long moment, then he replied in a lower, more meditative tone.

"No, I do not deny the truth which lies in foretelling. But it is an evil in this manner: should a man know that victory lies before him, then he shall be less desperate in battle; if he knows defeat faces him, then already his heart is that much gone out of him and he will be the quicker to cry off from attack. Therefore I do not wish to know what lies beyond this moment, nor do I wish to consult any augury, even those the Legions did in their day. So I think you are right, Myrddin of the House of Nyren. If that is the service you would offer me, I must refuse it, and it would be better that you do go to your own place.

"What you have done, laid the prophecy upon the forces of Vortigen in our favor, for that our thanks. And we shall strive mightily that the red dragon wins his battle, without sorcery. Call upon our people for a horse, for supplies, but get you from us and soon."

Thus Myrddin, who had gone out of the mountains a captive and a bewildered, frightened boy, returned into those fastnesses still a boy in body, but in spirit and mind another. For he who has called upon such Powers leaps in that single moment from youth to manhood, and is never afterward the same. He carried enough provisions in his saddlebag to be able to avoid the clan house, riding straight to the cave instead.

He loosed his mount in the small valley beneath the slope on which the cave lay and climbed to edge through the crack and come down into the place of the mirror. When he reached that point, he was aware at once that something about the cave had altered, though at first sighting all was the same—the lines of light still flickered across the installations, the mirror faced him as it ever had.

That strength of will which had sustained him through his journey—from the town where Vortigen had been driven into flight and where the forces of Ambrosius were now camped—deserted him. He sank down on the seat before the mirror, deeply burdened with the fatigue of his journey, empty-minded and spent.

Yet uneasiness pricked at him. Even in this secret place

all was not well. He fumbled with his saddlebags, found dry bread and a small leather bottle of sour wine. Dribbling the wine on the bread, he ate only because he knew that his body needed the food. It was not the hearty fare he had shared with the soldiers, but it was all he had now.

As Myrddin chewed he looked at the mirror, seeing his own reflection once again: small, dark, with tumbled hair, a face in which, now that he looked more carefully, the planes differed from those of his fellows. Had that difference come from his Sky father? He had never seen, among the wealth of pictures the mirror had shown during the years of his instruction, any other person.

Wearily the boy chewed and swallowed, but now and again he glanced around him. For, though he could see the cave plainly, more than half of it also being reflected in the mirror, the feeling that he was not alone persisted. It was like a trace of some scent on the air. So he found himself sniffing as if, like one of the great hunting hounds, he might uncover the intruder.

Once his hunger was satisfied, Myrddin rose to begin a thorough search between the squares and cylinders, tracing each possible opening between them back to the stone of the walls. There was nothing, no one.

But if the intruder was not here now, had there been someone earlier? Though how he could sense that he did not understand. Back once more on the bench before the mirror, he subsided, his head in his hands. For the time being he had lost that sense of purpose which had drawn him on, and he shrank dully from any thought of the future.

There was a sharp, ringing sound, as a piece of bronze might sing when struck by another bit of metal. Myrddin raised his head. The mirror was awakening—his reflection had vanished from its surface. In place there was the familiar swirl of mist. That deepened, thickened . . .

He was staring at a girl. Her body was held tensely and she had the attitude of one listening for a sound she dreaded. Behind her lay a countryside he knew well, the slope which reached to the cave entrance.

But this was no maid from the clan house! Her body was very slight and thin, not yet showing the curves of womanhood. Her skin was pale, the color of sea-bleached ivory, against which her hair was a cloud of dark, but a dark in which queer red lights played as if the sun sought out its match in it.

Her face was nearly triangular, the cheekbones wide apart, the chin almost pointed. Myrddin realized suddenly that the planes of that other countenance were similar to his own.

She wore a single simple garment fashioned as if a square of green had had a hole cut in its center, through which she had thrust her head, and then she had drawn in the folds about her middle with a wide belt which was formed of chains of a silvery metal braided together. Ankle boots latched with the same metal covered her feet. But she had no bracelets or necklaces.

Now she raised long-fingered hands to push the wind-tossed hair away from her eyes and at that moment she no longer gazed about her but stared straight from the mirror at Myrddin. He was startled, half expecting her to see him. But there was no flash of recognition in her eyes.

Simple as was her garment, young as she appeared to be and odd as she looked in the wilderness of this mountain place, yet there was about her an air of authority such as the daughter of a chieftain might have. Myrddin pushed forward on his bench, intent on conning her features, for she interested him strangely, more than any girl or woman he had seen. He wondered who she was and how she had come to be on the mountain. Was she some visitor at the clan house? Yet never did the girls wander far from that haven of safety, not in these days when the land might well hold war bands on the prowl.

It was then that the voice which was so familiar to him but whose source he had never discovered, unless it issued in some manner from the mirror itself, spoke;

"This is Nimue and she is Merlin's bane, for she is of the Others."

"What others?" Myrddin was jolted into demanding. The mirror voice still called him by that strange name. He had come to accept it, but to himself he was always Myrddin.

"Those who would not raise man again," returned the voice flatly. And after a moment's silence it began anew:

"Listen well, Merlin, for the evil approaches and you must be armed against it. In the ancient days when our people came freely to this world there arose a mighty nation, great beyond the dreams of men living now. That

knowledge which was of our gathering we offered freely
to your people, those who could open their minds to it.
And men prospered. Their daughters wived with the Sky
Born. Children born from such unions were mighty heroes
and people of Power. Nor did we then realize that within
your species lay a flaw.

"But there were others like us who also took ships between the stars. And it was not to their minds that those
of your kind should rise to greatness and knowledge. Thus
they came secretly into your world and there they found
the flaw, that your kind were prone to violence. They then
used this flaw to their own purposes. And there followed
such wars as your breed now has no knowledge of. For
such were fought with lightning drawn from the skies and
forces which overturned mountains, making land into sea
and sea into land.

"Many of us died in those battles and those we had
taught died also. Then the Dark Ones withdrew to the
skies once more, exulting that man would not rise now to
threaten their own rule, but would remain a brutish thing,
unlearned and unlearning. Some of our children survived,
and they attempted to keep alive the knowledge. But everything they had depended upon, such machines as you
see about you now, had been swept away in the disasters
of the earth. Metal could not be fashioned and man once
more turned to stone and the bones of his prey for tools
and weapons. Those who had begun their lives in great
cities ended them in rude caves, with nothing but their
hands and such knowledge as they could remember locked
within their heads.

"Those of us who would have come again could not, for
the lovers of the Dark controlled the roads between the
stars. And if we ventured forth we were harried and destroyed. So passed ages beyond counting by your species.
To all things comes a time of decay, however, and our enemies began to dwindle, though we, too, had lost very
much. But we had not forgotten those of our own left
helpless on this world and, gathering all that we had left,
we fashioned certain ships which could cross the void.
These had to be small and so could not transport us, but
they could carry certain elements of life within them. And
if any reached its goal, what it carried could start the
renewal of our race. We launched these seed ships with

hope, for the ships of the Dark Ones had not been seen in our heavens for a long time.

"At last one of our ships came to earth. But the beacon which drew it here was very old and the forces within it so limited that it was by happy chance only that it was still alive enough to bring the seed ship down.

"Thus were you born, Merlin. And you are set an early task, for we must have peace in which to grow again. To enforce this peace you are to be our hands and our liege man. Now the beacon which brought that first ship here is dead. But there stands a greater beacon in this land, one which if properly set alight once more will draw all of our fleet to it. And to rekindle that is also your task.

"There is now this threat: even as we left beacons to bring us once again into your world, so did those Dark Ones station alarms and similar drawing points. And one such has been alerted. From the seeding left within that has come this Nimue. She seeks to keep you from your task. Be warned, for all the cunning of the Dark Ones is being taught her. And she will have forces which may in the end match your own. She has already come here, drawn by the energy of this place, though she has not found what she seeks, for the defenses placed here still hold high. But she will search you out and what you will do she will try to undo, to keep man lesser than what he can be.

"Two duties have you, one to bring full Power back into the Great Beacon. And that is a mighty task, for a part of what was once there has long since been taken overseas to the Western Island. Some who had a faint remnant of the old knowledge recognized the Power in it and wished to try to use it though, having only a small part of learning, they could not do so.

"Your second duty is to provide such a leader for this land as to bring all its present quarrels to naught, and establish a time of peace in which we can come again, meeting with man and working together.

"These are what you must do, and Nimue will prevent you if she can. Be warned, Merlin, for you are our hope and the time grows short wherein this may be accomplished. Fail and the Dark shall utterly encompass your world and man shall be left to brutish life without the sun of knowledge!"

The likeness of Nimue faded. In her stead was another

picture, that of a place of great standing stones, some capped with huge lengths from one rough pillar to the next. And Myrddin knew this place, not from his own seeking, but because in the years past Lugaid had spoken of it.

It had been built by those fabled strangers who had held this land before Myrddin's own people had spread across the seas and settled here. It remained a sacred place, not only for its forgotten builders, but for those who had come later. Here were tied certain powers of the sun, so those with the knowledge could venture here and learn secrets of the stars. Even now men who yearned for enlightenment dwelt nearby, and it was here Myrddin believed Lugaid had gone after the death of Nyren.

"This is the Great Beacon," intoned the voice. Then that picture wavered and was gone. Myrddin sensed that he was now totally alone, his tasks having been made plain to him, the warning given.

The boy had much to wonder over. How could he hope to return a stone as great as those he had looked upon, by himself, from the Western Isle? He knew it was impossible. To enlist others in such action also seemed impossible. Who now, in the midst of war, with this country torn asunder, would listen to him? Nor could he tell the whole story, for it was, he decided shrewdly, past the credence of all but those such as Lugaid.

Lugaid . . .

Myrddin wondered what influence the Druid could wage with the kings and leaders of the host. His own memory of the man suggested that Lugaid was not one to be regarded lightly. But whatever he was now right in that accounting or if he had just built Lugaid up in his own mind, he could not tell. However, it would seem that his first step was to go to the Place of the Sun and there seek out the Druid. Also, seeing the actual site was better than envisioning it in the mirror.

Having thought out his plan, the boy sought an opening between two of the boxes and, wrapped in his cloak, settled himself to sleep. He slept but his dreams were troubled, for it seemed that he was shut into a great box, yet the walls of that box were as clear as a mountain stream, and through them he could see what happened.

Nimue stood before the box and she was laughing. Her hands moved in that sign of protection against sorcery which he had witnessed so many times in his childhood. He knew that he was her prisoner, yet in him was a mighty need to break forth and be about some demanding task.

Though he beat on the unseen walls of that box until his flesh was sore and bloody, still he could not win his freedom. And always he was haunted by the knowledge that he was failing in something of great and lasting importance.

Then the dream changed and there was Lugaid before him. The Druid lay sleeping on a bedding made of deerskin and dried leaves. But Myrddin stooped above him and laid his hand on the sleeper's forehead between his eyes. And he heard himself say: "I shall come."

At his words Lugaid's eyes opened to meet Myrddin's gaze. There was recognition in the Druid's face. And he spoke in turn, or at least his lips moved, but Myrddin could catch no meaning though he strained to hear.

Between them rose a wreathing of mist. Lugaid, seeing that, shrank away, motioning with his hand as if he would ward off some evil. The mist twisted to form a shadow face. Once more Myrddin saw Nimue laughing. Then he awoke.

He had half expected to find that strange girl standing over him as he had stood over the sleeping Lugaid. But he was alone and only the steady hum of the squares on either side of him broke the silence. But he knew well what was to be done. He must go to the Place of the Sun and make sure during the going that he was not trailed by anyone.

First he must have supplies and a sword. Though he was no trained warrior, he knew a little of the handling of a weapon and he was going into debatable territory where a lone traveler could have his throat slit for either the mountain pony he rode or the cloak on his back.

So, leading the horse he had brought from Ambrosius' camp, Myrddin went down the mountain ... to find desolation. For fire and sword had been here, days ago by the coldness of the ashes. Fighting nausea, he searched among the ruins, avoiding charred bodies, the dead men who had defended the walls. Too small a handful.... He wondered if Vortigen's kidnappers had been part of a larger band with orders to make very sure the clan of Nyren was wiped from the earth. There were only one or two women's bodies, and he guessed that they and the children had been taken off for sale as slaves.

But he found Julia. She had a broken spear still clasped in her death hold. By the signs she had died quickly; of a sword thrust, he thought. Bleak-eyed, he brought together the dead he could find into a shed still left standing. Bags dribbling grain lay there and of those he built a bier on which he put those of the kin, Julia at the very end.

Then he sought out a tinderbox and coaxed a spark to fire the bier, for he did not have the strength to bury them decently and he could not leave them for the car-rion-eaters. As the flames rose, he gathered together some moldy bread, a hunk of mouse-nibbled cheese and a water bottle he would fill at the stream. He did not look again at the flames reaching skyward. All he had known in the past was gone. No evidence of his childhood was left him, only the will to bring about the orders given in the cave.

So Myrddin rode away into a bitter dawning where the storm clouds were fast gathering. He breathed deeply, trying to drive from his lungs the smell of the clan house, just as he endeavored to close out of his mind what he had found there.

Even through the rain he rode forward, welcoming the wash of the storm against his body, because this was a thing of nature and not some ugliness of man's actions. And he wondered about the story the mirror had told. Had it really been true that man had known peace and such knowledge to maintain it with his fellows? If that was true, and he had no reason to doubt what he had been told, then if he could do anything to help return to that golden age, he would do it gladly.

Within him grew a deep hatred, not of those who had wrought the destruction at the clan house, for that was the nature of raiders. But rather his mind raged against those others who ranged the stars and had such powers as he could not even imagine, and yet who would withhold from man the wisdom to make him more than brute beast.

Were the Dark Ones jealous of the others, those who had chosen the way of earth? Or was it fear that moved them? Did they foresee that mankind was their enemy in some manner even as the wildcat and the hound were ene-mies from their births? If that was so, what quality could possibly lay within man to awaken a fear so deep among those who were his great superiors? Myrddin longed to be able to ask all this of the mirror. He would when he returned.

When he returned. . . . ?

He must twist his thoughts away from all such speculations, concentrate instead on weaving such a course toward his goal as would throw off any hunters. Because he was not trained in such evasions, he must make doubly sure that he did all he could.

So he kept apart from any dwelling, unless it was one of those ruins that men had abandoned long ago. Twice he spent a night in one, fireless and lightless, yet marveling at the building which still had signs of refinements of living that had never been known in the clan house. The boy stretched the food he had brought as far as he could and then snared a rabbit. At least he was woodsrover enough to do that, and bring down a duck with a slinger's good aim.

The meat he ate raw, forcing himself to such grisly meals because he dared light no fire. And never was he entirely free from the fear that he might indeed be followed. Twice he hid deep in bushes, his cloak tightly wrapped around his mount's head to stifle any whinny, while parties of horsemen trotted by. He thought they were levies who followed Ambrosius, but he could never be sure and wisdom told him to avoid any possible discovery.

Then, with the ache of hunger acute in him, and the drive of his own uncertainty heavy on him, Myrddin came at last to the plain and saw before him, as if wrought by some giant, the great standing stones. He had reached the Place of the Sun.

5.

Myrddin huddled in his cloak. Outside rain dripped from the roof of the rough hut, but within was a fire and between his hands a wooden bowl of steaming rabbit soup thickened with herbs. The door of the hut was only a curtain of hide at which the wind twitched now and again. He squatted in a daze of fatigue, still too tired to try to eat, though the smell of the food brought saliva flooding into his mouth.

Lugaid did not break the silence but sat cross-legged, fingering a fold of a robe now gray instead of white, one which was clumsily patched and much frayed. He who had once been given the seat of honor in the clan house was now like any beggar haunting the roads where men passed. But there was no beggar's whine in his voice, and the eyes which watched Myrddin were both serene and shrewd.

"Eat and sleep," the Druid said. "There is nothing here to threaten a man."

"How do you know that I am threatened?" Myrddin swallowed the soup he had scooped up in a wooden spoon.

"How did I know that you would come?" countered Lugaid. "The gods give men ways if they have the wit to use them. Did you yourself not forecast our meeting?"

Myrddin, remembering his dream, nodded. "I dreamed . . ."

Lugaid shrugged. "Who can say what is a dream? For it may well be a message sent or received. I think," he added slowly, "that you have learned very much, Son of a Stranger."

"I have learned . . ." Myrddin sipped again at the soup. He wanted to pour out all that had happened to him in that hidden cave, yet there was still a bridle set upon his tongue. Perhaps he would never be able to share what he

50

had discovered with anyone on this earth. "I have learned what has brought me to this place, for there is a task to be done here." At least he encountered no hindrance in saying that much.

"That I also knew. But not within this hour must you begin it. Sleep when you have eaten, for rest is also something which must be given any man."

And the sleep Myrddin had on the pile of leaves and hides within Lugaid's hut was dreamless, bringing no threat to make him restless. He woke to find the rain vanished, the sun full on his face. The hide of the doorway had been looped back to let in the day.

Through that door he could also see some of the standing stones of the Sky People, ring upon ring. And they were more strange than any ancient building of man, even those deserted ones in which he had taken shelter during his journey here. Between two of them now moved a figure robed in white. As it came closer he saw it was Lugaid, his beard, now whiter than his robe, untrimmed and growing down to his waist cord, while his mane of hair touched his shoulders.

Yet the Druid did not move like an old man, but rather with the firm step of one still in middle years. In his hands he carried a bag from which protruded leafed stems of plants. Myrddin guessed that he had been harvesting wild herbs and growing things, as he had often done when he had lived at the clan house.

The boy shook off the cloak which had been his covering. In place of the chill which yesterday's rain had brought, the sun now gave a gentle warmth. He was grateful as he stretched his cramped arms and got to his feet, ducking as he went out of the doorway of the hut. The passage was a low one, even for his slight height.

"Master," he greeted the Druid.

Lugaid shifted his bag. "You call me master, yet you are no follower of mine. There is something you want." The old man smiled. "Aye, you would ask something of me, and yet you know not just how to frame the words. But seek not for the pretty phrases. There need be no ceremony between us. I gave you your name on your birthnight."

"Aye," the boy repeated. "The name you gave me, Myrddin, I have heard it was once granted to a god of hills. There is another name which has also been set upon me, that being Merlin."

"Merlin." Lugaid said it slowly, as if he was trying the sound of it. "It is no name of the clan. Yet if it was granted to you, then it was done for a reason. So, Merlin-Myrddin, what is it you ask of me?"

"To gain me the ear of Ambrosius the Roman."

There was no astonishment to be read on the face of the Druid. He asked quietly: "For what reason do you seek the favor of Ambrosius? And why not speak for yourself?"

Myrddin answered the second question first, swiftly baring his story of Vortigen, the prophecy and his interview with Ambrosius thereafter.

"And you believe that he will not listen, thinking your wish smacks of sorcery? Does it?"

"If the old knowledge is sorcery, yes. But for this must I have his favor: a stone must be returned to this Place of the Sun, a stone which raiders carried to the Western Isle. It must be reset in its proper place."

Lugaid was nodding slowly before he had finished. "That tale I have also heard. But Ambrosius is one who deals with the things of this world, what can be seen, held, heard, tasted. Legends will not move him. However . . ."

"You know a way to reach his favor in this matter?" Myrddin's voice rose a little as the Druid paused.

"Perhaps. Even the Roman emperors of old had monuments raised to the triumphs of their arms in wars. And truly this stone is rightly of Britain, stolen from us. Were Ambrosius to win a notable victory, then, in the flush of rejoicing, he might be approached on this matter."

"That will need time. Fortune. Chance . . ." protested the boy.

"Youth is ever impatient. I have lived long with time. Enough to know that you must make it your servant, not let it be master. There is no way you can do this thing otherwise. For you cannot move a stone such as these"— the Druid waved his hand to the rings behind him—"except with men, a ship and warriors to clear a path for you. Do you believe those of the Western Isle will easily give up what they believe to be a powerful trophy?"

Myrddin strode back and forth, impatience eating at him. He had little faith in the Druid's suggestion. It rested on too many strokes of fortune which might go either way. Yet for all his tutoring by the mirror, at this moment he could see no other choice if Lugaid would not help him. Going again himself to Ambrosius after the firm dismissal he had received would gain him nothing.

He came to a stop and placed his hand on a tall blue stone set in the outer ring. Somehow through that touch there flooded into him a sense of age so great that it awed his spirit. Small crystals, pea-sized and cream in color, were sprinkled over the bluish surface. And it towered so that in the shadow of its bulk he felt dismay. He did not know the size of the stone he must seek, but if it were like this one, then half a hundred men, a hundred even, might not stir it.

No, Myrddin took hold on his confidence. Men with all their strength might not stir these from their beds. But the beings who had built this place had their own secrets and the mirror had given him some of them. Doubt now made him wish to try that power.

He looked beyond the stone he touched. The next in line had fallen and lay with tough, withered grass rising about it. He reached for his belt knife. No staff could serve him, not even one such as Lugaid carried cut from wood, even though that wood might be the sacred oak. His tool must be metal, and one which would give forth the right ringing tone.

Unsheathing the knife, Myrddin stooped to set its tip against the fallen stone. He began to tap, slowly, with a certain rhythm. And, as he tapped, he voiced the guttural sounds which the mirror's voice had made him repeat over and over again until he could give them the right inflection.

Faster and louder grew the tapping. His throat ached a little as he strove to utter sounds almost beyond the range of his own vocal chords. Suddenly he was aware that another chanting had joined his, that Lugaid was facing him across the bulk of the stone.

Tap—tap—his hand moved so fast, building up the sound's measures—thus and thus and thus—Myrddin's face grew shiny with sweat, his arm was weary, yet he would not surrender to the weaknesses of his body. Tap—chant—tap—

He was so intent on what he did that the first movement of the stone caught him nearly unaware. It was stirring in the furrow which its weight had caused when it toppled generations ago, stirring as some animal aroused from a long sleep.

Tap—chant—

The rock was rising, he had not been deceived! Yet he could not hold it so and, as his hand dropped, his wrist weak with the effort, the megalith settled back into its groove. Myrddin sank to his knees beside it, drawing his breath in long gasps, the strength gone out of him. If he had tried to move at that moment he would have measured his length beside that of the stone.

"Well done, Sky Son!"

His ears rang but not enough to deafen them to Lugaid's words. The Druid also leaned against the stone on the other side, gazing at Myrddin in astonishment.

"But," he continued, "you must have a better tool than a knife for this work." He swung around, still resting one hand to steady himself against the stone. "And you may gain it, if you are strong enough in spirit."

"Where?"

"From the grasp of those gone before." The Druid pointed to the low ring-mounds beyond the circle of stones. "For such did they work with in their own time. And when they died their tools were buried with them, for they were not to be fitted to the hands of lesser men."

"To take from the dead!" That part of Myrddin which was of his own world revolted from the suggestion. The dead were jealous of their treasures. Men must be very reckless, and without normal clan feeling, to break the rest of those gone before.

"You only take what they would give you if they were alive to put such a tool into your hand," Lugaid replied. "There are those resting here who are of Sky Blood also. And when a man dies, he lays aside one body for another, as worn-out clothing is dropped and forgotten. There are no guardians here, only methods to prevent such tools from coming into the wrong possession."

"But—" Myrddin struggled up, wavering, needing to cling to the stone to keep his feet. "A man could search a lifetime among all these graves and not find the right one."

"Like calls to like," Lugaid replied calmly. "Look." He touched the neck of his robe and, from beneath that covering, drew out a tiny bag of linen stained with sweat as if he had worn it a long time. He loosed the drawstring, which was also the thong to hold it suspended, and into the palm of one hand he shook a scrap of metal which gleamed almost with a jewel's fire. "Take it, feel it," he ordered. Reluctantly Myrddin held out his own hand, felt the Druid drop that scrap into it.

Then he brought it closer to his eyes, rolled the fragment across his palm with a fingertip. The thing was not bronze, he was sure, nor had it the softness of pure gold. With that coloring it could be neither tin nor iron nor silver ... perhaps like bronze it was a mixture of more than one metal, but if so he could not guess which. In color the scrap was a very light silver, yet across it, small as the piece was, there played a rainbow of colors, changing with the movement of the bit.

"That is of the Sky People," Lugaid told him. "We have not handled such material since the age before the world turned over. But if those who wrought this Place of the Sun lie here, then this shall let us know where any of its matter lies hidden. As those who have the gift seek for water with a rod and their own senses, so can this be used." He pulled up the hem of his robe and carefully unraveled a thread from its frayed edge. He tested the thread's strength by jerking it between his fingers.

Next he carefully tied it to the small fragment of metal and wound the other end of the string between two fingers, then held out his hand so the metal swung freely below. "Thus do we seek," he said.

Together they prospected the ring-mounds. Some were shaped like disks and some were circles, broken at one side or the other. They climbed each one, Lugaid's hands outstretched, the fragment dangling from the thread.

By nightfall Myrddin's confidence was broken. He was near to denying that there was any hope of Lugaid's device showing them some strange other-world tool. Yet the Druid seemed quietly content with their labors and his spirits, when they returned to the hut, were unshaken.

"If not today," he said as he fed bits of leaves into a pot he hung to boil, "then tomorrow."

"And tomorrow and tomorrow ..." the boy commented sourly.

"If necessary." Lugaid nodded. "Myrddin-Merlin, above all else you must learn patience, for you seem lacking in that. But so is ever the fault of youth."

"As you said before," Myrddin commented as he fed

their small fire with another stick, "I must wait for Ambrosius' possible favor, I must wait for searching by metal,
I must wait—perhaps too long!"

"I do not ask for the reason for your need." Lugaid
stirred the pot with vigor. "But now I do ask the need for
haste."

"There are two things I must do," the boy said, "though
why these have been laid on me, I do not know. I did not
ask to be born of a Sky Lord." He sat back on his heels,
staring moodily into the fire. "Little have I had of my heritage except trouble upon trouble."

"No heritage is free from that," observed Lugaid. "If
you were to lay aside your life's labor, then what would
you choose? The sword of a warrior with perhaps a quick
death, achieving nothing by your dying but the cutting
down of the life of another?"

Myrddin thought of the clan house as he had seen it
last. That was the fruit of war. That was the way of brute
man, the way to which his people were condemned unless
there was the promised change. He had no choice, being
who and what he was, except to carry the orders and the
burden laid on him by the voice of the mirror.

"I must do what I must do," he said heavily. "And if
this waiting is a part of it, then I must endure it. But I
have also been warned." He wondered if he could find his
tongue free to mention that other to Lugaid, since so
much of the mirror's knowledge was locked within his
silence. "There is"—he discovered that he could continue—"another abroad whose mission is to defeat what I
would do."

"One of the Dark Ones," Lugaid agreed.

Myrddin was surprised. How much did the Druid know
of that?

He saw Lugaid smile. "Ah, it is true that here"—he
tapped his forehead with one finger—"I have the lore of
old. Those who would be of our number must study the
lore for twenty years. Never can it be put in writing after
the manner of the Romans, but rather kept from one generation to the next by memory alone. Aye, there are the
Dark Ones who in the Sky times brought full measure of
trouble upon our world. That they, too, have their servants—what could be more believable? So there is a Dark
One sent to defeat you. Do you know the manner of the
enemy so you can be warned?"

"She is a girl." Without closing his eyes Myrddin had a sudden vision of Nimue standing on the mountainside, her fine hair lifted playfully by the wind, her gaze as intent as when the mirror had first shown her to him. "I know only that her name is Nimue, though of what clan or tribe or where she may be . . ." He shook his head.

"Nimue—a name of Power, for it was one given in the old days to a water goddess. I shall remember."

They ate in silence, each occupied with his own thoughts, and just as silently they lay down to sleep. Yet Myrddin felt a companionship which he had lacked before and a sense of well-being he had seldom known, except perhaps in the cave of the mirror. Nor did he dream.

As the sun broke on the next day they were back at their search. This time Myrddin went with more eagerness. Lugaid's belief in what he was doing seemed to be catching. And if patience was what he himself must cultivate, then the sooner he was about that, the better.

The sun was hot overhead as they climbed a ring-mound slightly larger than its neighbors. And that sun was reflected in small glitters, for the metal bit had begun to swing, moving ever faster. Lugaid laughed.

"Did I not promise that like would greet like? Here is given proof, boy!" He stamped the heel of his sandal on the turf which roofed the mound. "Beneath this lies what we seek."

He tucked the fragment into its hidden pocket and hurried back to the hut, returning with a bronze ax. "Since we lack a proper spade," he said, "this must serve, this and that knife of yours."

With a strength which belied his appearance of age, Lugaid straightaway cut into the root-bound turf. It was hard work, and they took turns at using the ax and scraping away the loosened soil with knife and large bowl. By sundown they had reached a length of massive stone which must roof in the grave space. Lugaid was clearing along that, seeking the end where they might find an opening.

The sun had gone; twilight was creeping in. Lugaid stood within the trench they had cut.

"Light! A torch! For we cannot leave this to the night!"

Myrddin straightened, his earth-stained dagger in his hand. He tossed aside another bowl of earth. Inwardly he knew that the Druid was right—they must not leave the

opened barrow during the night—though the human part
of him shrank from invading a place of the dead during
the hours of darkness.

Yet he laid aside his clumsy tools and hurried back
across the end of the blue stone circle, dodging among the
megaliths until he reached the hut. The fire, well covered,
still had its coals alive. The boy thrust two torches into the
embers, then swung them around his head, letting the air
feed their flames into life.

One in each hand, he hastened back intent only on
reaching the barrow. But his concentration was suddenly
broken by a sensation of alarm. Though he looked from
right to left and back again, he saw no movement among
the stones whose shadows were beginning to reach like
groping fingers over the earth. This wariness might only be
because of what they were going to do. He went more
slowly, however, and, as he went, he kept careful look
around him.

Once more at the digging, he drove the pointed ends of
the torches into the earth. By their flickering he could see
that Lugaid had not been idle during his absence, for the
end of the stone block had been reached, and now the
Druid was cutting his way down deeper to reveal whatever door might once have existed.

There was another stone set there, smaller but upright,
and it yielded to their combined leverage with the ax,
though the tool's metal broke into two pieces as the stone
moved. Myrddin squatted down, his smaller body better
fitted to the opening. Lugaid grasped the nearer of the
torches and brought the fire closer to give him light.

There were things within: jars, a brace of spears and
something wrapped in a covering which puffed into dust
when the air reached it. But Myrddin did not want to look
at that. Instead he searched for the gleam of metal, and
the fire suddenly revealed it.

With infinite care the boy thrust his arm in the opening
and groped until his fingers closed on something cold and
solid. He drew it toward him, bringing a sword out into the
light of the torches.

The blade could only be of the same alloy as that scrap
Lugaid treasured. Unpitted by time, straight and smooth
as if it had been forged within a year, it answered the
flames with a rippling of rainbow light. The hilt was wound
around with wire and a great dull jewel crowned the pom-

mel. Carefully Myrddin passed it to the Druid and then began pushing back the sealing rock with frantic haste.

"We must hide this," he panted. "Out there"—he did not turn his head above the trench they had tunneled—"from out there, we are watched!"

He heard the hiss of Lugaid's breath.

"Then take you this, boy, and go! Leave me the light. I shall close the barrow. But this must not be risked!"

He held out the sword and Myrddin took it once more, wishing he had his cloak to wrap that length of blade, for it seemed to gather light from the torches and reflect it again like some kind of lamp.

Holding the weapon tight against him, he ran down the side of the barrow, heading for the hut. And the knowledge that one watched among the stones was so clear that he expected, every step of his flight, to have a challenge hurled at him.

It could be some wandering tribesman, even a scout from a far-roving party of Saxons. And what he carried now, had they caught clear sight of it, would be booty enough to bring them down upon him. Yet he inwardly believed that the watcher was not any ordinary enemy.

He had left the door curtain looped up when he had gone for the torches. And that fire he had stirred to life was still flickering, making a well-marked oblong to guide him.

Myrddin was within ten paces of the doorway when a figure separated itself deliberately from one of the standing stones and ran fleetly toward him. The boy swung around to face that apparition. The hilt of the sword fitted into his hand as if the weapon had been forged for him alone. Its blade was far longer than the swords the Romans used, which he had seen among Ambrosius' host, more slender than those of any tribal making.

As he swung the sword before him the length gleamed, seemed to drip light and color. With it in his hand, Myrddin at long last knew what it meant to be a warrior, the fierce excitement that could grip a man with battle hunger. He did not realize he had bared his teeth, that he uttered a low cry.

But if he was prepared to blood the sword he had taken from the dead, he did not cut down that shadow unheedingly. For she stood within the full light of the doorway. And he knew her.

"Nimue!"

This time he not only saw her laugh but heard the ripple of that sound.

"Merlin!" There was mockery in the name as she said it.

6.

"Brave warrior." The girl's light mockery stung, setting him, in his startlement, a little off guard. "What would you now do, strike me to earth with that weapon of yours after the manner of fighting men in this dark land?"

Myrddin lowered the sword. She made him feel foolish, childlike. Since he knew her to be what she was, though, he must not let her remain in control of their meeting.

"Those who flit in the dark," he returned, "and come secretly so, must expect to see a bared blade awaiting them."

"Do you believe that iron will master me, Merlin? Do you still cling to the superstitions of your kind?" Her eyes glistened like a cat's in the light from the door. And she smiled. "Better waste your strength on such as them!" Nimue whirled and pointed back toward the stones from which she had come.

Things moved behind the rocks, things from a crazed man's nightmares. But Myrddin knew that they were not really there. Just as he had drawn on his own dawning powers to make the High King see dragons at war, so was she now striving to frighten him with illusions. As he looked at them and away again, they faded and were gone.

The smile vanished from her face and her lips flattened against her teeth. She hissed like a serpent or an angry cat.

"Do you think," she cried, "that you have *all* the learning of the Older Ones within *you*? You fool, it would take years upon years to even begin such studies. You are but a boy—"

"And you are a girl," he made steady answer. "No, I do not claim more learning than I have. But such play as that is for those who are totally ignorant."

She flung her head, so that her hair moved on her shoulders.

"Look on me," she commanded. "Look on me, Merlin!"

Her ivory skin shone with a glow of its own, her features altering subtly. Beauty flowed about her like a cloak. Suddenly there was the flowering wreath of the Midsummer Maiden on her head, the perfume of the blossoms reaching his nostrils. Her garment of green was gone, her slender body fully revealed to his eyes.

"Merlin . . ." Her voice was honey-sweet and low; it promised much. She came closer to him hesitatingly, as if she would touch him and yet some maiden fears kept her aloof. "Merlin," she crooned. "Put down that drinker of dead men's blood, come with me. There is more in this world than you have dreamed of. It awaits you. . . . Come!" She held out her hand.

Manhood stirred in him for the first time, hot and eager. He knew sensations he had never experienced before. The perfume of her flowers, the enticement of her body— his grip on the hilt of the ancient sword was not so tight. All of him which was of the earth wanted her.

"Merlin, they have deceived you," she said softly. "This is life, not what they would make it for you, shutting you apart from everything within you, straining now for freedom. Come to me, learn what it is to be truly alive! Come, Merlin!"

She raised both her arms, held them out to him, inviting his embrace. Her eyes were slumberously heavy, her mouth curved, waiting for his kiss.

"Merlin . . ." Her voice faded to a whisper, a promise of things he only dimly understood.

It was the sword which saved him. Its cold length brushed against his leg as he nearly dropped it. From that touch came a kind of shock which alerted him to her enchantment. He spoke only one word:

"Witch!"

Once more her eyes glittered. The flower wreath disappeared and she was again covered by her rough green robe. Now she stamped her foot and the hands she had reached out to him became claw-like, extended to rip the flesh from his bones.

"Fool!" she cried loudly. "You have made your choice and you must abide by it from this hour forth. Between us there is only war, and do not think that I will be a weakling as a foe! At each triumph you shall find me waiting, and if my strength does not prevail tonight, there will be other days . . . and nights. Remember that, Merlin!"

As she had come out of the night, so did she mesh back into it, mingling so quickly with the shadows that he could not truly have said where she went. And with her went that feeling of being watched. Now he knew that he was free, for a while at least, so he drew a deep breath of relief.

But he waited for a long moment, listening, testing with that other sense the mirror had taught him to use. No, she was gone. There was nothing here but that sensation of long-ago Power which was the nature of the Place of the Sun. For where men have worshipped with their whole hearts—where they have wrought things that are unseen, unheard and cannot be grasped in hand, only in mind and heart—there remains forever the breath of that Power, diminished perhaps by the long passing of time, yet nonetheless abiding.

Holding the sword with both hands, Myrddin entered the hut, set about building up the fire. He kept the weapon ever by his side as he sought out food, put some of the coarse porridge which was Lugaid's principal food in the pot to boil. As he worked he listened for the coming of the Druid, eager not to be left alone.

Not that he feared Nimue. He did not believe she could call up any strength to outweigh what he himself could summon. But her first attack was one he had not foreseen. He fought resolutely now against the picture which memory kept presenting of Nimue ivory pale in the night, of that slumberous, beguiling voice. Not for him was any woman, that he understood. He must have no ties such as were the right of his human heritage, lest those ties blind him to the purpose which was meant to fill all his days.

"Who has been here?"

Myrddin was startled out of his inner turmoil by that sharp demand. Lugaid had looped back the door curtain, stood tall and frowning within the opening.

"How did you . . . ?" the boy began.

"How did I know? By what Power I have learned! There is a hostile force awake this night. Yet it is not any guardian aprowl." The Druid's nostrils expanded as he turned his head slightly, half looking over his shoulder.

The skirts of his robe were heavily plastered with earth, his hands battered and bruised, soil caked under the nails.

"She was here, Nimue," Myrddin said.

"Ah, that is evil hearing! Did she see the sword?"

"Aye. She—she strove to bind me to her." Myrddin felt ill at ease, yet to share this with the Druid was to lighten somehow the burden of that memory, help to banish it from his mind.

"Like that, was it?" Lugaid nodded. "Aye, that would be the beginning with her. Perhaps if you had been older ... No, I do not think she could reach you so. But be warned, now that she is on your trail you will not find her easy to put aside. The Dark Ones have their own Power and the beguiling of men is a large part of it. Yet I do not think she can come nigh or weave her spells too well when you have a hand on that." He pointed to the sword.

"But as you have said, time may be growing short. I had not realized it. Thus I shall do as you have asked of me—I shall go to Ambrosius."

Myrddin knew a sudden surge of relief. He sensed how dangerous it would be to linger too long here where Nimue had tracked him. Yet this was partly his own place. He felt a strange kinship with the stones, as if they had once possessed some life of their own and had given him some heritage with them.

The boy slept with the sword against his body that night, one hand lying on its hilt. And if the girl who had come to him in the dark strove to weave any spell about his dreams, she did not succeed, for he did not dream at all. Instead he awoke with the day not only refreshed but more confident that what he must do would indeed be done.

Lugaid rode away on the pony Myrddin had brought out of the hills. The boy saw him go before visiting two of the snares the Druid had set. He was lucky; both held game. He toasted meat on an improvised spit and ate lustily.

Later he fashioned a rude scabbard from sections of tree bark bound together with rags torn from his cloak and so wore the sword constantly in the daytime. Its marvelous blade hidden from view, he slept beside it at night. For hours he wandered among the stones, setting his hands at times to one or another, feeling a kind of renewal of spirit rise in him from that touch.

For the first time he thought objectively about the training of the mirror. Much of what he had been told by that bodiless voice he could not use, for the metal wonders of the Sky People could no longer be made on his own world. These required too much in the way of special learning. What he had absorbed was, he guessed, only a very small portion of the knowledge which had once been common to his kind.

He could summon illusions as he had for Vortigen, hold them for a short space. He knew a little of healing, not only through the use of herbs from the fields and woods, but also by the laying on of hands and an ability to "see" the source of others' ills of mind or body. Thereafter, he might concentrate on rebuilding that which had been injured or harmed through sickness. But such an art required in return the belief of the victim that he could so be healed. And Myrddin doubted whether many now living could retain that belief. It was too close to what men looked down on, naming it sorcery.

He had been given the magic of tongues so that he could listen to the speech of a stranger and, by concentrating on the sounds, sort out in part the thoughts which had given birth to the words. He knew the magic of weightlessness—he had briefly applied it in this very place to the fallen stone—and he would have to draw on it in full if he was going to complete the task set him.

Now, as he wandered among the stones, he evaluated his learning critically. Perhaps he had more than Lugaid, but his knowledge was far less than it might have been had his race not fallen so far back into barbarism. He knew this, and it created a feeling of frustration within him. It was like standing in the door of a hall rich in treasure, knowing that the treasure was freely given to any man who might lay a hand on it, yet not having the power to cross the barrier between himself and the hall.

Yet he drew comfort from the stones, anticipation from the sword he wore with its bark concealment well lashed about it. And he often wondered for whom that weapon of the Sky metal had actually been forged. Had that other been one like himself, the son of no father? For the voice had shown him enough of the wonders of that other age to let him know that the Sky People did not fight so, man against man, face to face. Rather they commanded lightning flash and thunderbolt to slay horribly from a distance. He had shuddered and been vilely ill when the mirror had once reflected a clear picture from the final days when the world itself, so deeply injured by the wrath of being against being, had burst forth with inner flames. Seas boiled, mountains and land rose and fell as Myrddin himself might now idly toss a clod of soil about.

The boy longed to try the power of the sword and the chant, to return to its upright base one of the fallen stones. However, caution held him from such a trial. He did not know whether using his gift could recall Nimue, so he waited with a patience he schooled into himself for the return of the Druid.

It was spring now, though he had lost the strict measurement of days. The grass about the stones took on a new greenness, as fresh blades pushed up to hide the brittle skeletons of those frost had killed. He found small flowers budding, some already in bloom. Birds were in song, and twice he watched quietly as fox and vixen leaped and played among the stones. In himself there was a restlessness he tried to subdue. Twice he dreamed of Nimue, and awoke with a feeling of shame that his own self wished to betray what was the most steadfast in him. And always he watched the faint trace of path down which Lugaid had gone.

He counted off the days by putting small stones in a line from the hut door. And it was when he had put down the fifteenth of those that the Druid returned. He did not ride alone but headed a company of six spearmen of the tribes, who lagged behind as they approached the Place of the Sun, sending glances of uneasiness at the standing stones.

Lugaid gave a grunt of relief as he slid from the back of the pony. He raised a hand in greeting as Myrddin ran toward him, for that moment all boy in his excitement and relief.

"It is well?" he demanded as he neared the Druid. But there was no lighting of the other's face and Myrddin slowed, looking uncertainly beyond at the men who clustered now together, not dismounting, but rather looking like they would boot their horses into a gallop to be free of this place at the slightest excuse.

"Only in part," Lugaid returned. "Ambrosius is dead."

Myrddin came to an abrupt stop. "How did he die—in battle?"

"Not so. He died by the will of that she-wolf from

overseas, though her hand reached from the grave to do it. For she and her High King had perished in the flames of their clan tower only one day earlier. The fate she had sent to her enemy still reached him through the hands of one of her maids. The truth was known too late."

A death in battle, Myrddin thought, like his clan kin, would have been fitting. Such an ending as this was a blackness for Ambrosius, who had deserved a clean severence of his life's cord with good sword steel.

"Peace on him," said the boy softly. "He was one whose like we shall not see again." Something stirred in him which was perhaps a fragment of memory. But it was not yet time for that to ripen into action and it was quickly gone.

"Aye, he was a hero. And as a hero he will lie here!" Lugaid pointed to the Place in the Sun. "Your quest comes oddly to fruiting, Myrddin. Ambrosius' half brother now leads the war host. He is of the tribes in his ways and so would follow the old pattern. I have spoken to Uther, who men now call Pendragon, and he is willing that the Stone of Kings be brought from the hold of the overseas barbarians back to Britain again, that it may mark the grave of a hero."

Odd indeed were the quirks of fate. At that moment, great as Myrddin's desire was to fulfill the order he had been given, he wished as strongly that it might have come about in another way and that death had not been a part of it. He tried to remember Uther and summoned up only a fleeting mind-picture of a tall young man, his red-gold hair on his shoulders after the old fashion, his face ruddy, his mouth curved in laughter. But in that picture dwelt little of the force which he had felt in the dark, clean-shaved, Roman-seeming Ambrosius.

"We ride for the coast with this guard the King has sent. There shall be a ship waiting, and with it a company of warriors. For it may be that we must fight our way to the stone, buying it back in blood," the Druid was continuing.

Myrddin shook his head slowly. "I would we did not take it by force. . . ."

Yet he knew that in the end they would do whatever they must to get the Stone of Kings.

As they journeyed Lugaid told him more of the new ruler.

Ambrosius had never claimed that title, holding strictly to the one granted by the Emperor overseas, *Dux Britanniae*. But it seemed with Vortigen dead, his forces crushed or withdrawing sullenly from the field after an overwhelming defeat, Uther was willing to reach his hand for the High King's crown and no man protested.

"He has the tribes declaring for him," Lugaid remarked, "more so than they would for one of Roman blood. Yet those who followed his brother will also cleave to him, since he is now the only hope left. The Saxons have suffered such a pounding as they will not forget for a space. Still, I think Pendragon's men will ride often and swords will not rest long or easily in their sheaths.

"Uther has all the virtues, and also the faults of the tribes. Because he is a mighty fighter, they will follow him as they have always followed an open-handed hero. But such a hold on one's men is hard to keep. He lacks, I think, the deep-rooted fervor of his brother. Ambrosius knew only one task in all his life, to restore safe rule to Britain, though he was wrong in believing that it would come again from Rome. The day of emperors overseas is done. We fight our own battles and do not expect to see the Eagles march again along the roads they built."

"You find some flaw in Uther?" They had drawn apart from their escort and those warriors appeared very content to let them go at a distance, as if they did not desire close company with the Druid and his companion.

"No more flaw than lies in any man who is apt to follow his own desires too much. Just now Uther's desire is to forge a disturbed land into a peaceful one under his hand. Thus his wish serves a good purpose. But in the future . . ." Lugaid shrugged. "I do not try to read a man's fate too deeply; therein lie the seeds of despair. It is enough that he has given you your chance, Sky Son, to do what you feel must be done."

Myrddin was sure that Lugaid was evasive and had some uneasiness. He did not press. As the Druid had said, it was enough that Uther was minded to give them this chance to snare the King Stone.

They had a good wind to take them across the channel to the Western Isle. There they made harbor in a small bay with no sign of man. For the first day it was as if they traveled through a deserted land, though the men of the company were constantly wary and sent scouts ahead.

This was their power, that of battle, and they knew it well.

It was near noon on the second day when a scout came pounding back with the news that he had marked an ambush in a narrow glen. His wariness saved them, for the men dismounted and slunk through the countryside using any cover offered, until they were able to ambush those in turn and the battle became a bloody rout. Myrddin and Lugaid saw only the hurt bodies which they tended. But the trained attack of their escort brought in a prisoner of note.

He held his head high, though a gash in his face had opened like a second mouth and his sword arm was broken.

"Patch him up so he will live," the captain of their force advised. "For this is Gilloman who claims to rule that mountain land where the King Stone now stands. With him in our hands we can perhaps strike a goodly bargain."

But the young ruler spat on the ground at their feet and tried to laugh, though he could not do it well because of his hurt face.

"Are you giants?" he mouthed. "You do not look like giants, but like men even smaller than my people. If you strive to uproot the King Stone and take it hence you will fail."

"For that matter," Myrddin answered him, "we shall wait and see. But your hurt we tend now."

At first it seemed that he would struggle in their hands even though they meant him good. But at last he surrendered. Lugaid set the bones of his arm, binding the limb tight between two lengths of wood. And Myrddin put a plaster of herbs over the gash in his face. While he held it so the boy concentrated his will on the uniting of the torn flesh as the voice from the mirror had said how to do it.

And even if the prisoner did not believe, he looked oddly at Myrddin, saying: "What manner of youth are you? The pain is gone out of my flesh. There is true healing in your hands."

"It is my gift, even as battle might is your gift, King. And I would not have your death. Listen to a bargain: if I can move this stone, lift it from off the ground by the efforts of my hands and the summoning of my voice, then will you swear a truce for your people and let us take the stone to Britain without raising weapons against us again?"

Once more Gilloman strove to laugh. "No man living can keep that bargain. So if it is not some jest, then I give my bond of honor. Lift the stone by hand and voice and I shall bespeak my people. They will give you safe conduct to it. But when you fail, then stand ready to meet our attack."

"It is well," was Myrddin's answer.

Thus they rode across the country and on both sides, and behind and before, gathered those who had kind bond with Gilloman, ready to cut them down at the failure of the trial Myrddin had taken on himself. There came the day when he fronted not a single stone, but a dozen such, some set end in earth and towering, others lying prone. Yet he did not hesitate but walked swiftly among them until he came to one of middle size. It bore on its side a carving he knew well—the spiral circle of the Sky People.

He freed the sword from its covering of bark and the sun struck rainbows of light from it, so that he heard all those watching murmur. He raised the sword over the stone, not edge down, but rather so that the flat of the blade would meet its surface. Then he began to tap slowly while he chanted, this time finding it easier to reach those lower, more guttural notes which he sought. Faster grew the tapping, deeper the notes of his chant. And the flash of light from the moving sword veiled both blade and the hand which held it.

Now the sound of metal on stone was almost continuous, so that one could not detect the pauses when the sword was raised, so fast did Myrddin strike. And the growl of his chant mingled with the ring of the sword so that the sound made a whole which could not be divided one from the other.

The stone moved, raised from its earth bed. Yet Myrddin did not pause, only beat out his furious rhythm, singing stronger, deeper. With the stone so raised, he did not reach down to strike any longer, but his arm was held at shoulder level as he kept up the beat.

He began to pivot, moving slowly, scarcely a quarter of an inch at a time. The stone also swung with him until it was crosswise of the furrow in which it had lain. Now he took one step and another, and with him came the stone. He had no eyes for anything but it and the flash of the

sword. And in this moment he held back the weariness of
his body, putting all his will and determination into what
he would do.

On he moved and, through the air, well off the ground,
came the stone, controlled by the vibrations as the mirror
had told him might be done—given the right stone, the
right metal to use. Thus he passed from among the other
standing stones and brought his burden a little way down
the slope.

Then Myrddin lowered the sword and the stone settled
under it, lying once more on the earth. He raised his blade
and held it quiet and his voice, hoarse and strained, was
stilled. But he looked beyond the length of the block to
where Gilloman stood.

The face of the young ruler was practically covered
with bandages; above them his eyes were wide and filled
with awe. Now he raised his hand in salute.

"You have done what I would have sworn no man
could accomplish, save one of the God-born Heroes. As I
bargained so shall it be. Since the King Stone comes to
your summons it is free to go, and you and your men with
it. I know not the source of your magic, but I wish it well
out of my land, for it is hard to live under the threat of
such Power."

Thus did Myrddin win the King Stone without further
bloodshed. And so it was brought back to Britain, to rest
in the place from which it had been drawn so long ago. It
was raised openly to the glory of Ambrosius—yet
Myrddin knew that it had another use also, and one he
must strive to discover in the days to come.

7.

~~~~~~

Uther Pendragon was High King and there was a measure of peace in Britain. Myrddin stood in the Place of the Sun. Although the King Stone lay where it must be placed for the purposes of those he served—and he knew he served them blindly—yet his task was not finished. For Uther, as Ambrosius before him, was not the king he sought.

Lugaid had been right. Although Uther had the virtues of his warrior blood, he also had its faults. Quick to anger, his control over that anger was not contained with such iron bonds as Ambrosius had in his time set upon himself. Handsome, hot-tempered and hot-blooded, he was one to follow his own desires. Now he came riding out of the morning to front Myrddin across the King Stone.

He waved back his shield companions so that he stood alone and there was puzzlement open in his face as he faced the youth.

"You are he whom they call Myrddin?" he asked abruptly, as if he could not believe that.

"I am he."

"Yet you are but a youth. How can such as you be this prophet, this one who moves rocks by his will and the tapping of a sword? Who are you in truth?"

"I have been told I am son of no man," Myrddin returned. "As for my gift, it was given to me for a certain purpose, first that the King Stone return into its place for the good of this land."

Uther set his hands on his hips; his chin was thrust forward a little as if he were about to utter a challenge.

"Who are you to decide the good of Britain? You have not even bloodied that sword of yours in her service, if rumor speaks true." He nodded toward the blade, once more hidden by its bark trappings, where it hung from Myrddin's belt.

72

"The sword is not mine, lord. I only hold it guardian for a space. And my gifts are other than the gifts of war."

"I have heard that you prophesy. If that is true, tell me if Pendragon has won!"

"He has won," agreed Myrddin. "Yet shall the white dragon return and return again. Lord King, hammer this land into one kingdom, if you would rule in truth.

Uther nodded. "That needs no prophecy, boy. It is only what any man knows must be done. Tell me something which I cannot foresee for myself. My brother did not like sorcery, and those of the belief of the Christus, who now come into the land, say such is of the Dark and should be driven out. I am of two minds yet, boy. Tell me something I can believe and I shall give protection in return, a place for you at my hall, honor due—"

Myrddin shook his head. "Lord King, I am not for courts nor the honors you offer. Your brother once said to me that as a warrior I might ride with him, but as a prophet I had no place among his liege men. If you lean even the slightest on my words, then this fear of theirs will touch you also. It is better you have no such forces of dissension in your court. But you have asked for a foreseeing, and I shall give you one:

"You will breed an heir, but do this in a hidden fashion. And he will be such a king as this land has not seen since the days of the Emperor Maximus, perhaps even greater than that one who seized the Purple and made us safe for a space. His name shall be remembered through the centuries. And if he does as he is designed to do, then shall this land be blessed above all others of the world."

"Most men breed sons," Uther returned, "if they have not daughters. And who will come after me—that is of no matter now. Nor shall *I* know to prove you true or false. Do better than this, sorcerer, if you would show your magic."

"Lord King, do you expect me to summon a clap of thunder, or turn your men yonder into a pack of hounds? I deal not with what you call magic but with Old Wisdom. This much I can say: before next year winds to its end you shall have a use for me. When that moment comes let your messenger ride to where stood the clan house of Nyren and there among its ruins light a fire. I shall answer to your sending."

Uther laughed. "Boy, I cannot think what use I would have for you. It seems to me that your talents are small ones, mainly dealing with illusions and making men see what is not. You are right that my men are mistrustful of your magic and you are better apart. I do not know what manner of man you will make when your years are ripe, but I think that we cannot deal easily together, you and I."

He swept his cloak about him and walked away. Myrddin watched him go but in those moments he had a flash of vision. That tall man in his scarlet cloak, his bronze armor, was suddenly bent and shrunk, his face drawn and bluish, his strong-muscled arms hardly more than sticks over bone; death looked from his eyes. Not in battle would death come to Uther, Myrddin knew in that moment of other sight, but by treachery and slow degrees. And he would have called after Uther in warning, but he knew any words he spoke would be shrugged aside.

He sighed, thinking his a perilous gift if it would show him what he could not aid; he would be better off without it if he could see a man's death lying behind his face and had to keep still about it. But he did not turn away at once from the King Stone, rather rested his hand on its surface and wondered mightily what there was about this one stone, out of the many in this place, that made it so necessary to the purposes of the Sky People. The mirror had told him it was a beacon, but he could not understand its properties as such. He only knew that it held within it the same feeling of leashed energy he had sensed in many of the other stones of this place.

Lugaid was waiting for him when he trudged back to the hut. The Druid had made a bundle of Myrddin's few possessions. He held the pony bridled and ready for riding.

"You must go."

The abruptness of that startled the boy.

"Why?"

"There is a seeking now reaching toward this place. You have done what those of the Dark did not want you to, therefore they may well seek to end your life before you can accomplish anything further. Last night there were Shadow Dancers among the circles. As yet none has the power to take substance from the stones to build a body. But I think they shall return as long as you linger here. And with each of their visits they shall grow stronger, until they can indeed prove a threat against body as well as mind.

"I have not asked you the source of the power you have learned to use. Nor, I think, will that be given me to know. But now I warn you, Myrddin, go to that place and thereby renew your own strength. For that which has taught you must have defenses beyond the weaving of our race and, I hope, may be impervious to penetration by the Dark Ones."

"Come with me!" Myrddin said impulsively.

The Druid shook his head. "To each his own. What you have found is for your use alone because you are of the breed you are. No, I shall remain here."

"And the Shadow Dancers, then?" Myrddin turned to look down the avenues of standing stones. Under this sun there were slight shadows reaching from the foot of each, that was true, but there was no threat or mystery in them. He knew what Lugaid spoke of those things which Nimue had threatened him with on the night of their meeting.

"I am no fit prey for them, being of little account in the game they have been sent to play. Just as I am of little account in what you must do."

Myrddin thought of the loneliness of the cave, its nearest neighbor being the destroyed clan house, which he never wished to look on again.

"You are not of small account to me," he said. "To live only with the wild things among the high places, that is little to look forward to."

"There speaks fear," Lugaid replied sternly. "Each man walks his own road in his life; only a few times may he reach out and in truth touch another. You, being who you are, must accept that you stand alone in this world. If you would have company of your kind, then do what you are lessoned in doing."

So Myrddin rode from the Place of the Sun, leaving behind him a newly set stone among the many, and holding in him the stark knowledge that indeed he could look for nothing but loneliness, as was the lot of one who would use the Old Power. He went back to the hillside with its cleft entrance by ways which were little traveled.

It was far more difficult for him to force an entrance to the cave this time, for his body had grown. At length he won into the inner chamber where the installations still clicked and purred. Tired in both body and mind, he settled down before the mirror.

"You have returned," the voice observed, speaking as monotonously as ever. "And that beacon is now in place. So far you have answered to your birthright."

Myrddin did not know how the mirror could know of his success, unless, by some art similar to sorcery, it picked the thoughts from his mind. And he did not like that suggestion. Was he only the servant of this alien thing, a slave not allowed any desires or actions of his own? Ill then was his birth, for no man should be born subject to a destiny he could not choose nor change.

"It is done," he answered the mirror voice tonelessly.

"Rest, and wait," chimed the voice in return. And at once it seemed to Myrddin that he was freed from some compulsion he had not even been aware of carrying. He blinked and stretched like one who had awakened from a long sleep filled with dreams. Then he turned and edged out of the chamber of the mirror, filling his lungs with the fresh air of the mountain winds.

He did not return to the ruined clan house. Instead he fashioned a small hut, partly of stone, partly of branches. The high point of summer came and he busied himself with the matter of food and stores for the winter. He found herbs and growing things which he could harvest; and he hunted a wild cow, perhaps lost from the ravaging of the clan house, killed it and smoked the meat.

When the ravens gathered to pick the hide he had flung over a bush, a wild cat and her kitten moved in to dispute their ownership by feline hissing and growls. The ravens screamed their battle cries in return, greedy for all they could get. Myrddin watched the engagement until the hide was picked clean of all remnants of flesh. Then he scraped and worked it as best he could. Thereafter he left the offal of any animals he took in hunting for his feathered and furred neighbors.

It was a strange life, far removed even from the comforts the clan house provided. He grew lean and spare, taller, darker of skin where the sun burned him. There came the day when he used the newly honed edge of his belt knife to shave down off his lip and chin, at the same time hacking away his hair so it grew no longer than his earlobes.

His tunic and breeches were too small so he fashioned

new breeches, awkwardly, from the crudely tanned hide, using the thicker portions to make sandals. He tore the sleeves from his tunic and wore it loosely around the upper part of his body.

Now the short summer was drawing to a close. He must prepare for the cold months. Though he hated the task, he climbed each morning after sunrise to a point from which he could look down at the clan house. He was too far aloft to see much of the ruin and desolation which had taken the domain of Nyren, but he made sure that the signal he had asked of Uther was not set.

Almost reluctantly he also made visits to the mirror, but there were few times when the voice spoke to him and some of the questions he asked went unanswered. At last he was driven to chanting as he worked, fixing in his mind the lore from past learning sessions and exercising a voice he had little use for.

One day he found one of the raven kind with its foot trapped in a twist of briar, croaking its terror to the world. Freeing the creature in spite of its frenzied pecks, some of which drew blood, he found its foot broken and tended the bird as he would the victim of man's blood lust.

When at last the raven mended, the bird seemed unwilling to depart wholly to the wild. It would often fly to a perch near the log Myrddin had drawn up at the door of his hut and which he used for a work place, weaving baskets from osiers brought from a mountain lake, grinding some half-wild grain from a weed-run field.

Myrddin named the raven Vran and was surprised at the creature's response to his own tentative offers of food and his attempts to echo the bird's harsh cries. After a while, when he appeared from out of the hut in the morning, Vran would wing to him, darting down to perch on his shoulder and cackle in softer tones, as if in some unknown speech, into the boy's ear.

That winter was harsh and Myrddin, on the days of the worst storm winds, withdrew into the cave of the mirror. He had to pry and pick away at the crevice to force the doorway, his shoulders had grown so squared, his height increased. Vran disappeared, seeking out some shelter of his kind, and the boy missed his company.

He did not approach the mirror, for he felt a certain constraint now, as if this were not the time when he was to use the installation from the stars. In fact some of the lights across the cubes no longer appeared. He wondered, almost with a stab of panic, if they would ever work again, or if the mirror was growing old after a fashion, its power waning.

The days were no longer marked by any numbering of time. Myrddin had tried to keep a calendar of stones as he had by Lugaid's hut; but after a storm had dislodged a score of them and he could not remember their exact number, he did not attempt to renew them. There were days when he ate only one light meal and drowsed away the rest of the hours in a lethargy which was not normal.

At least no one troubled the peace of the mountain. In all the time since his return he had seen no human being. Nor had his special sense warned him that he was being watched, as it had when Nimue had stalked him.

He wondered where she was and what she might be doing. The uneasiness of that wondering aroused him to the thought that perhaps he might be well engaged in trying to track her, just as she had tracked him. But when he at last asked that of the voice of the mirror, the answer came quick and emphatic:

"Do not approach any who serve those Others, for they will lead you to battle and the time for that is not yet."

Myrddin was about to turn away from the question bench when the voice spoke again:

"The time is nigh now for your second task. Listen well. There must be a child born, even as you were born, one of our blood, unflawed. But all men must believe that he is of the High King's begetting. When you are asked to aid Uther in this matter, you shall use the powers given you. Let the King believe that he lies with the woman of his choice and enjoys her favors for a night. Let the woman believe that she entertains her lord. But within her chamber you must open the window and leave her alone.

"Thereafter, when the child is born, you must take him, telling the King that he will be in danger, for there are those who want their ruler to have no true heir. And you must hide the child carefully, as a fosterling, with a lord to the north, one Ector. Let that one believe that you have fathered the babe. For he is one who knows of the Old Race and you shall give to him the sign of recognition. In his veins, though much thinned by time and many generations, is a portion of our blood and like will greet like.

"Be ready when the King's messenger comes, that you may do this thing. For this child shall be the hope of your land, and our hope also. Only when a king of our kin reigns here in peace will the bonds be strong enough to bring about our return."

"When shall this happen?" Myrddin dared to ask.

"With the coming of spring. Use now your powers of illusion, work with them day after day, until you can use them as easily as a well-trained warrior can wield his sword. For such are your weapons and only by them can you fashion what we must have."

So Myrddin woke from the dreamy acceptance of passing days, one so like another that he could not have said that was yesterday, this is today, this tomorrow. And he flexed his powers as a fighter flexes his muscles before a contest.

He created his illusions on the nearby hillside, making them as lifelike as he could. One day he had a dark and foreboding forest around the entrance to the cave. The next he banished the darkness to lay down a fair meadow in which the flowers of early summer swayed beneath the caress of the wind. Then he fashioned people. Nyren walked there, his war cloak swept back, the chain mail rings of bronze sewn on his leather jerkin, shining brightly. He smiled as he came, raising his hand in friendly salute.

The struggle to hold such an image so that it did not appear as a shadow but as a living thing was the hardest task Myrddin had yet to learn. It tired him more than had his ordeal of raising the King Stone in the Western Isle. But the more he used that power, the more his strength grew, the more solid and lifelike became his illusions. Yet he could not be sure that he could hold them as well for others as he was able to do for himself.

Then he used Vran, who fluttered back to him as the spring advanced. He pictured a sheep butchered and skinned on the ground and the raven, with an ear-splitting shriek, settled on it, strove to tear the flesh. Then, giving a honk of surprise, the raven wheeled upward again when the sheep faded into a bush.

Daily Myrddin tested and wrought his illusions until the morning when, climbing to his point of vision, he at last saw smoke rising from the destroyed clan house. Waiting only to take up the bark-wrapped sword, he strode quickly down the faint path he had never wanted to travel again, to see through the gap of the smashed outer gate the men who stood by the signal fire. One of them he knew—Credoc, Uther's own shield man. That he should be sent on such an errand made Uther's great desire obvious. And Myrddin realized that the time had come of which the voice had warned him.

He knew that to these men in their rich cloaks, their fine linen tunics, their wealth and ornaments, he must look like a beggar of the wilds, a woodwose or some strange thing out of the hill legends. But he came proudly, knowing that only he could foster the King's desire, even though he would do it by trickery.

"You are Myrddin?" Credoc's disdain was plain to read.

"I am. And the High King wishes my services," Myrddin answered composedly. "The life in the hills, my lord, is not a soft one."

"So it would seem!" Credoc did not quite sneer openly, but his eyes and tone condemned what he saw, though Myrddin cared nothing for that.

But he was more suitably clad, in fresh tunic, cloak and trousers of clan check when he rode into the King's city. Years of neglect, other years of Saxon raiding, had done much to reduce to ruin what had once been a goodly port. But certain buildings had been repaired and the largest of these was snug-walled. It even had a look of splendor on the inside, where hangings of needlework covered most of the deficiencies.

Myrddin was taken to an inner chamber. Uther sat on the end of a bed whose tumbled coverings had not yet been straightened, as if the ruler had just risen from sleep, though the morning was well advanced.

"Ho, prophet." Uther drank from a silver-mounted horn cup and then passed that to a waiting boy, signaling him to refill it from a jar of foreign wine. "You spoke the truth on the day of our last meeting. I have indeed found a use for you. And if you serve me well in this, you may name your own reward. You," he said, turning on the others in the chamber, "get you hence, all of you. I would speak in private to this prophet."

"Lord King, he is a self-confessed dealer in magic," Credoc protested.

"I care not! Such magic as he has wrought to my knowing has been for the good of this land. Not notably so, of course, but at least to no one's hurt. Now leave me."

They obeyed, with visible reluctance. But the High King waited until they had gone before he spoke, and then only in a low voice which would not carry to the walls of the chamber.

"Myrddin, you dealt once in illusion, as you told my brother. Saying that men see what they want to see. Have women also this failing?"

"It is my belief that they do, Lord King."

Uther nodded vigorously. He was smiling, taking small sips from the refilled horn. "Then I wish you to create an illusion for me, prophet. Lately was I crowned here before the host of those who have long followed me. And not the least of those lords is Goloris out of Cornwall. But he is a man of age, still sturdy enough to answer the war horn most likely, but yet not one to satisfy a young wife as he should. And he has such a wife, the Lady Igrene, near a daughter to him by years. This lady—she is the fairest I have ever seen. Though I have bedded many women—and all of them came to me willingly enough—yet never have I seen her like! When I tried to speak her fair she would have none of me, but rather tattled to her lord so that he most rudely withdrew from my court, saying no farewells, in such a manner as to put shame on me!" Now Uther's face flushed and he spoke with his lips tight against his teeth in anger.

"No man or woman shall so shame the High King, that others may titter behind their hands! I have already sent my guard into Cornwall to make that plain to Duke Goloris. But his lady—aye, that is another matter. I would hold her within my arms so that she may know how a king can love. The Duke has been enticed from his stronghold but the lady is safe, he deems, within. Now tell me, prophet, how can I come to her bower or she to my chamber?"

"You spoke of illusions, Lord King. There could perhaps be woven an illusion so secure—for perhaps the space of a night—that the lady would think her lord had returned to comfort her. Yet it would only be the outer semblance of the Duke. . . ."

Uther threw back his head to utter a roar of laughter. He was, Myrddin saw, well heated with the wine. "A famous jest, prophet! And one which pleases me. You swear this can be done?"

"For a short time, Lord King. And we would have to be close to the Duke's hold. . . ."

"No matter!" Uther waved his hand. "In my stable are the fleetest horses in this land. If need be we can run the hearts out of them."

As the High King commanded, so might it be done. Myrddin found himself clinging to the back of a larger steed than he had ever known, riding at a reckless pace through the twilight; they passed on even through the night, for the moon swung high enough to give them wan light. He did not consider the good or ill of what he would do, but rather what could come of this if he was successful. Another Sky Son would be born, one like himself, always in half exile in this land. And at that he knew joy, for he had learned the bitterness of loneliness throughout his years.

Let the child be born and taken to Ector—then perhaps he himself would be free. He longed as fiercely for that freedom as any slave wished his chains to be loosed.

Thus in three days they came to a fortress by the sea and found hiding places in a copse. Myrddin pushed forward alone to look down on the keep Uther wished to invade and, in the silence of the spot on which he sheltered, he began to ready his powers for the greatest feat of illusion he had ever tried.

8.

The night was cold, unusually chill for Beltane Eve. There was a crisp wind off the sea, whose thunder-break of waves Myrddin could hear even through the thick walls of the fortress. He himself was feverish as if some rheum of winter troubled him as he crept along the passage, unsure of his powers even yet.

Uther and his men slept back in that hidden camp. It had been easy enough to introduce the herb powder into their single bottle of heather mead, for the strong flavor of the drink covered the lighter taste of the sleep herb. And he had implanted the illusion dream in Uther's mind with all the skill the mirror had taught him.

But now he traversed passages where twice he had to raise screens of illusion to distort sight and leave him free. The strain was telling on him. In the chamber ahead ... He paused within hand-touching distance of the curtain that cloaked its entrance, began once more to create his dream weaving.

When it was as strong as he could summon, he drew a deep breath and walked forward, lifting the right edge of the curtain and stepping boldly through. If he worked his magic correctly, the woman within would see only what she looked to see, the unexpected return of her lord.

In his hand was the tiny packet holding the rest of the sleep draft. Get her to swallow that on some pretext and his task was done.

A lamp of the old Roman design flickered beside a bed fashioned like a richly carved wooden box with its lid removed. However it held no occupant. Instead the woman stood looking out of the window at the storm-roiled sea, a cloak about her slim shoulders covering only part of her nudity. She turned swiftly as Myrddin's boot rasped on the stone.

Her startled look was gone in an instant. She smiled hesitantly, as if not sure in what mood the intruder came.

"My lord! But . . . how come you here?"

Myrddin gave an inner sigh of relief. So the illusion held—she saw whom she might expect, the Duke Goloris.

"Where else would I be?" he asked. "Fair lady, this is no night for wars or sword-dealing."

She came away from the window, dropping the edge of her cloak. Now he could see that indeed this one was fashioned for the joys of bedding, although he could look on her without that stir of confusion he had felt when Nimue unveiled her body in invitation. She was indeed beautiful, this Duchess Igrene, but it was a beauty one might view in the Roman images of their goddesses. Now she regarded him with a small, almost secret smile, and he guessed that in some things she could rule her old lord as completely as Uther wished to rule Britain.

Make an end to this play, something within Myrddin bade him. In this room, which was scented with woman and a life he knew nothing of, he was as uncertain as a stag who suspected a trap. His hand went out to a small side table on which there providentially stood a tall bottle of glass brought from overseas and two beautifully decorated goblets.

"The night is cold," he said. "I would have wine for the warming."

Igrene laughed low and sweetly. "There are other ways of warming one, lord." Slyly she motioned toward the bed.

He forced a laugh of his own. "Well enough. But first, pledge me in a cup, lady. Then we shall perhaps try your way to see which is best."

She pouted, but waited until he had poured a measure of wine into each goblet, then docilely accepted the one he held out to her. He pretended to drink, but she emptied her cup in a couple of swallows.

"My lord, you are not usually so behind in such matters." She came closer so that the flower scent which clung to her skin grew stronger. Making nothing of her nakedness, she raised her hands to unbuckle his cloak. "Lord, you are not yourself this night. . . ."

Myrddin wanted to jerk back, away from her reaching hands. By sheer will he kept still. Setting aside his goblet, he caught her hands and held them tightly clasped within his own, watching her with an anxious eye.

Now he caught and held her gaze. The playfulness faded from her expression. Her face smoothed, as if she no longer saw him in truth, but some vision which stood between them.

Gently, after a long moment of that locked gaze, Myrddin drew her to the side of the bed, settled her within it. Her eyes were still on what only she saw. Lying back among the pillows, she made no move as Myrddin left her.

The window was already well open to the night; the curtain of hide and the shutter meant to keep out the chill were both pushed far back. He made sure they would remain so. The woman on the bed muttered drowsily, her words not meant for him but for the vision he had planted in her mind.

Outside there was a fluttering sound. Myrddin averted his head and went swiftly from the chamber, threading his way, his heart beating fast in spite of his struggle for control. A guard stood at the postern and yet did not see the slight man who flitted by.

When he reached his previous observation point, a height above Goloris' hold, Myrddin turned. The moon was bright and clear. Some distance away flames leaped, where the lesser folk were celebrating Beltane. His night had been well chosen: only a small fraction of the keep's inhabitants would be within the walls tonight.

He could not see the window which lay to the seaward side of the tower. What happened there now was not his affair, he must only preserve the hallucination with Uther. With a heavy burden of weariness resting on him, Myrddin made his way back again to the hidden camp and sat for long hours there by the sleeping men.

With dawn Uther stirred. Though he opened his eyes he did not look about him with any recognition. Instead he got to his feet like a dazed man, his hands reaching forth to grasp something which was not there.

Myrddin scrambled up quickly. With the very tip of a finger he touched the king's uplifted head, directly above and between the eyes. And from his mind flashed the signal he had waited so long to give.

"Awake!"

Uther blinked, looked about him in the gray light. He yawned and then saw Myrddin. A frown knotted between his eyebrows.

"So, sorcerer, it would seem your magic works!" He spoke with a sour note in his voice. "You have done as you promised." There was no triumph or satisfaction in his tone. Instead his eyes avoided Myrddin's and he turned his shoulder to the younger man, shutting him out, or hoping to.

And Myrddin realized that, having slaked his lust, as he believed, Uther now felt shame for the act. He would not welcome in his sight the one who had aided him to an action he wished to repudiate.

"If I have done as I promised, and to your satisfaction, Lord King, then let me depart. For I have no liking for courts," Myrddin wearily made answer. He had half expected that Uther would turn on him, but not so suddenly. And he did not want to lose the High King's favor entirely, for this night's work was not yet complete and his further part required some thread of connection with the court.

"Well enough." Uther had turned completely away. He did not even glance in the other's direction, but regarded his sleeping men. "Ride where you will, when you will."

Myrddin accepted the dismissal with a dignity of his own, not bowing his head in any courtesy he did not feel, but rather walking back to where their mounts had been tethered. There he loosed his pony—for that means of returning to his own place he believed Uther owed him—and he rode away, without a single glance toward the King, nor beyond to where that keep rose beside the sea. But he was no more than over the crest of a small hillock when he heard the thud of hooves, saw a man riding at the best speed to which he could push his foam-bespattered mount.

"The High King?" he shouted at Myrddin. "Where is Uther?"

That anyone would know of this secret expedition was a vast surprise to the youth. Yet so certain seemed this rider that Uther was in the neighborhood that obviously whatever message he bore was of the utmost urgency, enough to break the veil of secrecy.

"Why do you seek the High King?" Myrddin demanded. Any change in the state of affairs was of importance for his plans also. "Have the Saxons sounded their war horns?"

The man shook his head. "Duke Goloris—he was slain in battle yesterday. The King must know—"

Myrddin pointed to the way he had come. "You will find the High King thereabouts—"

The messenger spurred on before he had even completed his sentence. As Myrddin kicked his own horse into a steady trot, he considered the importance of what he had just heard. Duchess Igrene would learn only too soon that her lord had been dead before that hour she would remember on Myrddin's implanted orders. And Uther would now find his way clear to take openly the woman he had professed to find desirable above all others. What bearing would such a marriage have on the life Myrddin was certain Igrene now bore within her body?

Would the High King, relying on his own memory, accept the child to come as his own? And what would happen if and when Uther discussed this happening with the Duchess? Myrddin had read the King's self-disgust clearly in the few words they had exchanged. What would come out of that shame?

There would be more than half a year to pass before he could learn that. His own task had been made clear. The child born of this night's work was to be hidden—hidden in the north with one who still had a fraction of the Old Ones' blood and who would be alerted with certain words Myrddin could utter. He saw no reason why he should not make his preparations now, so he did not turn back by hidden tracks to the cave and his solitude, but rode north.

The Ector he sought, he discovered some weeks later, was lord of a small holding which lay high among crags and steep valleys. He was esteemed by his neighbors, but never mixed much with them except in times when they must unite for mutual defense. And his people were noted as being extraordinarily averse to letting strangers settle among them. Ector had taken his own cousin to wife, for his line was ever known to wed within certain bonds of kinship, and he was a young man.

Myrddin pieced together this fragmentary information from hints and bits he heard from traveling merchants, now beginning to venture forth again as the Saxon menace was kept under control: from a smith who had spent the winter season working in Ector's hold but was now on the road that he might go to his ailing mother, from a bard traveling for the mere pleasure of finding new places. He was pleased with what he heard.

Ector was accorded by all with a keen wit and battle

wisdom which had aided in keeping the district free of
raiding Picts down from the north. His wife was a follower of the overseas faith, one of those they now termed
Christians, and she had given refuge to an elderly priest of
that god who was a noted healer. Though Ector kept his
territory jealously inviolate, he was not one to draw sword
without good cause, and those within his small holding
were as prosperous as any could be in these troubled days.

When Myrddin at last came to the narrow pass which
gave opening into Ector's domain he found guards there.
They were civil enough, though they detained him in their
camp while one of their number rode on to the clan house
with a message. Myrddin had drawn on a scrap of skin
the spiral which was the sign of the older days and said he
had private words for their lord.

He waited until nearly sundown before the rider returned, giving him free passage within Ector's land and
ready to be his guide. He found the lord of the holding
waiting for him as he came into the central courtyard of
the clan house. For a single moment of painful memory it
was as if he had come home again and all the heavy years
had been erased.

Just so had Nyren stood, his head bare, his features welcoming, to greet a guest in the times past. As a servant led
away his weary horse, Ector's hand touched his arm
tightly. And Myrddin, seeing that they were nearly alone,
repeated his words in a whisper.

Ector's hair was as night-dark as his own. And his lips
were clear cut, his nose narrow and high-bridged, his face
long, shaping a pointed chin. It was like seeing his own
countenance, somewhat older, and with slight differences;
Ector's face was enough like his own, even to the curiously marked eyelids which made the eyes appear almost
triangular, so that they could be close kin.

"Welcome, brother," was Ector's reply, nor did he appear startled in the least at Myrddin's whispering of words
so old their real meaning had long since passed from the
minds of men. "The kin house opens to you."

In this part of his planning Myrddin's path was made
easy. Though neither Ector nor his lady had had any contact with the Sky People, yet the tradition of such folk
had lingered strongly in their clan history. They accepted
without question what Myrddin could tell them. Though
he did not explain the circumstances surrounding the babe

he would find a refuge for, yet they were ready to aid him. Trynihid, even if she might follow in truth the new faith as preached by Nuth—a gentle, middle-aged man who tried to heal bodies as well as lighten minds with his teaching—was still of the kin clan and nodded her own head when Myrddin spoke of the importance of keeping the child safe.

She moved slowly, her own belly swelling with the long-wanted and hoped-for heir to Ector's holding. And she rested her hands on that swelling as Myrddin spoke of the safekeeping, nodding her head.

Seeing her in her quiet happiness made Myrddin uncomfortable, and he kept from the upper apartments where she sat when there was any leisure in the clan house. He had never been attracted to any of the ladies he had seen at the High King's court, nor to any girl of the clan house. Only once had desire stirred in his body: when he fronted Nimue in the night and she had challenged him to be a man to her woman, young though they were then.

The happiness of Trynihid and the care her lord wrapped now about her was a new thing to him. Because there were traces of the old inheritance in both of them, he felt more deeply akin to them than he had in any under his grandfather's lordship. There was a warmth of belonging between these two which was like the life-giving fire of winter—yet to him such comfort was denied.

He grew restless and yet somehow he was tied to this place, and to leave it for the gaunt loneliness of the land about the cave was more than he could face. He went with Ector into the fields and helped to number the flock, doing all a smallhold lord would. And he worked steadily with his hands, tiring himself as much as he could, so that, exhaused, he fell into deep sleep at night.

News came with the return of the smith. And Myrddin listened eagerly. The High King had indeed taken a wife— the Duchess Igrene. Yet he did not live with her, rather she dwelt among the holy women of the new faith, for she bore a child which was her first husband's. Until she was delivered of that, the King would not truly claim her.

So the illusion had held with the Duchess, Myrddin thought. And Uther must have done nothing to challenge her belief. This would work better for his own need, for Uther would not want the coming child about the court.

Fostering was honorable, much used among people of higher birth. Even a king would send forth his sons, not only to have them away from the temptations which would easily surround them in his own house, but to protect their very lives. There was always a jealous claimant to believe that by a private killing the path to rule would be made free and easy.

He must ride south before the winter really closed in on this harsher northern country and seek out Uther. Once he had used mind-bending on the King and had succeeded. He would be a poor man of Power if he could not do so again—to the benefit of the plan in which he was a part.

During the summer Myrddin had again undergone one of those swift changes of body which came to him in place of the more smooth flowing growth of those of pure human blood. He was taller, a little heavier of shoulder. Catching sight of his face in a newly burnished shield, he was more than ever struck by the resemblance to Ector, though his face was less softened by the passing of emotion and his eyes were always half hooded, as if he kept them as weapons in reserve. His beard was sparse and did not grow fast. When he shaved he did not need to touch a blade to his skin again for several days. But work under the sun had somewhat browned his skin and given him new strength of hand and arm.

Before the Feast of Samain he rode forth from the holding, bearing the good wishes of these distant kin, well clothed if plainly, his sword now decently sheathed in leather, not in a patchwork of bark. Ector had been awed by the sword, yet he would not even put a hand to its hilt, saying that such blades of old were well known to tolerate only one master.

"Aye," Myrddin had answered. "Yet I am not the master, Ector. He who comes will carry this into battle. I am but his servant in this as in other things."

He led a pack pony with full supplies, for he determined to move south by the lesser known ways, letting no hint of his coming reach Uther, if possible. To take the High King by surprise would better open the way for his own desire.

Riding at an even pace, he made the rest of his way back to the cave, though he was twice delayed by storms which lasted more than a day. Snow lay white there as he climbed the path his feet would always find, whether the eyes of men could see the way or not. There was a raucous call and a huge black bird coasted down to flap about him. Suddenly losing guard over his features, Myrddin held out his wrist and called joyfully: "Vran!"

Vran it was, planing in at once to settle claws on Myrddin's glove, turning his head this way and that to eye him, croaking all the time in a coaxing way as the creature had learned to do when it begged for bits of meat.

"But give me time, Vran," Myrddin promised, "and you shall be fed."

The bird fluttered up to perch on a stone and the youth rummaged through his pack, bringing out a chunk of smoked pork which he tossed to the ground, only to have a black explosion of feathers fall on it.

There was no indication that any had been this way during the months of his absence. And he had come for only one reason. Myrddin unbuckled the belt which supported the sword and, taking that inside, hid the weapon in the darkest corner of the cave behind the largest of the installations. He noted that the majority of those were silent now. Only one still had a run of lights back and forth across its surface. For a long moment he stood before the mirror, seeing only his own reflection. Truly he looked older than his years now—a man as old as Uther had been when he had last seen him. His face was secret, closed, and the soberness of his choice of tunic and cloak made him a dark and brooding figure. Perhaps this was how a sorcerer was meant to appear in a world which relished light and color, the glitter of gems and the burnished wealth of gold.

He went again into the outer world. Vran was working on a few last beakfuls of the pork. And Myrddin found another lump for the raven before he mounted.

"Little brother," he said, and at his words the raven stopped its fierce tearing of the meat, looking up at him with beads of eyes which seemed more knowing than any Myrddin had ever seen set in a bird skull. "Farewell, keep safe. When I return you shall feast again."

So promising, he turned the horse toward the valley of the clan house, tugging at the lead so the pack pony followed.

It was well past Samain and the winter wolf had fastened his cruel ice jaws on man's world when Myrddin came into the room where High King Uther sat by a fire which roared mightily and yet gave little heat beyond the small radius of the hearth. The King was alone as Myrddin had guessed, for the symbol he had sent was one which Uther would know and, knowing, he would not want any to share his inner secrets.

"So you come again, sorcerer," was his curt greeting. There was no welcome in either his face or his tone. "I have not summoned you."

"Events have summoned me, Lord King," Myrddin returned. "I served your desire and asked for no payment—"

Uther set his horn of wine down on the tabletop nearby with force enough to make its metal binding ring out. "If you value your life, sorcerer, keep a still tongue in that ugly head of yours!" he flared.

"I speak not of the past, Lord King, that is your own affair. What I must ask is of the future."

"All men whine and beg at a king's throne. What are your demands—gold, silver, a lordship?" Uther sneered. Yet his eyes were uneasy, wary, as if he did not like what he saw when he looked at Myrddin. He was even a little awed by the other's composure.

"I want a fosterling, Lord King."

"A fosterling—" Uther's mouth gaped wide in startlement. Then his eyes narrowed threateningly. "What plot is this, sorcerer?"

"No plot, Lord King. There will be a child born shortly to one whom you greatly love. This child is a threat to you in a small way. To have such ever under your eyes—"

Uther pushed up from his chair in a half-leap in Myrddin's direction. His hand had swung up as if to smash full into the younger man's face. Then he stopped, mastering that flare of rage.

"Why do you want this child?" he demanded harshly.

"Because I am responsible in part for its birth, Lord King. I am a man of the Power; as such I betrayed much I believed in to aid you on that night. Now in conscience I must pay for my interference with events. The child will be safe; it shall be gently fostered. Men will forget it lives. There will be no more whispers in your court. You and your lady queen will be lighter of heart. If it remains here, though, there will be those who would use the child as a tool for revolt. Those who followed Goloris are not all dead even if they are now silent."

Uther's face grew thoughtful. He strode back and forth along the edge of the hearth, his face tense with concentration.

"Sorcerer, there is wisdom in what you say. I would have this coming baby apart from the court, both for the sake of my lady and for its own safety. As you have said, there are those who have not taken kindly to events in the past. Perhaps if the child is male they will cherish the idea of a new lord in years to come. My lady believes it is— she thinks—" Uther's voice sank. "She sometimes thinks it was forced on her by a demon in her husband's guise. She fears its coming as if it will be born a monster. Take it if you will, sorcerer, and do not let me know where it will be fostered, or by whom. It is better forgot for the good of all."

"Well enough." Myrddin relaxed inwardly. He had carried his point without tedious argument. "I am lodged at the Sign of the Rowan. Let me know the hour of the birth and I shall come and go—no man or woman being the wiser."

At Uther's assertive nod he left the room. There was much to be done. For all his power and knowledge he could not travel north with a newly born infant in the dead of winter. But he had deliberately chosen his inn with an eye to that matter. The wife of the host had recently given birth and was suckling a fine healthy child, the place was clean beyond most of its sort and Myrddin had the means within himself to silence questions and provide answers men could be brought to believe. Now he only had to wait.

9.

The message came to Myrddin on the eve of the Feast of Briganta. He had already made his own provisions for the care of the child. In the slave market he had ransomed one of the small, dark, Pictish women taken on a raid across the ancient wall of the Romans. She had borne a dead child three days earlier and was so sunk in despair that the dealer asked no great price. But Myrddin, using the powers of the mirror, was able to communicate with her, promising her eventual freedom if she would take care of the baby he would bring her. She might not have believed the truth of his promise, but she did not protest when he took her back to the inn, asked that she be given water to wash and then provided her with a plain woolen tunic and a cloak perhaps warmer than any she had ever known.

The child was a son, even as Myrddin had been sure. And, since there had been no name given him, just as Lugaid had once named him, standing in place of the father who should have held the babe in his arms, so did Myrddin look down into that small red face and call him after the name the mirror had spoken: "Arthur."

Three weeks later he hired a horse litter and made contact with a levy of men riding to reinforce the northern borders, that they might ride with a measure of protection through lands which were still debatable. Thus they journeyed to Ector's holding where he was welcomed as kin come home. Ector pressed Myrddin to stay there also. But such an uneasiness had ridden with the younger man since he had left the King's house that he would not agree. The sooner he was well away from here, the less chance there would be of any secret man of the King or the King's enemies tracing Arthur.

Myrddin doubted that Uther would mean the boy any

94

fatal harm, but the High King would doubtless be a happier man if he should lose this unwanted child overseas. And there were still many ties with families in Lesser Britain. Among those Uther could find someone to hide Arthur past any finding.

"When he is ready for schooling," Myrddin had returned in answer to Ector's urging, "then shall I come." For he was certain that Arthur must be given those same sources of knowledge which had shaped his own life. "Until then, forget that he is not truly of your blood kin."

And Trynihid, holding her own son Cei to her full breast, smiled.

"Kinsman, he shall abide safe."

Ector nodded vigorously. "Blood oath on that if you wish—"

Myrddin smiled in return. "Kinsman, what need of oaths between those of one blood? I have no doubt that you will make him a true fosterling of this house."

Thus he rode in the early spring, heading south, but setting to a path which would take him again to the Place of the Sun, for he was very lonely. Perhaps in Lugaid he could find a certain companionship. Such a way would also confuse his trail for anyone who followed, for he could not rid himself of the feeling that he was indeed the object of a hunt.

The King's men, he believed, would be more open in their seeking, if Uther had changed his mind. No, this was more subtle, like being pursued by a shadow, a cloud, something he could not seize on nor confront, but which was there. And he knew only one who could command such a shadow—Nimue.

There could be, he speculated, some way in which each use of his powers might be made known, wherever Nimue hid to weave her spells. And, because he had no inkling of the depth of her knowledge, a prudent man would assess her skill at maximum in order to go prepared. So his haunted feeling as he rode north meant that she had now learned of Arthur.

His first fear lay with the child. If, when he himself traveled forth from Ector's land, that sensation of being watched vanished, then it must be the child who was in danger. Learning that, he himself would return immediately to make other plans, set up such protective barriers as he could. But, to his relief on that point, he went accompanied by the invisible watcher.

Now he searched the land around as he rode, set up certain mind-alarms of his own each night while he slept, lest he be ambushed unaware. Still there came no attack, only that continual foreboding feeling. . . .

He thought he could perhaps throw it off when he reached the Place of the Sun, remembering that sense of renewed power which had flowed into him when he touched those tall-standing sentinels of a lost age. How strong was Nimue? So much depended on the answer to that question. And what moves had she been making over the years since their last meeting? For he was certain that she had not been idle.

So he came into the giant circle of standing stones and there dismounted and stood to watch dawn banished by the rising sun. He had been right: here he was free of surveillance for the first time. Yet he knew he must not allow Nimue to be baffled long; there was always the fear in his mind that she might backtrail—that she would strike at Arthur. Above all else, Arthur must endure!

Myrddin crossed the turf to the hut Lugaid had built. He urgently wanted the advice the Druid might give him, the feeling of one comrade on his side if a strange battle was to be enjoined. But even before he reached the crude building he saw that its roof of branches was broken, that it no longer was the home place of any man.

"Lugaid!" He could not choke back his own despairing cry, though the name seemed to ring far too loudly in the air. The hide curtain was gone from the doorway, so he could look into the cramped single room. No one had been here for a long time.

A little forlornly he stooped and went in, kicking at the powdery ash which had been a fire. The bronze cooking pot, the wooden bowls and spoons were gone. There was nothing left to say when or where the Druid had left. At least Myrddin could read no sign of violence—Lugaid had not fallen prey to any roving war band or slinking outlaws such as might visit this deserted place.

Slowly the youth returned to the King Stone, setting his hands palm-down on its rough surface. This was indeed a thing of power! Within him he could feel his own energy and will rising to blend with the emanation from the stone.

That confidence which had ebbed when he found Lugaid gone came back to him.

There were things he could do here, certain forces he could evoke, which he thought would make Arthur secure, remove from his own journey that watching presence. And those he did, using word and thought, a certain rhythm beat on the rock face with the blade of his belt knife. He felt the answer from the stones, the gathering of what was like an invisible war band. And he marshaled that force, aimed it—released it like an arrow from a bow toward the north and Ector's small valley.

Then he was tired, drained. He dropped down in the grass, his shoulders against the King Stone, his eyes on the sky where clouds whiter than the whitest linen sailed slowly and impressively to affairs outside the understanding of man. Beyond the clouds, beyond the higher sky, lay other worlds, many more than a man might count. Life inhabited those distant worlds—though the mirror had shown him little of that and only fleetingly. Yet, if the Sky People returned, their ships would be bridges to those worlds. Would he have the courage to voyage outward, seeking another sun? He did not know, though the idea excited him. How long would the waiting continue?

Men thought in years, in seasons; the Star Lords in centuries. Man's life was short. How long was that of a Star Lord? Perhaps three, four, a hundred times that of man? At the moment he felt all man, awed, a little afraid of those who would come to his summoning if he could fulfill everything the voice of the mirror asked of him.

Myrddin slipped into a half-sleep as his pony cropped the new-springing grass around the stones. In that sleep his imagination woke and showed him even stranger things than the mirror had ever hinted at. Yet there was nothing threatening in those sights, unearthly as they were. He only felt wonder and delight.

Cities—such cities!—with shining towers of rainbow glass reached high into skies that were not the blue of the earth he knew. And some others were set under the restless waves of seas, sharp pinnacles, as red as the precious coral he had seen shown by merchants from the southern lands. Yes, he could imagine the cities, but he could not bring to life the people who had built them. Perhaps man could only see life equal to his own image. That was the fatal shortness of man's sight.

The sun passed behind one of the clouds; more were gathering. Myrddin was roused by a wind with a sharp promise of rain and storm. He caught at the reins of the pony, started back to the hut which had been Lugaid's. He sheltered there that night while wild winds raged across the land. Twice he cowered as lightning struck with explosive force against the King Stone, as if that rock drew the full fury of what lashed across the sky.

He had weathered such storms before, but it seemed to him that he had never faced one with such fury wrapped within it. He plugged his ears with his fingers, closed his eyes—still he could not escape either sight nor sound. There was a strange odor in the air.... This was the force men could never hope to control, now gone mad and striving to wipe the earth clean of life.

In spite of his fear Myrddin was also gripped by a wild exultation which made him wish to run out into that chaos, leap and shout, abandon all to become a part of the fury, free himself from restraint, of his mind's control.

But in the morning there was nothing to show the passing of such force. Not until he had ridden outward from the circle did he see trees overthrown, their roots pointing accusingly like crooked fingers at the sky from which their deathblows had come. In Myrddin there was a new kind of peace. The storm might have drawn with its disappearance all his unease, his fears. He still had some of the freedom which had grown in him during those dark hours.

His sense of being spied on was also gone with the storm. Yet he took no chances and approached the cave only after some days of travel by a circuitous route, using the caution he had always maintained. This time Vran did not greet him, even though he whistled for the raven and laid out an offering on the ground. In fact he became aware, as he watched and listened, that there was an odd silence over the slope. There were no other birds. Even the wind had ceased to blow here.

He listened not only with his ears, but also with that mental sense. The very absence of any life was in itself a warning. And he could guess what might have happened; he had been too sure he had thrown off that questing. The mind so engaged had not wasted time trying to trail him, instead it had come straight here!

Nimue!

He stripped saddle and bridle from the pony and turned

the animal loose, trying to conceal any outward sign that he was conscious of what might soon face him here. He decided, after several quick glances in that direction that the crevice entrance to the cave was undisturbed. Stones he had piled there to hide the opening had not been moved. It was the sword which lay at the back of his mind now. He was sure it would be impossible to transport any of the space things from here—they were all too large to be drawn through the crevice. How they had entered into the mountain he never knew; perhaps they had been left there through the centuries.

But the sword was a different matter and Nimue knew that he possessed it. It could well be that she wished to take the weapon from him. He shifted his plump saddlebags to his shoulder, went to the crevice. This Nimue knew also, so he was betraying no secret. But let him get inside and she would discover that she had been left behind. He well understood that the mirror had its own safety devices and that he alone was able to approach it.

He worked quickly, refusing to turn around, to look over one shoulder or the other. There was a growing pressure on him, a command—but not to the extent that his own will could not counter it. As if he could hear her laughter ringing again, he believed she was watching—waiting—applying the burden of her will, intent on making him obey. But she was too confident, too sure of her own use of the power. He must not be so overconfident in return; rather he must be wary.

Perhaps she had easily been able to compel obedience by use of the same hallucinations which he had employed to his own purposes during the years. Now her confidence was supreme, because she had not previously met resistance such as he could offer.

So far he had not resisted because his will marched with hers: she wanted him in the cave, he wanted to make sure that the sword was safe. The last stone was aside; he stooped to wriggle through. Once more he discovered that not even the enlarged entrance was big enough to admit him without a struggle. His tunic tore on hip and shoulder and skin beneath suffered painful grazes.

The cave was deeper in gloom, with only one small line of lights alive. Myrddin dropped his saddlebags, went directly to the niche where he had concealed the sword. The wrapped bundle lay there in safety, but he stripped off the sheath to make sure that the blade still rested within. In the dark it shone with a wan light of its own, and he held the hilt in his right hand, ran the fingertips of the left along that smooth length. Like the stone, this touch reported to him the feeling of unleashed strength, of energy which might be released on command. This was more an object of destiny than just a tool to move the King Stone. It had a future use also, and that he would learn in time. But now it was safe and he wound the wrappings about it again hiding its luminosity.

"Merlin!" A voice, but not the familiar one.

He rounded the nearest square to look into the dark surface of the mirror. There was a strange silvery sheen across it and in the midst of the eerie light stood Nimue. She was now a woman and that quality in her which had moved Myrddin at the Place of the Sun was stronger, far stronger. He was dazzled by the woman who looked at him as if she were indeed behind the mirror, her eyes meeting his.

"Merlin!" Now she made his name not a demand for attention, but a soft greeting which stirred an answer within him. Breed called to breed in spite of all he knew.

"Alas, poor Merlin." Her voice held no mockery, though he might have expected it, rather a touch of pity. "You have entered the trap and it is sprung. All your meddling with the affairs of man—and woman—will be put to naught by time itself. Clever are those who fashioned you to carry out their actions, be their hands and feet in this tormented land. But not quite clever enough. They set guards about their mirror and everything else they landed from star voyages, but perhaps they did not know that guards can be placed around guards. Merlin, you have gone to earth like the fox which is hunted, but unlike the canny fox you will not come forth again!

"I have set an outer force field to keep you in and you shall abide there until your human part fails through hunger and thirst. This deed is terrible, aye, but worse would you in time bring to pass if you are not so halted. Your Arthur will live, but he will be no more than any other man. Thus falls to dust your dream of kingdom. He will never claim a crown, and death unknown will also be his portion. Farewell, Merlin. It is a pity we could not deal together as distant kin should."

She was gone in a flicker of light. Myrddin had flung

out a hand as if to try to arrest her disappearance, though he knew that the real Nimue had not stood so, only a sending she had released. Now he whirled and in a minute was at the crevice.

The opening was there, he could put an arm into it. Yet before his fist was out into the open it met, with a shock of force, an invisible wall.

Two more testings, top and near ground level, made it plain that the barrier formed a tight plug. He wasted no time in useless physical struggle. Only the mirror might have an answer for this and he returned to it in two strides, crouched down on the viewer's bench he had so often occupied in the past. Gazing intently at his own reflection, he thought his problem, aware, though he knew not how it was done, that his query or plea for aid registered somewhere.

He saw the installation, so long dark and quiet, waken to life. Then the mirror voice spoke:

"The force field is too strong to break ... now. And it is true that you wear a body which was not fashioned to withstand much physical stress. But for that there is an answer. You will sleep, Merlin, and during that sleep all body processes shall be slowed down. Thus, when the moment comes that time thins the field, you can awake and issue forth once again, alive and whole. This is the manner by which such can be accomplished."

His own face and body were not gone from the mirror this time, but he saw himself going to a long, low machine at the far end of the row. There he pressed his hands, fingers deep into small holes. The lid of the machine rose on upward-reaching pillars. Then the man he watched stripped off his clothing and he climbed through the wedge between the chest and lid to lie down. The pillars slid toward the cave floor, sealing him in.

Myrddin shivered. He could not doubt the wisdom of the mirror and the voice. Yet this way seemed to be entering his tomb while he still lived. To follow such action needed all the courage he could summon.

The mirror had cleared again. He saw only his own form as it was, while he reluctantly rose to his feet. Slow starvation, death by thirst—or the offer of the tomb? The chances were very slim on either side. But because he trusted the mirror he followed instructions now.

That long box opened as he applied the pressure, just as

the mirror had shown. He stared down into the interior as the lid rose. Within was a rosy glow, pale, but strong enough to reflect on his hands. And the bottom was awash in a liquid from which came a pleasant, aromatic scent. He stripped off his clothes, piled them to one side and slung a leg over the edge of the box. The liquid was about his ankle, rising up his shin; it was warm, soothing somehow.

He pushed through the rest of his body, settled himself at the bottom of the box. Now the liquid washed over his chest, caressed his cheeks. And that was the last thing he remembered, except that the lid was settling swiftly downward to lock him out of the world.

There were dreams, strange dreams of cities whose like he had never thought could exist, so high did their narrow buildings tower into the air. Men flew in things which were not birds, but made stiffly of metal cunningly fashioned. The dreamer sometimes abode for a small time in the body of one or another of those men, though he was then beseiged by thoughts so different from his own time that he could not understand them.

Even as these men flew about the clouds, so did they travel in turn beneath the surface of the sea. It would seem that no secret of their world was hidden from them. Yet they were unhappy, restless and much troubled, and Myrddin soon shrank from any contact with their minds.

There came a time when the world itself went mad. Howling winds broke the cities, did such damage as no normal storm could. Waves rose mountain-high in the sea to crash upon the land, sweeping the remnants of man's world into oblivion. Mountains breathed forth flame, great gouts of molten rock flowing down their sides. When that met the waters of the insane seas, steam formed so thickly as to blot out both land and sea, and hide the heavens.

When there was an end at last, the drowned, scarred land was changed, had new bays, new rivers. Some of its substance had been lost to the eating of the sea, but in return it had gained in other places steaming spreads of stinking mud which had once been water covered. But man had survived—in some manner a handful of men survived. Shocked, mind-deadened, they crept forth into the new world. A few could remember earlier times, but only in fragments. The others were near imbeciles, wanting only to eat, sleep and sometimes mate brutishly with less grace than any beast.

They were lost indeed, that remnant and they sank back farther than animals. Some preyed on their fellows to fill their bellies, killing their quarry with rocks. A few strove to cling to their memories. Some of these had wit enough to draw apart, to establish themselves in areas they could defend against the mindless brutes. Once more came a slow, very slow climb upward. Truth became legend overlain with imagination; later generations had no belief that man had ever been other than what he was in their own time. But there were always some who remembered better, whose tales from one generation to the next were clearer, less embroidered.

Myrddin dreamed and dreamed again. His was a breed which clung to life, which might be defeated but which was never wiped away. And among man were always to be found the dreamers, the seekers. . . .

There was a loud sound, like the ringing of a great mellow-toned gong. Within the box Myrddin stirred. His breathing, which had been so slow, began to quicken. The liquid completely covering his body was draining away. His eyelids fluttered.

As if that small movement was a signal, the columns which supported the lid of the chest began to climb steadily upward. His eyes opened and he uttered a feeble sound. His limbs felt stiff, no stiffer than if he had spent a night in the open. And his mind was returning fast to the here and now.

Was the voice right—had the force field been weakened? He crawled out of the box and stood upright, feeling dizzy enough to clutch at the edge of the lid. Around him the installations were afire with a beading of flickering lights. His body dried quickly. That moisture which had filled the box rolled from his skin in large drops, leaving little dampness behind.

He looked for his clothing. But when he stooped to pick up his tunic the linen was yellowed, so frail it tore as he pulled it on. Time—how much time!

Dressed again, he came to the mirror. How long had he slept was the foremost thought in his mind, how long?

The voice, as strong as ever, answered that thought.

"Sixteen of the years of this world, Merlin. But the confining field is now shattered. You are free. And that one who set this upon you can do no more, for her powers were greatly drained by what she did. Now she moves in other ways for your defeat. It is time that you take up battle."

He stared at his own reflection. Sixteen years! But he was perhaps only a year or two older than he had been when he entered that box! How could such a thing be?

"It preserves life, Merlin. However, think not of the past. You must be about your mission. And that is to see Arthur truly king of Britain."

"Uther?" He made a question of that name.

"Uther dies. There are great lords about him—two have married daughters of his body. But he has had no sons, no sons save Arthur whose claim you must make. Though you have not done for Arthur what was planned, taught him as you were taught, yet he is of Sky Blood and so ours, not theirs. Put Arthur on the throne, Merlin, and Britain shall have a High King whose name will be spoken by men for more than a thousand years."

Myrddin nodded slowly. Arthur and the sword, they must come together. It was this thought which had lain far at the back of his mind since the time Lugaid and he had found that wonderously wrought piece of Sky metal.

"Arthur and the sword, with you behind him, Merlin. This is the task for which you were conceived and no greater one can be faced by any man living. Arthur and the sword . . ."

10.

Merlin stood looking down at the great camp where chieftains and petty kings flew their battle standards over brightly walled tents. He was no longer Myrddin, he must remember that. Now he wondered if any of those gathered here would remember him. Sixteen years—Arthur was man-grown and he had had no part in his teaching. Wholly of this earth would be any wisdom the boy had. But there was nothing to be gained by looking over one's shoulder with regret; facing forward with wariness and hope was all that was left.

His time-tattered clothing had been changed by chance for a long wool robe such as bards wore. And he had allowed his beard to grow, though the hair was sparse enough not to impress unduly. He had found the robe in the baggage of a dead man lying beneath the summer sun, his horse cropping nearby. Three Saxons enriched the ground with their blood, escorting the stranger as a warrior should go. Merlin did not know who that benefactor had been, or why he had been so ambushed. But he had given the unknown spirit thanks for the horse and the robe folded into a bundle, and he had buried him face to the east under a morning sun.

He had met scores of travelers approaching this temporary capital of Britain. For Uther was dead for a handful of days, but the High Council had not yet named his successor. Having learned plainly how affairs stood, Merlin set his own plans accordingly. Now he studied with narrowed eyes the arrangement of the camp. The banner of Lot who was wed to one of Uther's daughters—that was very prominent below. And there was the Boar of Cornwall—now upheld by a son of Goloris who was not in the legal line of descent, but about whom Cornish men rallied. Merlin saw other devices which he did not know, but he could guess that every lord here had come with at least a faint hope of advancement.

He searched for the one important to him, the Soaring Hawk that was Ector's badge. At last he sighted it, not among the inner circle of the great lords, of course, but in the company of King Urien of Rheged, that northern kingdom which had held stoutly through the years to prevent the Picts from ravaging far south of the old wall. Circling off the dusty road, Merlin made his way toward that tent.

Before it stood a young man trying on a jerkin on which rings of bronze were tightly sewn, one against another. His head was dark and for a moment Merlin was nearly startled into hailing him by name. Then the youth raised his head and looked full square at the newcomer and Merlin saw in him a much younger Ector.

"Lord Cei," he named the boy by guess. "Is Lord Ector within?"

"My father has gone to the Council of the Dukes," Cei returned, eyeing Merlin with what might even be disfavor. "Have you a message for him?"

"We are kin, distantly," Merlin answered. Cei had a certain arrogant cast of countenance which had never been his father's. "Aye, I have a message for him." He longed greatly to ask for Arthur, to know how the fostering had gone through his years of imprisonment. But now he knew better of Cei than to bring that query into the open.

The son of Ector approached stiffly to pay him the courtesy of the house, holding the reins while Merlin dismounted. Perhaps because of his plain robe, with the dust of the road thick upon him, he made little better than a beggar's appearance. But he accepted the boy's attentions as rightfully his due, as indeed they were.

Within the tent they passed out of the glare of the sun. Cei ordered a manservant to bring wine. He eyed the long package Merlin carried which was the safely trussed sword, but had better manners than to ask any questions as Merlin settled on a traveling stool with it across his knees close under his hand.

"How does your father and your lady mother?" Merlin had spilled a few drops of the wine to the earth underfoot as was the custom of the clans, and now sipped appreciatively at a better vintage than he had found in any inn.

He remembered wistfully now his summer spent in the safe valley, and how he had labored beside Ector to gather the earth's bounty.

"My father is well. My lady mother—" Cei hesitated a moment. "She died of the coughing sickness last winter, stranger."

Merlin's hand shook. So much he was remembering now; of Trynihid's pride when she carried her son, of the closeness between her and her husband. Grievous must have been the blow for Ector.

"May happiness of the Blessed Isle be hers. . . ."

"We follow the Christ here, stranger." Cei replied with a sharp note in his voice. "You wear the robe of a brother of the Church yourself, why do you speak then of the Blessed Isle?"

Still a little confused by memories and a sense of loss, Merlin looked up at the youth in near bewilderment. "My robe is but a borrowed one." He gave the first answer which came into his head. "I am a bard."

The longing to know of Arthur was so great he could hardly control it. Except for Cei and two menservants he had glimpsed, there appeared no others here. Had they left Arthur back in the valley? If so his plan was defeated before he could even bring it into action.

"Cei, where are you, boy?"

That voice was the same. Merlin started joyfully to his feet as Ector entered. But this was not the Ector he had known, and fronting a stranger made him uncertain for a moment or two so he stood open-mouthed, staring like any loutish slave in the fields. The slim body he had known had thickened and gray streaked the dark hair. The face it framed was tired, with the look of a man who had to force himself at every sunrise to a day of duties he hated, and could look forward to no true rest even when that day was done.

But the eyes which met Merlin's were the same. First they mirrored puzzlement, then recognition. But surprise overrode both of those.

"You are alive!" Ector broke the tense moment of silence. "But why did you not come?"

"I was imprisoned," Merlin replied. "Only lately have I won my freedom."

"You—you are changed. But you have not grown old, only—only strange," Ector said slowly. Then he seemed to recollect that other ears were listening and he turned to his son. "Do go and find Arthur and bring him here. This lord is one he should know—"

When they were alone Ector continued: "The lad has done well enough. But, when you did not return as you had said, we could give him no more learning than we gave Cei. I know that this was not how it was to be."

"You have given him the best you had. How can anyone fault that?" Merlin returned swiftly. "The failure was mine, not that I could have foreseen it. But tell me now, what of the Council? Have they set yet on a choice of king?"

Ector shook his head. "It is a perilous wrangle, for there are those who back Cornwall, and he has shown himself a good commander in the field. Then there are those who hold by Lot because he has wed the King's young daughter, and he is a man of no little ambition. They may pull Britain in two between them before we see the end of this. Urien broods and plans, though he has not shared his plans with me. And the Winged Hats raid as they will. It is the bad days come again, but there is no one commander with power enough to seize the rule without dispute from the others."

"With power . . ." Merlin repeated. "But if one were to give him the power. . . ? It seems that I have come at a moment which must be seized quickly, lest all we hope for go down into the darkness. Listen, kinsman, Arthur is of the Pendragon blood. He is Uther's son, though the High King would have him live in hiding lest he be plucked away in childhood by just such lords as this Lot and the rest. And for him I have also the Power, or at least a symbol of it." He turned eagerly to snatch up the wrapped sword. "We must arrange that he accept this openly before all who think to rise to the throne."

Suddenly he became aware of Ector's silence. Glancing up, Merlin saw a white horror on the other's face.

"What is it? Is he maimed, unworthy in some manner by clan laws?" Merlin was chilled by the expression he saw.

"He—" Ector moistened his lips. "He is a comely lad and— By the wounds of the Christus, had you only told me!"

"What has happened to him?" Merlin dropped the sword, reached forward to close his hand about Ector's arm. Now he shook the northern lord, as if by force he would have an answer out of him.

"Uther—he brought to court some of his baseborn get. And one of them—Morgause—she was old for her years, hot-eyed for any man. She—she enticed Arthur to her bed a week ago!"

Merlin stood as still as one of the pillars of the Place of the Sun, his mind moving swiftly. Arthur was not Uther's son, but if he made plain the real circumstances of the boy's birth would one of these lords follow him? No, there would be prattling of night demons who begat him, and the same aversion Merlin had met himself in days past. Yet for a man to lie with his sister—that, too, would put a stain on Arthur for his lifetime.

"This Morgause," he asked, "is she wed?"

"Not yet. The King was dying but when rumor of her conduct reached him he was greatly angered. He summoned a lady who was much with him because she had great healing arts—the King died slowly of a wasting sickness. Into her hands he gave Morgause, though the girl was not mindful to go quietly. They say that she was taken away by night, bound and gagged, within a curtained horse litter. And no man knows where."

Merlin gave a small sigh of relief. "Is it generally known that Arthur was the cause of her going?"

Ector's frozen cast of countenance lightened a little. "No. She was free with many men. Uther himself found her in bed with one of the guard. He knew her nature. And he swore he would not have her an open shame in his court."

"Then we are safe." Merlin gave a sigh of relief. "There may be rumors, but with the wench out of sight they will soon be out of men's minds. It remains that Arthur must rule. I have been given the sign,"—and his fingers moved in that old secret twisting—"that this is ordained. Now it is in my thoughts we may accomplish this so . . ."

He gathered up the sword once again and began to pull away its wrappings while he talked. And he saw that Ector seemed to forget the shock which had disturbed him so profoundly, that he nodded his head in agreement as this point and that were swiftly outlined.

"Remember," Merlin warned when he had finished, "Myrddin is dead, Merlin lives. Arthur is best unknowing of his true heritage for now, since he has not had the training of his kin."

"It is—" Ector was beginning when the flap of the tent was raised and a youth burst in with exuberance, as if he had been running to the encounter.

Looking at him, Merlin knew a shock nearly as deep as Ector had experienced earlier. This—this could not be Arthur!

The lad bore no outward signs of the Old Blood at all. Taller than Ector and Merlin by several inches, his hair was the red-gold of a tribesman; his face lacked the hooded eyes and high-bridged nose, the secret-keeping mouth Merlin fully expected to see. This young giant was cast in Uther's image. But how could that be? There was an openness about his manner, about even his features, which Merlin could not reconcile with the Old Heritage at all.

"Lord," the boy said, smiling sunnily, "Cei said you would speak with me—"

"I wish you to meet this lord." Ector indicated Merlin. "You were my fosterling because of him, and he has something of great import to tell you."

Merlin moistened his lips with the tip of his tongue. His eyes refused to accept this handsome boy as the Arthur he had thought of since his birth. Had he looked like the Old Race, then he himself could have confidently told the boy as much of the truth as he deemed necessary. But now, his instinctive wariness when confronted by so apparent a tribesman wavered.

"Lord?" The boy turned questioningly to him. There was an eagerness in his eyes. Perhaps all these years he had hoarded questions which could not be answered by his foster father. It would only have been natural for Arthur to wonder about his parentage. And he had had no mirror to make plain his destiny.

"I am Merlin, and I am a follower of the old knowledge." He watched closely for any reaction, any hint that this unlikely Arthur had deduced he himself was not full kin to those about him. But there was only wonder to be read in the boy's expression. "You are of kingly blood. . . ." After the affair of Morgause it was perhaps better not to make too close an identification with Uther. "In fact you are of the kin of Ambrosius and of Maximus." And, Merlin's thoughts added silently, of a breed

far greater and older than either. "In your childhood there
were those who believed you too near the throne. Thus it
was considered better that you be fostered far from the
court. Since Lord Ector is kin to me, and into my hands
you were entrusted, it was to Ector I took you. But the
plans we held then were not accomplished. It was set upon
me to teach you the old knowledge. However, I fell into
the hands of an enemy and have only lately been delivered
from the prison in which I was held captive.

"But this I would tell you, Arthur: there were prophecies made at your birth and before your birth. High King
of Britain will you be . . ."

The boy had looked puzzled, now he laughed. "Lord
Merlin, who am I to claim the throne these great lords
now wrangle over? I have not a single liege man at my
back, nor tribe kin to raise my name."

"You have something greater than an army." Merlin
had to believe what he was saying, he *had* to believe that
the mirror had led him aright. "And that is command over
a Power which was, is and will be. That you shall prove
before the sight of all men when the morning dawns. No."
He held up his hand to halt the questions he saw the other
would ask. "I shall not tell you how this may be done.
You will come to the testing innocent of all knowledge, so
that no man may afterward question the result. But only
you who were born to do this thing can achieve it."

Arthur studied him soberly. "You plainly believe what
you say, Lord Merlin. But to be High King in Britain is a
task few discerning men would thank you for. Those who
reach now for the crown see only that and not the heavy
burden it carries for its wearer."

Merlin felt a lessening of his doubt. If this boy could
understand that, then indeed he had some of the Old Race
in him. If only he might have been taught! But that time
was past. Now the end lay within Arthur's own character,
for good or ill. And by Ector's account there had already
been ill.

Ector spoke to Merlin. "I shall tell the Council. There
will be those who will raise the cry of sorcery—"

Arthur made a sudden movement. "I am no party to
sorcery!" he stated firmly.

"There is no sorcery," Merlin replied. "There is only a
knowledge which most men have forgotten. And if any

remember enough, then perhaps they may win over you. But it has been prophesied that only you shall reign."

He held stoutly to his faith in the mirror. If that was shaken he had no secure anchor in his life, and all he had done had been meaningless. The Star Lords must have foreseen much when they had prepared the way for this hour to come.

But he was also chilled and had a queer feeling, as if he had lost something he had long treasured. His hope of finding a strong kin in this boy who had been fathered, even as he had been, by the strange beings who strode easily from star to star, that withered into dust. Even the tie he clung to when he met with Ector, tenuous as it was, was lacking here. There was no feeling of inner recognition between Arthur and himself.

Now the boy shifted from one foot to the other, looked from Merlin to Ector, as if he awaited only his foster father's permission to be gone. When Ector nodded, he vanished so quickly it was easy to read his relief in being away from this stranger whom he might distrust more than trust.

"I have been thinking." Ector became brisk, as if he, too, sensed a certain atmosphere of strain. "There is a stone nearby—I think it might be one of the Old Ones— well placed for our service. But will they listen to you?"

"They will," stated Merlin grimly and briefly. "Now let us to this stone of yours."

Ector was right, it was indeed a standing stone, very like those in the Place of the Sun, except this one happened to be alone. Perhaps it marked some long-ago victory or defeat. Power was still generated by some great deed within it, sensed when he ran his fingertips across its surface. Right for his purpose indeed.

Merlin freed the sword from its wrappings and, placing both hands on the hilt, set its point to the surface of the stone. Slowly, in a low voice, he began the chant, not to induce a stone to rise this time, but rather to open a gate for the metal resting against it. He put all the concentration he had learned into this deed, shutting out the world, leaving just the stone and the metal which he would make obey his will.

The point of the sword bored inward, as if what it rested against was not hard rock but far softer wood. Inch by inch Merlin strove to work the metal into the stone.

When it was a third embedded his arms fell to his side and he swayed, would have crumpled to the ground if Ector had not caught him.

"The ancient knowledge is a fearsome thing, kinsman." He steadied Merlin's body against his own, his arm tightly about the younger man's shoulders. "Had I not seen you do this deed I would not have believed. But Arthur does not know the words of Power. Can he indeed draw it forth again?"

"It is so set that only he can do so," Merlin said faintly. "He is of the race who have power over stone and metal, though he knows it not." He made a strong effort, drawing on his own last store of energy. "Now we must see that the lords are made aware of the testing."

Afterward Merlin was never to remember clearly how he confronted that assembled company. He only knew that within him that night there was an upsurge of Power so that men listened—even though he wove no illusions—listened and believed. With torches in hand they went to the stone and there looked at the sword buried in its harsh body. Thereafter they agreed that the test Merlin proposed would be their first effort to select a war leader. Even though they might well believe that no one of their number could pluck that metal forth, yet something in them yielded to Merlin's fervor.

He himself was so wearied that he fell rather than laid himself down on the bed of cloaks and coverings which Ector provided in his own tent; he then passed into a sleep untroubled by any dreams, as spent as a man who has won a victory against overwhelming odds.

In the morning Merlin ate and drank what was given to him, tasting nothing, chewing and swallowing without knowing what he did, so centered was his whole energy on what was to happen. Later he took his place by the stone with an impatience he found hard to cloak with the outward-seeming dignity and foreknowledge which his role of prophet demanded.

They came, those of the most consequence first. Lot of Orkney stood, his face a fox's mask beneath fox-red hair, his eyes sliding from one man to another as if he would so weigh the importance of each man to his own cause.

But under his hand the sword did not stir. In fact he jerked his fingers quickly back from the hilt as if they had been licked by fire. Goloris' son out of Cornwall tried, and the others, so many that their names began to mean little to Merlin. Most were tribesmen, but one or two must have been of Ambrosius' old army, for they were clearly of the Roman breed.

Next came the younger men, some boys who had barely taken armor. Their attempts to draw the magic blade were more intense, as if they believed where their elders were of two minds about it all. Cei's dark face was the only one Merlin recognized. He had always been too much apart from court and camp to know many.

But he held his breath as Arthur, the sun turning his hair to a gold as clear and bright as that from the Western Isle, stepped forward at last. Then within Merlin's mind word fitted itself to word in a smooth, long-practiced pattern, though he spoke not aloud.

Arthur wiped the palms of his hands across his thighs as if they were damp with sweat. His tunic was as sun-bright as his hair, and the light seemed to draw in about him in a dazzle of flame. Or was it only Merlin who saw him so?

The boy closed a tight grip on the hilt of the Sky Sword. Merlin saw the rippling of muscles as his tunic tightened on shoulder and arm with the effort he put forth. His face was utterly serious. If no one else in this throng was wholly sure, Arthur was.

There came a protesting, grating sound. Slowly the sword loosened, came forth from the slit in which it had been set. Merlin heard the indrawn breaths, the gasps from those who watched. They had all tried—they knew this deed to be impossible—yet before their eyes Arthur was accomplishing that impossible feat.

He gave a last tug. The hilt fitted his hand as it never had Merlin's narrower, long-fingered one. The blade was a fire as he gave a joyous laugh and swung it up through the air.

Merlin did not shout, but his words carried through all that company as if he had roared them forth full-lunged.

"Hail, Arthur Pendragon, High King of Britain, he who was, is and shall be!"

Awe conquered that moment. He saw even Lot's drawn sword give a warrior's salute to the chief. And Merlin felt the tension begin to ease out of him.

Then he chanced to glance at the gathering of women who stood a little apart. Queens and ladies had stood there watching, perhaps each hoping in her heart that the magic of this deed would favor her lord and that she might reign with him. But among them . . .

Merlin's hands, hanging by his sides, clenched into fists, though he might have guessed she would be here, and in some trappings of state this time, no rough green square belted about her now. No, she was tall for a woman, and slender, with a grace which made most of her companions seem like women who labored in the fields. Her robe was green, right enough, but it was richly worked in fantastic patterns, and the thread of that working was silver, just as there was a silver circlet about her dark head, one which bore a green stone to rest in the middle of her forehead.

Her eyes met his and he saw a small, secret smile form on her lips. Straightaway all his feeling of accomplishment was threatened, he was on the defensive. If he only knew what powers she could summon! The mirror had said that in using her energy to imprison Merlin in the cave she had nearly exhausted what force she could summon. However, just as that field had waned over the years, could Nimue not in turn have regained at least partial command over what she had lost?

The lords of the company were coming to Arthur, to swear their faith to him. Merlin saw Ector, as always a little apart. Two strides closed the distance between them.

"Ector," Merlin said in a voice masked by the clamor of those greeting Arthur, "who is that woman, she who is turning away now?"

He must know what standing Nimue had at court, how much opposition she might be able to summon, either openly or more subtly.

"They call her the Lady of the Lake. For she has a hold of her own, one people say was once a temple to some strange goddess who ruled springs and rivers. But she has great power of healing and has dwelt in the court lately tending Uther until his death. It is she who bore away Morgause, and perhaps keeps her in that tower which is her own. Men credit her with the old learning. Yet if she is of the kin, never has she moved to claim it with such as my own clan."

"No!" Merlin exploded. "She is of the Dark Ones, Ector, and her true name is Nimue. It was by her will that I have lain in prison. We must set watch on her, for she will

mean Arthur no good will, mainly because he is what he
is."

But they were too late, for, when Ector had summoned
two of his trusted valley men to set watch upon the Lady,
they found her gone, no one knowing where. And Merlin
was left with a shadow of fear of what might come to
color his days and disturb his nights.

11.

Merlin stood once more within the Place of the Sun. Lugaid's hut was just a tumble which could no longer be discerned as any habitation of man. He wondered, not for the first time, where the Druid had gone—if he was not indeed dead. He shivered as if some foot had pressed on his own grave barrow, and the loneliness which always lay in wait beyond the circle of his will stirred like some beast crouching ready to attack. Ector—Ector had gone down beneath a Saxon ax, two or three battles ago.

Time had become not a matter of the counting of seasons but rather of battles, for Arthur was the war leader whom they had long sought. He had in him more skill, even in his youth, than Uther had ever summoned for ridding Britain of the invaders; he had more flexibility than Roman-trained Ambrosius had been able to employ in his handling of the jealous, quick-to-anger clansmen.

His answer to the inroads of the Winged Hats had been cavalry—the Black Horsemen of the borders. Horses of the Friesian breed, larger and heavier than the native ponies, which had been auctioned off nearly a generation earlier when the cavalry left the wall, mated to the also dark-coated Fell Ponies of the north, producing a wiry and strong mount, able to carry a man wearing chain armor. The horses themselves also wore protection of stiffened leather oversewn with metal links.

The Saxons, in spite of their reverence for white horses, which they sacrificed to Wotan on suitable occasions, were not the horsemen most tribesmen were. And a quick cavalry charge, tearing into massed footmen, became Arthur's way. Ambrosius had done well in his time, holding back the invaders, pushing out those Vortigen had welcomed as a buffer against Scotti and the Picts; Uther had held precariously to the gains his brother had made. But

117

Arthur was ever pushing at the Saxons, forcing them back
and out.

More and more of them had taken to their dragon-
prowed boats with their women and children, their possessions; they headed overseas, away from Britain where the
continual harassment of Arthur's men kept them living
with spear and ax to hand, with no surety at the rising of
each day's sun that they would be alive to see its setting.

In so much had Arthur won.

Merlin dismounted by the King Stone, his shoulders a
little bent under his white robe.

He rested both palms on the surface of the block. How
young, how filled with excitement and triumph he had
been on the day it was set here! He had won so easily
what he had given his life to obtain. A stone ferried back
across the sea, planted in the earth of Britain—an act too
small to be deemed a victory.

Now he sighed wearily. He had made Arthur king, yes.
But the Arthur who now sat on the throne was not the
king of his dreams, nor his labors. He listened to Merlin
with courtesy. Sometimes—only sometimes—would he
listen with agreement. The priests of the Christ were also
near at hand. And they turned on Merlin when they could
with a gabble of sorcery, raking up once more the old
tale that he was demon-sired.

It seemed to him now that there was always a subtle
flaw in all he planned. Only three things had he done without mistake: brought this stone back to its rightful place
where it could serve as part of a future beacon, freed the
Sky Sword and put it in Arthur's hand and raised Arthur
himself to the throne.

But Arthur did not have the learning which the future
of the Sky People depended on. His character had been
formed by others. And Merlin had long since learned that
Nimue had her own ways of countering all he would do.

There was the matter of the Queen. Merlin's mouth
twisted in a grimace as if a mortal pain had struck him
with that thought. A king's daughter, of such beauty as
made men's breath catch in their throats when they first
looked on her—outwardly a worthy mate for Arthur. Inwardly—what? A toy, a doll, a woman so obsessed with
her own kind of power, of the body alone, that her eyes
were never still when she was in company; rather they flitted here and there seeking out each man to see if he was

smitten suitably by her grace of face and form. That was
Guenevere.

And Merlin scented suspiciously something about her
that was of Nimue, though he had never seen the Lady of
the Lake since she had turned smiling from Arthur's
triumph with the sword. So long ago . . .

Merlin rubbed his hand across his forehead. He felt a
great weariness of spirit, together with a foreboding he
could not understand. Twice he had made the pilgrimage
back to the cave, but the mirror was silent; he had not
tried to break its silence, drawing instead what force lay
within himself to carry on.

Still he dreamed at times, and those dreams were able
to nourish his will. He saw the cities which rose in the sky,
the men who mastered the ability to fly, fashioned the
land itself to suit their will as a potter slaps and pinches
clay into a new form. He saw what man could create, and
then he awoke to the squalor and the degradation of what
man had come to in this age.

He had wisdom to offer, but who would accept his
counseling? Arthur—when it suited his own plans. Others—a few who came to him for healing. But the majority
listened to the priests from overseas, looking on everything
that was not favored by their preaching as the outpouring
of evil. How and why had he come to this low ebb?

He stood apart now as if encased in uncracking ice. He
could feel compassion, but he was more kin to the beasts
of the fields and the forests than to man. And always the
loneliness gnawed him.

His very appearance set him apart, for it seemed that
he did not age greatly now that he had reached man's es-
tate. He prudently used the arts of herbs to alter his face
and hair, bringing about the effects of encroaching years;
otherwise his continued youth would also awake hostility
in men who feared most of all the failing of their own
powers, the approach of age which meant death in the
end.

Cold and dark—

Suddenly Merlin shook his head, stood straighter. He
was letting his own uncertainties defeat him. Arthur was
firmly on the throne of Britain. The King had forged that
peace with the sword Merlin had put in his hand. No man
could seize victory unless he had first tasted defeat. This

was the hour at last, the hour toward which all his own
life had been directed!

He looked about him with renewed vigor like one awakening from a dark dream. The stones stood tall and strong
here, ancient as their setting had been. What had the mirror ever set in his mind—the Power that was, is and will
be! And the "will be" lay before. He would bring Arthur
here in spite of all the priests from overseas, take him on
to the mirror. Why had he allowed shadows to lie heavy
in his own mind, whisper dispiriting thoughts in his ears?
He was Merlin of the Mirror, perhaps the last man of this
world to hold so much of the old knowledge! He had
wasted time too long. Now that Arthur did not need to
hunt the invaders from his land he would be ripe and ready
for the task he had been destined for, just as Merlin had
been destined in turn.

It seemed to him as he threw aside that morbidity of
mind that the stones blazed royally under the sun, with a
flare like that of torches. They stood for torches in a manner, emblems of forgotten light in a dark world. He held
his head high, straightened his shoulders.

Why had he allowed the cloak of doubt and a premise
of defeat to rest on him lately? It was as if men's talk of
magic indeed held a core of truth and he had been firmly
encircled by some spell, just as he had formerly been removed from the world by the action of the mirror to
preserve his life. Flooding through him now was a realization of Power almost as strong as the day he had raised
the King Stone from its bed of earth on the Western Isle.

Yet he also felt a reluctance to leave, to start back to
the High King's fortress-palace. These stones were closer
to him in spirit than any man living. And he thought with
deep regret of how he had longed for Arthur's birth that
there might be one other to share the alienation he always
felt, most strongly when he was among a throng of men.

He whistled and the horse, which had strayed a little,
grazing on the ragged grass about the standing stones,
nickered an answer, trotted to him and butted its head
against Merlin's chest while he fondled its ears, the stand
of mane between. It was one of the famous black mounts,
larger and sturdier than the hill ponies Merlin had known
years earlier, and more docile, lacking those quirks of in-
dependence which sometimes moved the ponies to resent
the control of any rider.

After he swung up into the saddle Merlin still lingered to look on the stones wistfully. He could see the barrow they had raised over Ambrosius, that dark, forceful man who had endeavored so hard to bring back the past because only in its ways could he see any security.

Uther did not lie here. The foreign priests had claimed his body, set it under the floor of one of their rough-walled churches which had been erected on the site of a Roman temple, the very stones of that temple riven and reset to the service of this new god.

Merlin could see also the barrow they had invaded to bring forth the sword. Who had lain there? One of the true Sky Men who had come to death so far from his home? Or one like himself, a son of a mixed union? Merlin would never know, but now he found his hand rising in a warrior's salute, not only to the man called the Last of the Romans, but also to that unknown one of a far earlier age.

As he rode out of the Place of the Sun he buttressed his own resolve. He would appeal to Arthur, take him to the mirror. Arthur was far from a stupid man; he could tell the difference between ancient knowledge and that which ignorant men of this age termed magic.

Also it was time, surely it was time that Merlin put the King Stone to its intended use. There was a certain object in the cave of the mirror. That must be brought forth, placed under the stone meant from the first to be its guardian, and then—then the summons would go forth!

Ships from the stars, ships which themselves were older than man could reckon, would come in answer. Once more men would rise to conquer sky, earth and sea! The glory of that belief exalted him, gave warmth to melt quickly the ice encasing his hopes. Man stood on the first step of a new and glorious age.

So was he borne up by his thoughts during the long journey back to Camelot, and his night dreams were the brightest he had ever had. Arthur and the mirror—the signal and the stone—

Days later Merlin rode up the rise of the ring-and-ditch fortress which Arthur had held and reworked into the most formidable hold in all of Britain. The guards knew him well enough so that there was no challenge at the inner gates. And he paused only to change his travel-stained robe for one more in keeping with the splendor of the court before he sought out the King.

Arthur was inclined to be expansive. "Hail, Merlin." He beckoned across the center of the board which was one of Merlin's own ideas, a circular dining place where no quick-tempered chief or petty king could claim that he was slighted by being placed below another with a lesser claim for notice. Being round, none could say that his fellow was more advantageously placed than he.

"Hail, Lord King." Merlin was quick to notice a new face among the familiar ones. Cei was no longer at Arthur's right hand, though the foster brother, for all his uncertain temper, had been the King's comrade from the beginning. No, here was a new youth, hardly more than a boy.

Looking on the dark face of that stranger, Merlin suppressed a sudden shiver. If Arthur had nothing in his features of the presence of the Blood, this youth showed it more plainly than Merlin had yet seen it, except in his own mirrored face.

Familiar was that look, yet also strange. For the eyes which peered from under the veiling lids were hard, unreadable. Those sullen and watchful eyes were old beyond the apparent years of the boy's body; they more than hinted at some vengeance. . . .

Merlin took his imagination firmly to task. He should be glad at this moment that one of the Old Race was here. Yet there was nothing in the youth to which he could warm.

"You are in time." Arthur gestured and his own cupbearer hastened to produce another cup of hammered silver, fill it with the wine from overseas and hand it respectfully to Merlin. "You are in time, bard, to drink to the health of one of the Pendragon blood new come into our service." He nodded to the youth. "This is Modred, who is son to the Lady Morgause, and so my own nephew."

Merlin's hand closed tightly about the goblet. He did not even need that sly, darting look from the boy's eyes, a look which measured him in a way alerting him to danger, to know the truth.

Arthur's nephew? Nay, Arthur's son by that slut whom Nimue had taken into hiding. And by that single glance at him, Merlin was also sure the boy knew the truth—or the part of it which could cause the most harm for Arthur—

that he was indeed the King's son, and by a lady who was reputed the King's half-sister.

Merlin drank, knowing that his long training in hiding his feelings must now serve him better than ever before. "Lord Modred." He nodded to the boy. "The Pendragon blood is in honor."

"Aye." Arthur smiled. "He is in good time to blood his sword and show what mettle he has in him. For we have had the coast lights up along the Saxon shore. These war dogs yet sniff around for some mouthful of prey to snatch. We ride hunting again—"

The King's face was a little flushed, his eyes alight. Merlin, looking at him, knew that no argument he might use now would stop Arthur. He must set aside his own plan of confronting the King with the mirror, so letting Arthur learn his heritage and true purpose. And Modred ... Modred who was the King's son was fostered by Nimue. That Merlin also instinctively knew. She had had a long time, as earth men measured time, to prepare the shaft. Now she had launched it. To the malice of one who sees himself bereft of a rightful place, add the iron will of Nimue. She had a formidable weapon in this youth.

Though caution moved in Merlin, so did anger begin to rise. It was always Nimue and from the first he had been far too influenced by her good fortune. Now he would seek her out. And how better find a road to her than through this Modred who was her creature?

Merlin listened to the excited talk of a new expedition against the Saxons. But as he sat in his place at that round board he raised his eyes to the gallery of the great hall, there looking from one fair face to another. It was the boast of the Queen that she had in her train the most beautiful women of Britain, having no jealousy in any threat of comparison.

There sat Guenevere. Her richly embroidered robe was a clear yellow, like ripening grain. There was a thin crown of red gold on her hair, which was so near the color of her robe that hair melted into cloth and cloth seemed a part of hair. A heavy necklace of amber was around her throat, and earrings of that same mystic gem dangled against each cheek as she leaned forward, her eyes narrowly intent on—whom?

Merlin traced her gaze. She was looking at Modred and about her lips there lay a faint shadow of a lazy smile.

For a long moment Merlin studied her intently, for he knew that something lay in that look which he could not read. And his inability to do so was disturbing. That the women of the tribes were puzzles for him was perhaps a kind of maiming, though that thought was startling in itself and he did not have time to consider it now. He had believed Guenevere a doll, a plaything, without any thoughts which might be of service to his own goal. Was she more?

He was searching now for another face, however. So he turned from the bright sunlight of the Queen to the more subdued rainbow of her ladies. Some he knew by name, others were but flower faces which he had never chosen to study with as much interest as he now gave them. Nowhere was the one he sought. There was no dark lady as vivid, or perhaps more vivid, than the Queen. If Nimue had introduced Modred to the court, she had not come here herself, or else she chose not to attend this feast.

Slowly Merlin sought for her with that other sense which he rarely used in such a large company, mainly because it could be overwhelmed and lost when there were so many minds and personalities all emitting energies of their own. No, he would take blood oath his enemy was not present.

But her will was here, in the person of the King's "nephew." Merlin began to plan anew. He could not believe that this sudden news of Saxons at the coast signified any great difficulty. It would seem that Arthur himself looked on this ride as a diversion, a chance to show his new-found nephew the dexterity and invincible force of the Black Horse troops.

Now—Merlin knew it inside himself, swelling, pushing aside, erasing all the doubts of his half-human heritage—now was the time for him to do what should be done in this hour. Summon the Sky ships at long last—with or without Arthur's concordance!

He had withdrawn, even in the midst of the feasters, into his own thoughts. Now he was suddenly aware that the men about him were rising, calling on their armor bearers, making ready to ride. There was excitement in them, that fiery thirst for battle that always marked the tribesmen. He could feel the force of their emotions kindling an answer in himself. And he was quick to control it with that other part of him which was not of this world, but of the Star Lords; that part of him thought, planned and used invisible forces to accomplish its ends, not the sharp-edged primitive weapons about him.

There was one standing before him, looking into his eyes. Merlin, now alert, stared back at Modred.

"They call you bard." Modred's voice was low-pitched, to pass unheard in the clamor about them now. "They also name you sorcerer, son of no man." There was an insolence in his tone which would have brought any of the tribesmen to his feet, sword half out, ready to offer an open challenge in return.

"All that is the truth." Merlin was a little mystified by this open approach, though he had felt from the first that Nimue's man would in some way make plain his feeling.

"And how much of it is true?" The challenge in the youth's voice was even more marked.

Merlin smiled. "How much truth do any of us know concerning ourselves? Or are able to convey that truth even a little to others? We all have our own powers and forces, much or little. What matters is how we use the gifts and learning given us."

"There is learning from the dark as well as from the light," the other answered him flatly. "The High King listens to the priests of light, bard. The old days are done—"

Now Merlin laughed. The same battle fever which gripped those around him at the message that there were Saxons to be met arose in him, but for another reason. Nimue, through this youth, was delivering her challenge. And when it came to war, then his doubts vanished. He could draw on the forces he had used that day when the stone rose to his signal and moved. What had eaten him lately in this court? He was no useless tool; he was a commander of such powers as none in this hall had ever seen. Now his mind moved rapidly as he enumerated those powers in part, even as his surface thoughts probed at Modred.

"Have you never heard this, Lord Modred," he asked, making a mockery of that name, light mockery which the boy caught, for there was a dark flush rising under his skin, "that there is that which was, is and will be? I think she who taught you knew that promise well."

He had half turned away when Modred caught at the sleeve of his robe.

"You are insolent, bard! And what mean you by 'she'?"

Merlin laughed again. So Nimue had not been able to establish full control of this nursling of hers. He might look like one of the Old Blood but he had the ways of the tribes, with that spark of angry fire rising at the first crossing of mental swords.

"Boy"—he gave him no "lord" this time—"you have not learned manners, whatever else you have been taught." Merlin twitched the sleeve of his robe from between the other's fingers. "Most of all, you should learn the nature of your man before you speak."

Perhaps he had given the boy a hint too much with those words. But he was also of tribe blood and royal as Modred. He also thought that Nimue must not have done too well in choosing this tool for her meddling. He was not another Ector, nor even a Cei—he was partly a fool.

Merlin made his way through the throng of excited men. He had his own mission, now that he had at last made up his mind. However, at the door he paused to look back. Modred was still staring after him, and now the boy's hand lay on another arm, that of one of the priests from overseas. The priest's shaved face was alive with emotion and Merlin saw that Modred's lips were moving. That he stirred some pot of trouble, Merlin had no doubt. But what kind of trouble . . . He shrugged.

He went swiftly to his own quarters and put aside the bard's robes. Those white lengths made him too conspicuous. He pulled on a simple tunic over breeches, picked up a hooded cloak. Thus garbed, he found a fresh mount, filled saddlebags with bread and cheese from the kitchens where the servants milled about doing the same for the troops gathering at the King's orders. But Merlin rode out first, and in the direction of the mountains.

It had been several years now since he had taken this way, but he could never forget each twist and turn of its going. And the time he had spent living wild in the woods never departed from his mind either, so that he made small camps at night without fire, and was able to hide his going well, which had become habit with him.

The ruins of Nyren's hold showed now only as a single tumbled outer wall overgrown with bramble and bush. There were no longer any ghosts left there to trouble him. But Merlin halted for a long moment as he came near it, trying wistfully to remember how it had been when that was the clan home for one Myrddin.

Then came the upward slope. There he stripped his mount of bridle and saddle, hobbled it and turned the horse loose to graze while he went to the mirror. He picked free the stones of his door to go inside. The cave was very dim. Not one of the cubes showed any light, and he did not approach the mirror. This time he had no question to ask. He knew well what must be done.

Edging along the wall he came to a cylinder as tall as his forearm, as big around as a circle his two hands could make, thumb touching thumb, little finger against little finger. Stooping he gathered that up. Long ago the mirror voice had told him of this, of how it must be used. The instructions were as clear in his mind now as if they had been issued within the hour. This was the full purpose of his life. There must be no more hesitation, no more trying to work through men whose natures betrayed over and over the will of the Star Lords.

The beacon was lighter than he thought it would be as he carried it out into the open. He set it to one side, reclosed the door with the stones. He was not finished with the mirror. Arthur *would* come sooner or later, even as had been planned. There would be time for that. How long it might take for his message to reach the ships, he had no idea. Months, years . . . it was his task to keep Arthur king until that hour when those others would come.

Holding the cylinder close against him as one embraces a longed-for treasure, Merlin started down the slope.

12.

~~~~~~

There was no light this time when Merlin reached the Place of the Sun. The year was late, harvest was well in and cold bit fiercely at a man in the frost-tinged early mornings, the long dark nights. And the stones seemed to stand bleakly aloof now, as if they had withdrawn from all possible contact with the men of this earth.

If he still had the shining sword his task would have been comparatively easy. But now that was Arthur's, and Merlin must make do as best he could with his knowledge alone. As he penetrated the pillared circles he shivered with more than the reaching fingers of the cold wind. The kinship which he had always felt waiting for him here was missing, closed off like a door to shut out the unwanted in the dark of night.

Nor did Merlin lift his hand to caress any of the stones as he had been wont to do on his earlier visits here. Necessity drove him directly to the task. So he approached the King Stone where it lay, flanked on either side by the rude arches in all their strength.

Carefully putting down on the ground what he had carried through these days of travel from the cave in the mountains to this site, Merlin considered the stone.

It was plain that he could not merely set his burden out, enthroned on the stone, as he had once naïvely thought to do. Anyone passing here, shunned though the site generally was, might be moved by curiosity to inspect the beacon. No, it must be well hidden and his training told him exactly where: under the massive block of stone itself.

He had moved the rock once to prove his strength, therefore he could move it again, though the task was a formidable one without the sword. He had only the short blade of his belt knife and that was not fashioned from the wondrous metal. Nevertheless he must use it.

It was dusk when he had reached the stones. Their shadows cut deep, and there was something about those shadows. He found himself jerking his head around now and then to stare intently at one or another of the pools of dark. Though he knew that Nimue had previously used only such illusions as he himself could call up at command, still there remained a residue of the uncanny, the not-to-be-known in this place.

Merlin recalled what Lugaid had once said, that a temple where the worship of certain forces had continued for a long time absorbed into itself the power of belief rising from those worshipers. That power, too, could be drawn on by the men who know how to awaken it.

Only this was not a place of the night. It needed dawn or the full beams of the sun, which had long been honored here as a source of life, to bring forth its full energy. He must wait out the hours of the night. But he could use that time to prepare himself for what would be the greatest effort he had yet made, greater even than the parade of illusions which had brought about Arthur's fathering.

Picking up the beacon once again, he moved over to the tumbled mound which had been Lugaid's dwelling. There he made his rude camp, drinking from a small spring, now almost silted up again since the Druid had not come to clear passage for the water, eating the last of the provisions he had carried from Camelot.

Merlin settled then with his back against the half-toppled wall of rough stones and looked back over the Place of the Sun. As the light fast faded the wind came. When that blew around and over the pillars there rose a weird wailing sound; the imaginative might well read into it the lament of men and women now long vanished from the earth, yet still somehow alive and longing for a safe return.

Not for the first time Merlin wondered about the Sky Lords. What did they seek here that they were so determined to come again? If they were mighty enough to travel from one of those stars now shining above him to another, why could they not have found another world which would welcome them?

Was there some quality found only here which they

must have in order to endure as a race? Did they need mankind in order to survive? The mirror had been evasive whenever he had tried to probe into that. He had often been overwhelmed, when it poured forth information, with much he could not begin to understand because his world had no names for the strange artifacts, the complicated machines those others used with ease. But some of the most simple questions appeared in turn to silence the voice, as if it in turn were baffled by such searching on his part.

Though he did not close his eyes now, but continued to watch night engulf the Place of the Sun, Merlin was at work inside himself, drawing out scraps of knowledge, summoning energy to buttress all his power. This would be no fashioning of an hallucination, it would be a real act.

He was a general as supreme as Arthur, but his troops were not men. Down and down he delved into his own memory and mind. And then, with a sudden start, he recognized a picture which that memory supplied. There was Nimue in this place, her body white, her hair tossed by the wind. He could hear the honey smoothness of her voice, almost reach out to touch the hand she extended to him. No!

Resolutely Merlin fought that memory which was so troubling. He was a little apprehensive ... could he perhaps actually touch Nimue now by recalling her too plainly? Out of his mind—he must thrust her safely away.

The mirror, he must concentrate on the mirror, as if it stood full-length before him now. He grew calmer and his turmoil faded as he visualized the mirror. And its voice was in his ears so that he could sort out words, phrases, fit such together to reinforce his knowledge of what must be done here at sunrise.

He was no longer tired. Power was growing steadily in him, filling his body, his mind. He must hold it so contained until the moment came to release it to do his will. Time for darkness—time for light—but he did not mark the hours. Nor was he any longer cold. Power furnished heat in his body so that he threw off his hooded cloak in spite of the frost-breathing wind.

Chancing to glance down at his two hands resting on his knees, he was not surprised to see that his flesh was giving off a kind of glow. Why shouldn't it? He was afire with force, and now he had only to contain it until the moment to come. His lips moved but not even a whisper emerged from between them, only in his mind did the archaic words echo in the proper patterns.

Merlin rose when the sky grayed. Though he had been sitting through the night his limbs were in no way stiffened. He felt instead like a runner advancing to the starting post, eager to be gone. His left arm cradled the beacon against him. His right hand held the belt knife, drawn and ready.

Long strides brought him to the King Stone and he stood behind that block ready to face the rising sun. He placed the beacon on the ground between his feet. And now he stretched out his hand, began to bring the knife blade ringingly down on the stone, while from him poured all those words he had gathered out of memory, arranged in the right pattern, ready for this great moment in his life.

Beat—beat—ever increasing in tempo. The sky showed the forebanners of the rising sun. His voice sing-songed an invocation older perhaps than even the stones about him. Beat—chant—beat—

The stone—it was coming alive, reluctantly, heavily, in grudging answer. But it was coming! The beat had increased to a flashing of metal; sparks flew from that meeting of rock and iron. Merlin's voice rose as he called on the force which was imprisoned in the stone to answer to his will.

The block stirred, not as quickly as it had under the summons of the sword, but it was answering! His will harnessed the force—he raised the knife blade—one end of the stone followed.

His tunic clung damply to his body. In spite of the cold he was feverish with heat, sweat pouring from him. Up and up. Until that block stood on end. Then he said the single word he had never dared use before, one of the Great Bindings of Power. The stone remained on end, the place where it had lain was bare.

Merlin dropped to his knees. He began to dig with the knife point in the uncovered oblong of earth, working as fast as he could, for he had no idea how long that Word would hold an inanimate object. Dig, scrape loose the soil, dig again, deeper, deeper, faster—

At last he had the pit ready and he fitted the beacon into it, standing erect, its lighter end pointing to the sky.

Now he worked even faster, pounding back most of the
earth he had excavated, hammering the soil down with
both palm of hand and butt of knife. Finally he threw
aside the knife and, with his earth-stained, broken-nailed
hands, he touched the top of the cylinder at a certain
place, turned it so that the cover itself slid around to the
left under the pressure of his fingers.

Trembling from near exhaustion, Merlin threw himself
back from the bed of the stone. He got to his knees, looking up at the towering block. In his mind he released the
Word. The stone fell with a crushing force. He only hoped
that his pit for the beacon had been deep enough to
preserve it. But now he was so spent that he could only
lie, one hand against the King Stone, only half conscious
that he had finished his task.

It was the touch of the stone which aroused him at last.
He had always been able to feel the force imprisoned in
this mighty block, but this steady throb was new. Merlin
gave a cry of relief and joy as understanding reached him.
He had succeeded. The stone itself was charged by the
beacon—he had indeed lighted the way. But when would
the ships come? How far, how many, when?

He was too weak to rise to his feet at once, but sat
there, his head drooping on his breast, his hand resting on
the rock, aware most of all of that steady beat.

What roused him this time was an alert of danger, as if
some warning or foul stench had carried down the wind.
He groped in the withered grass for his knife, his only
weapon. Now he heard the thud of hooves, a shout which
could only have come from a human throat.

Saxons? Outlaws? He was sure only by that warning of
his heightened senses that those who came were enemies.
So he did not rise to his feet, rather crept on his hands
and knees into the shadow of a standing stone. From there
he could see the party milling about. They were not
advancing directly toward his insecure hiding place, he
thought they were reluctant to enter the enclosure of the
Place of the Sun.

One of them came riding swiftly from the direction of
Lugaid's hut, urging Merlin's horse before him. He could
hear their excited voices but not make out the words. He
was near enough, however, to see that the two who appeared to command the party wore the robes of the

priests from overseas, while their followers were plainly liege men to some tribal lord.

The priests were urging the warriors on. But, in spite of commands impatiently delivered, as far as Merlin could read their gestures, the tribesmen were not about to enter the ancient sacred place, which was a clue to their mission. For the oldest law to which all the tribes bowed was that no blood could be spilled within, no fugitive pursued into one of the Places of Power.

He was sure that he was their quarry but he could not guess the reason for their hunt. Arthur gave room at his court to the believers in the Christ and many of his people were worshipers, but he also followed the liberal policy established by Ambrosius, asking no man what god he paid homage to when he came armed and ready to join in the harrying of the invaders. There were still some of the old Roman breed who bowed knee to the Bull-Slayer Mithras, and others who served older gods of Britain.

Who had granted these hunters permission to come after him? Merlin would swear that it was not the doing of Arthur. Though the King had never been kin-close as Merlin had once hoped, he respected and sometimes listened to the man who had put the sword of Britain into his hand. No, Arthur would not turn against him. But someone had sent these hunters, and his guess fastened on Modred. Had the "nephew" come out of nowhere gained this much ascendancy at Camelot?

The priests were still urging on their followers, but the warriors drew back. So now the gray robes themselves came forward alone. One held aloft the symbol of his god, a cross of wood, and they were both chanting. Merlin saw that the sturdier of the two had drawn a sword, though that was foreign to the very teachings he was supposed to uphold: a man who was a priest was not a warrior.

Hiding like a hunted animal revolted Merlin so he now rose to his feet on the far side of the stone behind which he had taken refuge. When he stepped into sight he was as erect as a warrior awaiting an enemy's charge.

Now that they were closer Merlin could see their features and he recognized one. He was the priest to whom Modred had been speaking in the feasting hall at Camelot. So his suspicion was confirmed. This meeting was of Modred's doing.

"Whom do you search for, men of a god's service?" Merlin came into full view.

The one who held the cross chanted, in the tongue of Romans, an invocation against the forces of Darkness. Now he stuttered over a word, but continued his chant valiantly. His companion did not quite raise his sword. Though his eyes were those of a fanatic, he seemed not yet ready to ride down an unarmed man.

"Demon spawn!" he spat, his voice rising above the chant.

Merlin shook his head. "You stand now," he said quietly, "in a place which has known many gods. Most are now long forgotten, because those who called upon their names in times of peril are also gone. As long as men realize that there is some greater Power outside themselves, a force which will aid them to better lives, to good will, and to peace in time, so there will be gods. What matter if some men call that Power which is the greater Mithras or Christus or Lugh? The Power is the same. Only men differ, being mortal, while the Power was, is and will be—beyond even the death of this earth on which we now stand."

"Blasphemer!" was the cry from the priest. "Servant of the Evil One—"

Merlin shrugged. "You take upon yourself my role, Priest. It is for a bard to call names, though he does it with greater ease and skill, being well able even to insult kings to their shame in open courts when he chooses to sing them down. I have no quarrel with you. What I have heard of your Christus tells me that he is indeed one who holds true Power. But I say he is not the only one who has—or will. To each tribe of men a god arises in his own time. I salute your Christus as one who has seen the Great Light. But would such a one welcome the hunting of men who do not follow his road? I think not, for if he did, then truly he is not the Great One to whom all roads are made open and plain."

The older priest's chant had dwindled into silence. He studied Merlin with an odd appraising look on his old face, for it was a face wrinkled and much worn by time.

"You say strange things, my son," he said.

"If you have heard much concerning me, Priest, then you know I am a strange man. If you wish to match pow-

ers with powers—that is the game of a child who plays
with the truth and does not use it worthily. Behold—"

He pointed with his forefinger, moving it quickly from
side to side. Small flames danced for the space of three
breaths on the crown of four of the blue stones.

The older priest watched this with calm. His wild-eyed
companion flushed a deep red and cried out: "Devil's
work!"

"If that be so then, as evil yields to the force of good,
banish it, Priest!" ordered Merlin as again the flames
danced.

The priest pointed and spoke in Latin. But the flames
remained until Merlin snapped his fingers, when they vanished. Now the priest's face swelled with scarlet wrath.

"The nature of evil," Merlin observed slowly, "lies not
outside a man, but in. Within himself he makes room for
hate, fear and all the things which are spawned in
darkness. If he does not give such room, then he does not
give birth to demons. I use no force to harm and never
have. Nor will I do so. For if I put my talents to such a
purpose, then they shall in turn be lost to me. What god I
hail when I use his Power, that is my own concern. I
strive not to make any other man believe in him. It is
enough that I know such Power exists, that it was, is and
shall be!"

The old priest studied him for a moment and then said:
"Stranger, your road is not ours. But from this moment I
shall not believe what has been told us, that you are an
active agent of evil. You are sadly mistaken, and I shall
pray for you, that your mind may be turned to the truth
and away from the error you believe in."

Merlin bowed his head for a moment. "Priest, all
prayers made in good faith are noted by the Power. It
matters not in what name they may be said. I mean you
no harm, let it be that you shall say the same—"

"No!" The cry came out as if the younger priest were
strangling with anger, or perhaps some fear. "This demon
breed is a threat to all believing men. He shall die!"

He made a sudden lunge with the sword, not awkwardly
but with ease. Merlin thought that perhaps he had been a
warrior before he had put on the priest's robe. But Merlin was ready, for he had noted the small change in the
other's eyes. His own hand swung up, empty. The sword

was dragged to one side, as if caught by a giant magnet, to crash against the nearest stone. The blade shattered.

"Go in peace," Merlin said as the priest stared incredulously at the jagged scrap he held. "I say the truth, I mean harm to no man. But you would do well to ride from this place. For the old ban remains here: no man coming in wrath and with a bared weapon once lived within these circles. The worshipers who enforced that law are long gone, but there is still the force of their prayers. Go and be glad that the stones do not rise up to answer you in kind."

"Brother Gildas," the older priest said quietly, "under your obedience to God, do you come. This man walks his own road and it is not for us to question him."

Then he reached down and caught the dangling reins of the other's horse and turned away, leading the second mount behind him, while the rider sat silent as if shocked beyond speech. When they joined the waiting warriors the older priest gave an order. The tribesman who held Merlin's horse loosed it. And they rode away with a haste on the part of the escort which suggested that if the priests did not believe in the force of the ancient holy place, they certainly did.

Merlin watched them disappear. Again the great fatigue born from his efforts seemed to fasten leaden weights on his limbs. He must have sleep and soon. But would it be wise to linger here?

He thought that he could trust the older priest, and from the results of their trial of strength, he was superior to the other. Besides, it had been plain that the warriors were not minded to ride into the Place of the Sun to take him. He returned to the King Stone. The sun generated some warmth here and he had his cloak for a covering. Also the wind had died. He pulled together the coarse, dead grass to fashion a nest in which he settled to sleep.

It was late afternoon when Merlin awoke. The noise he had heard was the plaintive whicker of his horse. It had grazed its way among the stones and now waited nearby. The man wished he could fill his own belly so well. He had eaten the last of his provisions the night before and this was not the season when one could glean berries or herbs to stay hunger. He would have to try his luck in the old way of his boyhood with sling and stone, perhaps he could bring down a rabbit.

Selecting some pebbles which seemed suitable, he set out and found that his old skill was indeed not lost. But he did not leave the circle of the stones, building a small fire instead, striking sparks with a piece of flint and his knife blade. There, beside the King Stone, he roasted the rabbit, eating it down to the last fraction of flesh which could be sucked from its bones.

In spite of the dark Merlin went to sleep again in the same grassy nest as the shadows grew, united and spread darkly. It was as if in his mastery over the stone, his planting of the beacon, he had achieved the freedom of the circles; now there was nothing which could threaten him. And his sleep was without dreams.

Sun in his eyes awoke him. There was no reason to linger here. He had the impression that it would be long before the beacon brought any answer, but before he rode away he again laid a hand to the stone to assure himself that that steady beat continued.

He was riding to Camelot. Modred's setting the priests on him was such an outright declaration of battle that Merlin knew he must not allow it to pass. The youth must not think that he had won even in a little way, that he had brought about what might be termed Merlin's flight. And this time he could enter the court with an unfettered mind, ready to turn to his own purposes any chance which would bring Arthur to listen to him. He had set the beacon, and that great labor the mirror had placed on him was now out of his hands.

Before he reached the court he heard the news of the King's victory in the skirmish over the Saxons at the shore. He had guessed from the first that it had been a skirmish only, but even so small a victory, when Modred had taken part in it, would establish the boy well among the warriors.

Merlin had his own small chamber within the sprawl of the three-story inner building which was ringed about by a stone and earth wall. He went to it, stopping on the way only to order a servant to bring him a kettle of hot water for washing. For his clothing and his body were salty with the dried sweat of the ordeal at the Place of the Sun.

As he stood in the middle of his small room, he looked about him and felt an odd unfamiliarity with it. There were his containers of medicants, the bunches of dried herbs laced on thin thongs across the wall, the few books he had assembled, all in the Latin tongue. There were some queerly shaped stones whose oddity of appearance had appealed to his eye. But there was no wealth, no show or ornament or color. His bed was like a rough box with linens and woolens for covering, and there were no hangings on the walls, no cured skins for rugs. As he looked around him he remembered those other rooms—those of his dream cities and the wonders that furnished them, adorned their walls, covered their floors.

Would he ever see the rise of such tower houses again? Surely it must take a long time for men to learn enough of the long-forgotten knowledge to erect their like. Even if the ship came tomorrow, this year, it might be generations before that world would bloom again.

There could be only one hope left when it did, that it would not be the quarrels of men, or of Sky People, which would tear it once more into nothingness. For how many chances would the Power grant to his kind? There must be a limit in the end to the rise and fall of civilizations, nations, mankind himself.

And when the Sky People came, what if they met such as this Gildas? Could they work through or with such as he? Would they discover enough men ready to believe and to stretch out hands to the future? Or would fear and awe become terror, making ignorant men turn their backs on the offer of a new world?

Arthur—Merlin could understand now why he must win Arthur. Not because the King was a battle leader without equal in this time and land, but because he in himself was a symbol men would follow, listen to, learn from. Therefore, above all, Arthur must be prepared for the coming from the stars.

13.

In the end Merlin did not have to go to Arthur, for the
King came to him. There was a scratching at his curtained
door, an almost stealthy sound, as if the one who waited
there came on some secret errand. He reached out to
twitch the curtain aside and saw the High King, alone.

But this man was not that supremely confident Arthur
of the feast hall. Years had touched him since that night
when he bade Merlin drink to welcome Modred. There
was a tic by his left eye, and he looked as if he had parted
all company with sleep for days. Now he eyed Merlin narrowly, with a menace about him which the other could see
as well as sense.

Arthur turned sharply again after he strode into the
chamber, held up the curtain and gave a quick look right
and left as if he would make sure there were no lurkers
outside. When he spoke he had controlled his voice until it
was only a whisper.

"They have told me tales of you, sorcerer. And those I
did not believe. Perhaps it was because I was a fool and
chose weakly to shut my ears, since it was by your doing
that I came to be High King. Aye, that tale have I also
heard!" Hot anger glowed in his eyes, and the fingers
which rested on the hilt of the Sky Sword curled and
tightened there as if he would draw the blade forthwith.

"Now will I have the full truth out of you even if I
have to carve it from your living flesh! Aye, I am so
driven now, sorcerer, that even that will I try!"

"The truth of what, Lord King?" Merlin, too, sank his
voice. Mischief had been made, that was evident. And he
could guess who had so worked upon Arthur.

"Am I Uther's true-born son?"

Merlin's thoughts sped to a swift conclusion. He could
guess the shameful story which Modred might use as a

level against the King, against Merlin and against all the House of Pendragon.

"That is what he believed," he said slowly.

"Then—" the King's face was white with strain—"then Morgause—and I—Modred—" Suddenly a flicker of intelligence broke through. " 'So he believed,' " he repeated. "You choose odd words, Merlin. Can it be that his belief was not the truth? If so, who fathered me, for Goloris was dead a day before my mother lay with him she thought was her true lord."

Arthur made a visible effort at control. "I have heard a strange tale, Merlin. A claim has been made on me which can cover my name with black shame, set me before men as one worse even than that traitor Vortigen who betrayed his people to the axes of the Saxons. But it was you who took me as a fosterling to Ector, and it is only you who can know the truth. If I am Uther's son in truth, then I am foredoomed through my own lust to be one hunted out of the ranks of honest men. My honor is ruined and were I to give an order to the meanest kitchen slave he would spit at my feet. You say now that Uther *believed* I was his son. Give me the inner meaning of this. For I tell you I am near to drawing my own sword against my throat because of what has been told to me!"

Merlin pulled forward one of the stools. "It is a strange tale, Lord King, but it is the truth, and it goes back many years."

Arthur eyed the stool as if he had no wish to linger there. But he did sit down as he burst forth: "Get on to the telling of it, and quickly! If it can lift this burden of wrongdoing even a little, then—Speak, man!"

"You know what they say of me, and with truth." Merlin sat himself on the edge of the bed, still keeping his voice to a whisper. He was also alerting his inner sense to make sure no other was within range of his voice now. "I am the son of no man. . . ."

Arthur shrugged impatiently. "I know they name you demon-bred. But what has that to do with—"

"Not demon-bred," Merlin interrupted firmly, using his powers as he could to reach out to the King, make him listen. "My fathering was of the Sky People. Aye, there is truth in those old legends. The daughters of men once bore children to others who came from the stars above us. And from that mating arose a mighty race who fashioned such wonders as no man now can do more than dream of. But in the end there was a mighty war, one which did indeed rock the entire earth, so that land became sea and sea bottom land. Mountains rose from plains and all was altered so that those few who survived were like madmen and remembered very little of what they had been. They sank lower than the beasts of the field and forest.

"But those who had fathered them did not forget. And when that war which had carried them outward to the stars—for the Sky Lords had mighty enemies we knew not at all—was done, they remembered earth and longed for it again. Thus they loosed ships of the sky, and one such answered an ancient beacon set among our mountains. It carried the seed of the Sky Lords and my mother was the first to receive it into her womb—"

"You spin a wild tale," Arthur interrupted.

"Look well at me, King, into my eyes," Merlin commanded. "Do I spin you an idle tale or do I speak the truth?"

Arthur met his gaze squarely so that their eyes locked. After a moment the king said slowly: "Though this thing seems impossible, yet you believe it to be the truth."

"A truth I am prepared to prove," Merlin stated. "One of the duties which my birth laid on me was the fostering of a king strong enough to bring all Britain under his hand and keep peace. For the Sky Lords needed that peace when they could come again to us. Ambrosius was a great commander, but he could see peace only as the Romans had commanded and imposed it. Uther could deal with the tribes, but he was of their nature, having their faults as well as their virtues. He was a man of lusty passions and, where those were involved, he knew no self-discipline.

"It chanced at his crowning that he saw the Duchess Igrene and wanted her. So open was his desire that her lord withdrew from court, thus gaining Uther's displeasure. Goloris set his lady, as he thought, safe within his own sea-bound keep, one which had never fallen to an enemy, so well girt and guarded was it.

"Then Uther sent for me and ordered me to use certain powers to gain him his desire. I told him that I could weave an illusion which would make him Goloris in seeming for a night that he might enjoy the Duchess' bed. And I set upon him a dream that this was so, just as I entered the keep and bemused the Duchess with another dream. But what came to her was no man of our world; she conceived by the will of the Sky Lords.

"Uther knew shame and the Duchess, learning that her lord had truly died before he had visited her, was bewildered of mind to the point that she listened to the talk of night demons. Thus both were eager to give you into my hands.

"Ector had in his veins some of the Sky Lords' blood, though his descent from them was far in the past. He took you very willingly. It was set that I should school you, even as I myself was taught, in the lore which had come from our fathers. But I had—have—an enemy." Merlin hesitated. Need he now speak of Nimue? Perhaps he should so that Arthur would be warned.

"The Sky Lords whose heritage we share have their dark enemies also, of an alien breed. They wish that we not rise once more to rule here, but be forever plunged into the darkness which mankind seems ever to draw about him—the darkness of hate, killing, despair. Thus these enemies were alerted as to my birth, and they in turn produced my opposite, one who faces me ever with powers which may be as great as my own, or perhaps more. For we have never yet met in equal contest. This being, bred out of the Darkness, is she whom men call Nimue, Lady of the Lake."

Arthur's amazement was plain to read. "But she gave aid to Uther, she has sheltered Morgause, fostered Modred—" Then he stopped nearly in mid-word and his expression grew intent.

"Aye," Merlin pointed out quietly, "and this devotion to the line of Pendragon might well have two sides, Arthur."

The King's fist clenched where his hand rested on his knee. "I can understand your hint. You think that she has done so with a purpose which means no good to me. But as I have your word, I have her actions. She was your captor?"

"With the Power she gathered to her she kept me captive. For I was unknowing that she had found out my place of refuge until she struck. So I was held in bondage until the time of your crowning, High King. And that which you should have known from your childhood was lost to you. Then I learned what else had happened—that Morgause had tempted you—and, though I have no proof of what I say, I also believe that act was of Nimue's doing. She could well foresee that deep trouble would come of it. As now it threatens. She also made Modred her tool—"

"He is my son," said Arthur heavily. "In honor I cannot deny that."

"In body he may be your son," Merlin agreed, "but inwardly he is of the Dark. And should he set abroad this tale which so defames your name, then can he wreck all you have fought to win."

Arthur looked down at his fist; his face was ravaged, nearly as bleak as if his spirit was broken.

"How can I prevent it?" he asked dully. The first of his anger had burned out; now he looked out from a pit of ashes. "Will any man accept the story you have told me? They will rather prate of demons and all the old fears. And I shall fall from the throne as easily as a leaf is wind-whirled across the ground at the year's end."

"First," Merlin answered him, "you must accept your inheritance, though it comes to you late. I shall give you the proof that all I have said is the truth. This cannot be shared with most men, to that I agree. But with it to arm you, then there will be a way to defeat Modred and the one who stands behind him."

"This proof of yours. . . ?"

"Lies in another place, Lord King. One you must visit without even a shield bearer at your back. Alone with me."

"Leaving Modred here to spread his poison!" Arthur said.

"You will give Modred something to shut his mouth for awhile, and yet this act shall not be strange in the eyes of your men. He is of the blood of Pendragon, therefore you shall make him regent while you go. Yet take the precaution that he has no real bidding over your war lords."

"Aye, be sure I do not give him claws, as it were!" For the first time Arthur's expression grew lighter. "Now I must cast in my mind for an explanation of why I go forth from the court in such a manner."

"Lord King, there are old forts long fallen into disuse in the direction we must travel. A Roman road once ran by them from a good port. Since trade now waxes, what better reason could you find for seeing if this way can once more be put to use? Take with you the men of your own shield comrades. When we reach the point nearest where you must visit, you shall fall ill of a fever and be tended by me, perhaps by one bodyservant you can trust. Have you one in whom you can set full confidence?"

Arthur nodded. "There is Bleheris who came to me when Ector fell. He first taught me how to use a sword. Though the years begin to wear upon him, he is an apt holder of secrets."

Merlin cast his memory. Bleheris? There was a small dark man with tattooing across his forehead, not one of the tribes. He identified that vision from the past.

"The Pict?"

"Aye, he was won to Ector when he was not slain out of hand as he lay with a broken leg after a raid. And he married Flanna, who was my nurse. She chose to stay even after her service was over and Ector offered her freedom and goods, the same that you promised her. Bleheris is now my man, bound to me tighter than any battle comrade."

Merlin nodded. "We ride then at your will, Lord King. And bring with you an open mind, for you will discover that I have not told you even half of this story which concerns us both."

The tense anguish which had driven Arthur when he entered was gone from his face. In its place was rather an expression of anticipation, which was like the one he always wore before some trial of strength. But, as the King left the room, Merlin was left with much to consider.

Merlin had not expected Modred would blacken his own birth in order to bring down the King. Arthur's Queen had borne no children. Merlin half suspected that the fault lay with the King. It might be that the half-bloods could not breed with mankind now for some reason. His own indifference to any woman but Nimue pointed in that direction. Though Arthur's infatuation with the Queen had been marked enough, he was so often from court in the past that he might not have realized that their relationship was indeed sterile.

Arthur, without a direct heir by Guenevere, left only Modred of the old royal line. But that Arthur could beget a son outside lawful marriage on a woman of the tribes was a contradiction of Merlin's suspicions. He wondered if Nimue had had a hand in that conception, for she was certainly much about the court of Uther when that secret coupling had taken place, and had taken charge of Morgause immediately after Arthur had lain with the girl. Could Modred even *be* Arthur's son in truth, or rather again some halfling of the Dark Ones?

Merlin had sensed in him any trace of the Power which could not be mistaken by those of the Old Blood. No, he thought it likely that Modred was exactly what whispering tongues and Ector proclaimed him, Arthur's getting by his reputed half sister.

The boy could be threatening to spread such a story to bring Arthur to heel. If that were his game, though, it was none of Nimue's planning, for Arthur was no weak fool. He had been distraught, it was true, when the story was first thrown at him, but anyone in his position would feel shock and dismay. Now that Arthur had heard the truth, and would be shown the proof, he in himself would be immune to any demands from Modred. What remained to be considered was how far Modred would go to bring down his father. Was he too young and hotheaded to realize that besmirching Arthur would also mean disinheriting himself? For just as a king among the tribes could not show any physical disability, so neither could he have his name so shamed before those he ruled.

Modred was ambitious, of that Merlin was sure. He did not think the boy would foul his own nest; he wanted too much to be Arthur's heir. Only if the Queen should show signs of breeding in the future would he turn to telling all he believed to be the truth.

And by that time—Merlin's slightly hunched shoulders straightened—Arthur would be fully armed. Only let him front the mirror and listen. The real truth would make him free of such devious intrigue.

So Arthur named Modred as his regent before the court, though carefully setting such secret safeguards as he could to limit any plans the black-browed stripling might have. However, Modred appeared content with the deference shown him. Nor did he appear to notice Merlin's presence, though the priest Gildas frowned hotly at the bard from his place among those around Modred's throne.

When at last they rode out of Camelot, Arthur half turned in the saddle to look back at the rise of the palace. When he faced around again his face was grave.

"I know not why," he said to Merlin who rode at his left hand, "but it is as if the future lies hidden in clouds.

The sun now shines on us brightly, yet when I look back, a shadow gathers there."

"Uncertainty," answered Merlin, "cannot easily be thrown off. Perhaps you have learned too much, Lord King, in too short a time. But time can also be an enemy. There are many in this land who will not welcome any change, even the coming of a lasting peace."

"That too, I am beginning to understand. My war band watches now wistfully for some warning beacon aflame. It is as if they wish back the days when we were always in the saddle, sore, weary, half-famished, and with the enemy before and behind us. Death rode with us, yet they dwell on those days when they sit at the feast board; they boast of slaying and of the planning of campaigns. Even I cannot still a quickening of the blood when my hand fits about the hilt of my sword. We were born in war, we lived by war and if war is gone ... then we may feel purposeless and unneeded."

Merlin laughed. "But there is more than war to occupy the hands and minds of men, Lord King. I grant you that only by struggle do we reach our highest feeling of accomplishment, but that need not be struggle against another of our kind. Wait and see. There is much we can do which in time will make the Great Nine Battles of Britain seem the play of thoughtless children."

"Show me, Merlin, and you shall have my thanks. I think I was born for but one cause, to fight. And if I have not Saxons—and I shrink from thinking of any of my own rising against me—then give me a battlefield worthy of my ardor."

Arthur inspected three of the old forts, and at each he detached a certain number of his men with orders that they were to examine the usefulness of the sites thoroughly, reporting at his return whether these could be repaired easily and once more put to service. Thus it was that when they reached the fourth and last fort, before Merlin knew they must strike into the mountain ways, Arthur's company was much depleted.

There were no men of noble rank left in the shrunken band. The King had arbitrarily assigned all of them to overseeing the study of the other forts. The eight men who rode into the last section of tumbled wall and burnt-out interior were, Merlin could see—appreciating Arthur's astute selection—not the most curious nor resourceful, but rather those who wished no more than to take orders given by others, without any worry to themselves.

As they camped that night Arthur complained of an aching head. He ate very little of what Bleheris brought him and Merlin suggested that he go earlier to rest since it would seem he might have taken a touch of such a fever as accompanies a rheum.

Only to the Pict did the King tell the truth, that the chamber which had been hastily cleared and set aside for Arthur's uses must be as well garded as a treasure chest, for the King's absence was to be kept a secret. And the small dark man bowed his head in promise.

There was no moon outside that night, but Merlin knew that his sense of direction would draw him to the cave, just as a migrating bird is drawn even across seas on the path it must travel with the seasons. And Arthur was no stranger to the ways of ambush and scouting, practicing now, to escape his own band, all the craft he had used against the enemy. So together they worked from shadow to shadow away from the ruins of the fort, seeking the high hills which lay beyond.

Merlin believed the King's illness might be stretched to perhaps four days without the members of his escort growing restive and beginning to wonder why he was not seen, nor any messenger sent with news of his ailing. They were perhaps still a night's journey away from the height of the mirror cave and the darkness would slow them. But, through the night, he heard a soft laugh from Arthur such as a boy might utter, trying some reckless exploit of his own.

"This is like the days of my boyhood," he confided in a whisper as they reached the top of one ridge and lay belly-down to detect as best they could what might lie ahead. "Just so did Cei and I sometimes stray secretly afield by night. Though then we were not hunting what we hunt now. Merlin, if Cei is Ector's son, then is he not also of the Old Race whom you mention with such reverence? Could he, too, be part of this secret of yours?"

"If it is so willed. I do not choose," Merlin replied. "That which is from the stars does so. But we must press on, Arthur, for there is yet a distance to go and the night is short enough."

Not so short, however, that they reached the cave before a single streak of dawn swept across the sky, a sword

blade to part night from day. And Merlin, more by touch
than sight, worked at his improvised door, pulling loose
those rocks he always tried to arrange as if they had once
cascaded there from above. At last they were cleared, be-
stowed now also so that anyone who might stray into
these higher ways would not see them piled too straightly.

, Then Merlin took the fore and worked through into the
cave of the mirror. He was greeted there, not by the dusk,
but by a flashing of light, for all the squares had awakened, either during his absence or to herald his return. Arthur had greater difficulty in pushing his larger body
through, but when he stood by Merlin, the rows of flashing lights, the dark burnished surface of the mirror before
him, he said nothing. And Merlin, glancing sidewise, saw
that the King was seemingly struck silent with awe. Indeed, there was nothing here which was of the world they
knew.

"The mirror." Merlin laid his hand gently on Arthur's
shoulder, drew him forward to face that tall-standing
oblong of shining surface. As he did so he spoke formally:

"Here stands now Arthur, High King of Britain, who
was fathered and born to the command of those we
serve."

They could see their reflections in the mirror, though
these appeared to waver, perhaps because of the flickering
of the lights. Then Merlin felt Arthur start as, out of the
air above the mirror, came the voice in answer:

"The greeting of the kin to you, Arthur, who was, is
and will be, though you remember not from age to age
and thus are now blind to the past. This is one of the
hours in which you face a choice and must act for the
good of your people though, by the tricks of the enemy,
you have come late to this meeting. Watch, Arthur, for of
choices before you not only your destiny, but that of Britain will be wrought. Merlin, to Arthur alone shall this be
given, so he shall see, while you remain blind."

The bench slid forward as it had on Merlin's first visit
there long ago. Arthur seated himself as one in a trance.
To Merlin there was no change in the mirror. He still saw
only his own dark-browed, slow-aging face, Arthur's own
brightness of mien. But the King gave an exclamation and
leaned forward a little, his eyes wide, his lips parted as if
he were about to utter some cry of the same astonishment
that was imprinted on his countenance.

Merlin stepped back. He had been late indeed in carrying out this, the last of his duties. But perhaps not too late. Maybe by her use of Modred, which had sent Arthur to him Nimue had weakened her own control over the future. Otherwise the King might never have been persuaded to believe him. Arthur, haunted by the shame Modred seemed to put upon him, had been so readied that Merlin could lead him here easily.

He watched the King, whose eyes were still so intent on the mirror, who sat so unmovingly, that he might have been fashioned of metal like the objects about him and not of flesh and blood. Shadows of expression crossed his countenance, now and then expressing alarm or resolution. Whatever Arthur was learning from the mirror was slowly changing the King even as Merlin watched.

He had come to the mirror a mighty war leader, triumphant in the success of all his maneuvers in the field. Now he was becoming a leader shaped in another pattern. Merlin's own heart beat faster with excitement as he watched that metamorphosis. Nimue had failed!

The Arthur who would go forth from here need not tremble before any ill-speaking or shadow of the Dark. He was becoming the ruler he would have been if that fashioning of him not been delayed for all these weary years.

14.

Night and day passed, then another night before Arthur at last rose from the bench and turned to face Merlin. There was no light in his eyes now, rather the dour look of a man who must set his will to some great task and summon therefore all his innermost energy.

"You have seen. . . ?" Merlin asked.

"I have seen," the King answered. "If this is some dream, then at least I have seen enough to know that a man can live for and by such a dream." He hesitated. "But kin-brother, we are not like other men. There will be those who would turn their faces from any belief, even if they were shown something they could touch with their own hands. I——" He shook his head slowly. "A man can but try."

Merlin watched him narrowly. There was no exultation in Arthur, only a kind of grimness, as if he had accepted some burden which he must bear whether he wanted to or not.

"I wonder," the King said now, "if this time is wrongly chosen. Men have lived with fear so long that now they look on each new thing, every stranger, as a threat."

That question matched some of Merlin's recurring doubts. Had men come far enough yet to want to reach for the stars?

"Closed minds," Arthur continued. "Can you," he said, turning to Merlin, "believe that any of this"—he waved his hand about the cave—"will now be thought anything but the work of demons? You have known this since childhood. I come to it a man grown and tried, so that I can understand such fears. And fear leads to hate and destruction. Also, there is the Lady of the Lake."

"What of her?" Merlin moved uneasily.

150

"If she is the enemy, then we must know more of her, wherein lies the root of her own powers."

"She knows me," Merlin returned. "I have long been her enemy. If I sought her out . . ."

Arthur nodded. "Just so. But she served Uther well, being noted for her healing gifts. We have begun an imposture here with our excuse of fever which has struck me down. Well, can we continue that? I shall return to Camelot a stricken man and those about me will send for this Nimue. It will be your part, kin-brother, to be reviled as one who has boasted of cures he cannot make. Perhaps you must even be resigned to exile for a space."

Merlin had one objection. "Lord King. I know of this woman and I have tasted her powers. What if you cannot stand against her? Then indeed you shall be sacrificed and all our plans will come to nothing."

"That is a fortune we must dare. I see no other way to best her, for otherwise she will spin her spells and these will reach to enmesh us, as a spider web enmeshes the unwary fly, when we need to make some necessary move. Kin-brother, you seem unusually wary of this Nimue— why?"

Merlin flushed. "Is it not enough that she held me captime when I had need to aid you? The mirror has told me little of what forces the Dark Ones can command, but what I have seen of those has been daunting. To offer yourself as her prey might be the greatest act of folly in our world!"

"It may," Arthur agreed. "Still, I know that we must draw her from cover. Men say that no one can seek her out unless she wills it, that great mists curl around that ancient keep she has taken for her own, hiding her dwelling from the eyes of all. But if I can hold her at Camelot then you, with your greater knowledge of such forces, might well penetrate to that secret place of hers and discover just how strong is the support she can call on."

Arthur thought in terms of warfare. Merlin must reluctantly agree. however, that this risky form of attack just might succeed.

"Did you learn this from the mirror?" he asked in return.

Arthur sighed. "The mirror leaves to men their own choices. It can show what may happen, but that future constantly changes with the acts of man."

"That is true. Very well, it shall be as you wish, Lord King." But even as he agreed, Merlin remained uneasy. Arthur was the chosen King. It was for him to make the decisions now that he had learned his role, but he had not yet met the Dark Ones face to face, only seen something of their work in the affair of Modred. He did not know Nimue except as a healer and a figure of some mystery.

They worked together to close the cave and then took a secret way back to the ruins, evading two sentries. Arthur cursed them under his breath for their lack of attention. Bleheris awaited them in the inner chamber.

"It is well you have come, Lord King," he said with open relief. "The men grow restless. Twice Tirion has come asking how you do. He has threatened to send a messenger to Lord Gawain at the other fort—"

"I do badly, Bleheris," the King returned. "Listen well, shield comrade, this is what must be done. You will go out among the men and say that the fever which grips me is worse. Then Merlin will follow straightaway and order that branches be cut and a horse litter made. You will be ever by me, but when you fetch food or drink you will speak of my strange ravings and that I am fevered worse than you have seen any man before, that you are disturbed in mind because of this illness which has come over me. Do you understand?"

The small Pict looked from the King to Merlin and back to Arthur again.

"This is some battle ruse, Lord King?"

Arthur nodded. "But it is for a kind of battle which is not fought with swords nor spears. I must be returned to Camelot as one who is gravely ill, and only you and Merlin must tend me on the way, so that the truth may not be guessed."

Bleheris looked now to the curtained doorway of the room.

"Lord King, these men will be alarmed. They do not like this place. They have been speaking among themselves of the ghosts of old ones who do not favor the company of living men and who have thus struck at you. This talk can become dangerous—"

It was Merlin who answered: "Demon-attack, Lord King, might well serve our purpose."

Arthur's face was sober. "But dangerous for you, Merlin. Such whispers have always spread about you. They can say that this attack is of your doing if we speak of demons."

"True enough. However, such a report will serve our turn well. Let it stand. Go, Bleheris. Do not add anything to this talk of ghosts, but look knowing when you hear it, as if you could say more if you would."

The Pict grinned. "Lord Merlin, I do not know what game you and the High King play but if it is your will, I shall do my best to make it come right for you."

As Arthur had planned, so was it done. The High King developed certain symptoms induced by Merlin's herb knowledge, making him flushed of face, hot of skin. Bleheris reported that the men of the following were now convinced that their leader was demon-attacked and that they had begun to look askance at Merlin. The Pict was given his own instructions. Once they reached Camelot he was to whisper it about that only the Lady of the Lake, who had kept Uther visibly alive when all other healers had given him up for near dead, should be summoned.

The lords of Arthur's following were persistent, as each group joined the train on their return, that they see the King for themselves. But, when they did, the High King seemed to lie in a stupor; Merlin gave the impression of one who was gravely troubled, as if, in spite of his well-known healing knowledge, he was now faced by an illness he found baffling.

He was well aware that Cedric had sent a messenger ahead and he was not surprised when, just a half day's journey away—for they made that trip slowly, fitting their progress to that of the rough horse litter they had devised—the messenger returned with one of the gray-coated priests. To Merlin's relief it was not Gildas, though he was well able to read the hostility of the man. When the priest attempted to see the King, however, Arthur cried out that there was a new demon to torment him, and he acted so well the part of a man half crazed with a high fever that the priest was forced to withdraw.

The lords turned on Merlin, demanding an explanation of what fell disease had struck down the High King. He drew a long face and answered that there were strange emanations in ruins. Who knew what shadow things lurked where old evils had been done?

They came at last to Camelot and Arthur was carried inside and placed in his own bed. But when Modred and

Guenevere speedily came to him, he rose up and ordered them away as being traitors and murderers. Only Bleheris and Merlin seemed able to soothe him. And he did not make the mistake, even for a single moment, of dropping his role of a gravely ill man to exchange so much as a whisper of coherent speech with them alone.

The second day Bleheris moved to carry out his part of Arthur's plan. When he returned he slipped into the King's chamber like a small shadow among larger, ran swiftly across to kneel by Arthur's bedside.

"Lord King, I have spoken," he whispered, "even as you ordered. I talked of the Lady of the Lake to two of the Queen's maids, the man who waits on the Lord Cei who has just returned and others. I think they listened."

Arthur's head moved almost imperceptibly on the pillow to show that he heard and understood. Merlin gave a sigh of relief. It was good hearing that Cei had returned from a visit to Urien's court in the north. He himself had never felt the kinship with Ector's son that he had with his father, but he knew that Cei was completely loyal to Arthur, no matter how terse and rude he might be to others. Cei was also quickly jealous of any Arthur chose to favor, so with Cei on guard Merlin could go more light of heart to accomplish his own part of what they would do.

Now he bent over the King as if examining some small change in his patient. There were none to see, but his lips only shaped the words he would say:

"Tell Cei!"

Again the King assented. Perhaps he, too, felt the need of someone to take Merlin's place.

They waited for the fruits of Bleheris' sowing to ripen. It was in the morning of the next day that the Queen, together with Cei and Modred, pushed into the chamber. Merlin could believe in Cei's concern, but that of the other two he doubted. He believed Guenevere liked her crown too well to want to see another in Arthur's place, but Merlin had not even that small shred of trust in Modred. Modred would be for Modred. His attack on Arthur had already revealed how far he was willing to go—to achieve what? Nimue's desires? His own chance at the throne? Either motive would make him a fell danger.

But those two now left it to Cei to round on Merlin with the words he himself had been waiting to hear:

"It would seem, healer, that your powers are less than you would have us believe. Our lord does not grow better under your hands, but worse. Therefore we shall seek elsewhere for one who can return him to health."

"Aye." Modred interrupted with an arrogance that acted on Cei as a goad urged an ox to labor. "Good Brother Gildas is learned in the art. And since he is a servant of God, who better can cast out the demons which have entered the King?"

Cei glowered at him. "We have no proof of the powers of this priest of yours, boy." His tone was meant to crush, to relegate Modred to the status of a child.

"You—you forget yourself, Cei!" Modred flared instantly. "I am of Pendragon's own kin—"

"And I am his foster brother," returned Cei flatly.

None of the tribes had an answer to that, for the foster tie was counted in their world as strong as blood-kin. Before all of Camelot, Cei was as Arthur's birth-brother.

He turned his shoulder now on the youth, whose temper-flushed face was a mask of open hate, and spoke straight to Merlin.

"You have wrought no cure, not even a small easing of our lord's distemper. Therefore we have sent for one who can. The Lady of the Lake is well known to have great power over such ills. Did she not rid Uther of them when his sickness began?"

Merlin bowed his head. "I love our lord too greatly to speak against any help which may be given him. Therefore, summon this lady if you think her nursing the greater good."

Cei had an uncertain look for a second. It was as if he had expected a hot protest, and to get such instant agreement made him uneasy. Guenevere had moved forward to the bed; now she raised her head to look around.

"My lord, I have already sent a messenger to summon her. If any can raise my dear lord again from this bed, that one is she. As for you, bard, self-proclaimed healer," she flashed out at Merlin, "better that you get hence. Leave us. I command it!"

Arthur had closed his eyes. Now he gave a small groan. Merlin made as if to go to him but Cei stepped swiftly between.

"The Queen has said it. Get you gone, son of no man.

Your name has no honor here, and best you understand that."

Merlin withdrew. He did not care that his going seemed like the flight of one overawed by the company. It was much more important that he have no confrontation with Nimue. He could not tell how much she could read of their motives and plans if she faced him in person, so avoiding her was the way of a wise man.

Within his own small chamber he made ready for the task ahead. Laying aside the robe of his office, he put on once again drab journey clothes which would mark him perhaps no more than an upper servant of the court. Then he drew from his store of things of Power certain carefully thought-out selections. There was a piece of star iron, found when meteors fell to earth, and also a glassy dark jewel droplet from the same off-world source. There were herbs which he sifted a pinch at a time into a small linen bag, its drawcord long enough for him to wear it amulet-like about his neck. He tucked it inside his tunic against his skin, so that as his body warmed the bag the faint scent of what it held reached his nostrils, serving to clear his head, keep his senses fully alert. Last of all was Lugaid's legacy to him, that small fragment of metal which had been wrought in the long-ago and had helped to find the sword of Arthur.

These were not things of any "magic" as men thought of magic, but some had or should have an affinity with any off-world object. And as Lugaid had said long ago, "like seeks like." Merlin had also gathered over the years—with, he had always hoped, no notice—information concerning the stronghold of Nimue. He credited the tales of the enchanted mist which always enfolded it as being ordinary men's reaction to some hallucination; if that was the truth, such could not baffle him. That he had never ventured in its direction might be to his advantage now: Nimue could well believe he had learned his lesson so well that he would never try to match strength with her again.

Last of all he drew from a secret place behind his box-bed a rod twice the length of his forearm. Into the head of this he carefully fitted the gem of the stars, making sure that the prongs of metal waiting there encircled it past any chance of loss. Then he reversed the wand, weighting down the slightly larger butt with the pebble of meteor iron. Both in place, he laid the rod across his wrist, trying it at different places until end balanced end, and it remained level as long as he held his arm steady.

Once again he gathered a goodly pack of supplies from the kitchens and took a leather bottle with a shoulder sling; he did not fill this with wine nor cider but carried it to the spring where he tipped into it as much pure water as it would hold. So armed with his own weapons and provisioned for travel, Merlin set forth from the High King's court.

He fixed his mind as he went, not on the true goal of his journey, but rather concentrated on building about him a small trace of illusion, as much as would keep him from the notice or memory of any he passed. Confident in his power of producing hallucinations, he was content none would report him and, perhaps, his absence from Camelot would not be quickly noted.

He did not go directly toward the site he sought. Instead he started eastward, following one of the old Roman ways for some distance, until it met one of the tracks of a yet older people. There he turned, crossing land which seemed bare of man. Now Merlin released the illusion, made the character of the land itself serve him for concealment. At the same time he built another form of illusion, this one within himself. He purposefully did not think of Nimue, nor her tower; rather he held the thought to the fore of his mind that he traveled merely to another outpost of men.

Merlin had no idea what safeguards surrounded Nimue's hold. He doubted that they were the ordinary ones of high walls with men to defend them. His own cave possessed a distort which would make any invader not of the Old Blood uneasy and blind. And if anyone did persist, there was a device within which would bar the way. Merlin had not the least doubt that Nimue's place in turn had its own invisible guardians.

The defense of his own refuge, however, had not been proof against Nimue. Therefore, reason argued, hers should not be beyond his powers to solve.

By nightfall Merlin reached the edge of the wood which men called Nimue's first defense. There the old road curled around its edge as if, even in the dawn days of this land, men believed something uncanny lay in that forest.

Merlin drew back under a wide bush, not lighting any

fire, munching instead a small portion of bread wrapped around a bit of cheese, drinking sparingly from his water bottle. He sent out those invisible scouts which served his mind, reaching farther and farther when these scouts reported nothing but nature in the trees' shadow. At last Merlin broke that concentration and set his mental scouts on guard while he dozed in light sleep—he would not dare surrender to any depth of unconsciousness.

It was at the rise of a nearly full moon that he felt a stir which was not of any person, nor animal within the forest. This was the force that he recognized only too well, for it he could draw on it himself. Whatever sentinels served Nimue were now at their posts.

Merlin made no attempt to identify the nature of those beings, or lesser powers. He had no wish to alert them to his own presence by any touch of mind. What he did now, with care and all the skill he could summon, was locate each and mark where it was stationed.

Perhaps Nimue depended on some form of visual distortion by day and terrifying illusions by night, which would be a natural enough defense against most men. Finally he marked a slash a little to the west of him where a stream wandered through. It was not deep but of some width.

There was his door. For he knew, as true men did not, that water, flowing water, was a nonconductor of distorts and illusions. From this truth was born the ancient belief that certain evil forces might be stopped if the pursued were to cross running water.

He had his gate for the morrow, and now he knew where all the enemy sentinels near him kept their posts. Leaving his own thread of awareness on guard, Merlin lapsed once more into slumber.

The dawn light came and he crawled from the embrace of the bush. Once more he ate a little of his food, then set off westward until, before the sun had more than sent a warning of color into the sky, he reached the stream. A series of fording stones were set where the old road dipped to meet it. Merlin made no use of these, but waded out into the center of the running water as equidistant as he could get from each wooded bank.

He waded through knee-high water so clear he could see the stones below, the darting forms of water-dwellers. Before him he held as a balance the rod tipped with the two star gifts. This remained level until he was well into the forest itself, the trees arching above the wash of the water to form a tunnel of dusky green.

Every one of Merlin's searching senses was alert. He picked up the flickers of small lives which were part of this world, but no trace of those things which had been set to prowl the night. Suddenly the rod turned of its own accord in his grip, swinging in an arc to transpose itself end for end. The gem pointed ahead and slightly to the east. His alien gifts had served him well, pointing a direct path to Nimue's hold. Still he did not leave the water; he would stay with it as long as the stream ran in the same direction he wished.

The gem-point of his wand was slowly being pushed backward, until the wand once more formed a level bar. He had reached the place opposite the hold. A little ahead of him the stream made a right-handed curve also, so sharp a one Merlin did not think it had been designed by nature. Then, catching sight of some very ancient and moss-grown rocks squared and fitted together, he knew that his guess was right.

The path of the water here was much narrower, as if being forced through a sluice. It also had far more of a current rising up his body, resisting his advance, while the rush of its outflow had swept away sand and grit so that his boots slipped on stones set to line the way. Now prudence dictated that he move closer to one of the banks where he could grasp overhanging bushes and vines and so work his way along without risking a fall.

Merlin's advance was slow, yet he was not tempted to crawl out of the water which to him was a promise of cover, small as it might be. Now he could see the sun once more ahead, dancing on an expanse of water much greater than the outlet up which he pulled himself. Moments later he stood, sucking a thorn-torn thumb, looking out on Nimue's domain.

She was indeed Lady of the Lake. On an island to which clung only a ragged bush or two—all that could find root-room among the rocks—was a tower of stone so dark as to make one believe that the very passing of time itself had overlain it with a sable cloak.

In the lower story there were no windows, but, above that, narrow slits gave what must be very limited light to the interior. The stones themselves were not cut and mortared into place after the Roman fashion, rather they were the roughly surfaced rocks which were like those of the Place of the Sun, though fitted with such a cunning hand, allowing for all their natural oddities of shape, that they formed a most solid building.

From the tower, well to his right, there ran a causeway of the same rocks. It was broken in the middle and Merlin guessed that the dwellers in the tower—whoever or whatever they might be—had some way of temporarily bridging the gap, so that drawing away the bridge gave them protection.

The water of the lake itself was odd, giving off a shimmer of light which Merlin knew was part of a strong illusion. Doubtless to anyone not versed in the use of such things, the whole lake and the tower might be shielded in an impenetrable mist, just as tales reported was so.

He studied the tower, seeing no sign of life about it. As it now stood it could be a long-deserted ruin. Yet in his hand the wand quivered and fought against his hold. If he loosed it he believed it would be drawn across the water to a strong power source. Now it was his task to span that gap with more than his wand—his whole body.

To his left, however the quiver of the water's surface grew more pronounced. Merlin had a sudden warning. He splashed up onto the bank, watching warily that agitation of the lake. Out of the water reared a monstrous head, jaws agape and dripping, showing fangs as sharp as any sword point.

15.

This was no illusion. The monster beast was real, though not of any breed he had seen. Merlin recalled some of the information taught by the mirror, that there were many worlds coexistent with this earth, and the walls between them sometimes thinned. By chance, or by some swift loosing of force, a life-form from one might well be drawn into another; hence the tales men told about loathy worms and dragons slain by courageous human heroes.

Trespasser in this world though the water thing might be, it was not the less dangerous for being transplanted. And Merlin did not doubt that the lake-dweller was part of Nimue's defenses.

The thing moved shoreward with disconcerting speed, its dagger-jawed head held well above the surface of the lake, an ominous hiss puffing with foul breath from its mouth. Merlin twirled the wand in his hand, spinning it with nearly the same force he had used when beating the blades on the stones.

The creature's eyes, set far back within pits of the narrow, scaled skull, no longer stared unblinkingly at Merlin. They were held instead in fascination by the whirl of the wand. He knew a small relief: the thing was not too alien to answer to controls he had perfected long ago among the woods creatures.

Now the monster's head swayed a little left, right, left, right and there was no more interest in Merlin but full attention for the whirl of the wand. Having so caught and held the thing, he probed what mind it might have: alien and deadly but not intelligent, thus open to his own attack.

As Merlin might build an hallucination for a man, he strove now to set the creature under his rule, and that proved easier than he had hoped. Though he began to

161

lessen the swing of the wand, the monster did not move. Its head still swung and its eyes were dulled as if, in a measure, it were now blind.

Merlin took a chance and stilled the wand, waiting, poised to begin again should the lake thing move. But it did not. He sent a last command winging to its strange brain. The coils on which the head was reared began to slip down beneath the waters and at last ripples closed over it.

He had thought of approaching the island by swimming, lest any scouting of that broken causeway bring attention from the tower. Now he knew better than to try. He did not even have any idea of how long the serpent thing could be held in mind-bondage. So he strode as swiftly as he could along the shore toward the end of the causeway, not neglecting as he went to keep an alert watch on both land and water, as well as leaving his mind open to any emanation from other guards.

At the shore end of the causeway he paused, looking across that middle break to the island. The glare from the water was unusually dazzling—perhaps some safeguard had been triggered by his presence here and was striving with all its might to bewilder and bemuse the invader.

Under his feet was a trace of ancient way. A well-used road had once run to this spot. But his wonder grew as he looked at the tower. For all the kinship of the stonework to the megaliths of the Place of the Sun, this had not been any stronghold of those he knew—or sensed—in the latter place. It was almost as if this dark squatting building had been summoned into this world from another, like the scaled thing of the lake. Even looking at the heavy lines of its walls disturbed Merlin.

Could it be a distort of some kind which reached him so? Merlin did not know, but he had no wish to invade either island or tower. However, wishes did not rule him.

He began to whirl the wand once more, holding it out at nearly arms-length from his body. If his defense was working as he hoped, no watcher in the tower could see him clearly behind that flashing rod. His mind-probe picked up nothing ahead. There was only a blankness, which in itself was wrong.

Now he had reached the edge of the break and saw that there were scars on the old stones. Merlin thought this proved his guess was right: there was some way of bridging this gap which could be laid down and taken up again. But he could not allow himself to be defeated by a length of open water.

Looking down, he could see fallen stones, green with water slime. Some did break the surface, though their tops were wet and also slimed. Merlin measured their setting critically with his eye.

The shimmering of the water was very thick here, but not enough to veil those possible stepping-stones from him. To take that path, though, he must put aside his own defense by the rod and thus expose his coming to any watcher in the castle. He considered the problem and could see no other answer.

Merlin tied the wand fast to his belt with cords—tight enough to insure he could not lose it—for he would need both hands free now. Finally he swung himself over the edge of the break, dropped with all possible caution to the top of the first water-washed rock.

He kept a wary eye on the water itself. If there were any more monsters in this lake, this was the proper place and time for them to make their presence known. The surface of the water shimmered so much he could not see what lurked below it.

The next rock was green with slime, and it was more than a possible stride away. He would have to jump that gap—the quicker he moved the better. Merlin leaped, his feet skidding, but he went to his hands and knees, clawing for a hold so he would not slide into the water.

Disaster had been so close his mouth was dry and he was shivering. He had kept his perch; the next rock was not so far away. Also, though its top above the level of the lake was very broken and rough, that stone was drier.

It took resolution to move on to that perch, however. And, when the second stone teetered under his weight, as if about to turn over and fling him into the water, Merlin fought fear once more. This block would be hard to take off from and, though the next was far more level, it was slime-streaked.

Somehow he made the step once more, his heart pounding, as the broken rock swayed with every movement. He squatted on the third stone to get his breath, glancing around for any hint that he might be the quarry of some other foul creature.

The last jump landed him at the foot of the other side

of the break. Now he stood on a small outcropping of stone, hardly wide enough to hold his feet. His face was only inches away from the wall he must climb. He reached above him, not daring to stretch his head far back to look up, hunting holds for his hands and feet.

He found them and pulled himself up. When he edged over the top of the causeway he lay for a moment, willing his heart to beat normally, his will to establish control over his emotions.

Then he got to his feet. Before him was a doorway but no door was shut against him. Instead there was what seemed to be thick darkness between Merlin and the interior, as if indeed some night cloud had been fitted there to keep out the light of day.

Merlin untied the wand from his belt and held it in his hand with the gem upward. It pointed toward the doorway of its own accord, pulling the wand straight in his grasp. Though he needed no assurance, he could tell by the action of the star stone that like indeed called to like and what was in the tower was not entirely of his earth.

As he walked steadily toward that dark-curtained doorway he feverishly sought to discover whether any new guardian lay in wait beyond. Did Nimue have henchmen and women to serve her, perhaps plucked like the serpent of the lake, from some other world or time?

If there were other guards they had some defensive cover which was not for his understanding, because he could pick up no trace, nothing similar to the haunters of the woods. He stood before that curtain which swirled and billowed within the opening, and in that instant he was aware that Nimue needed no locks or doors. This cloud stuff was as efficient a barrier as solid stone would be. Try as he would, Merlin could not advance another step.

He was not ready to concede defeat, however. Instead he drew forth from his belt pouch the last of his armament, Lugaid's scrap of metal. This could be bent if one exerted pressure enough, as well as will. Now he pressed it as tightly as he might about the gemmed point of his wand, until the stone was covered with a cap of shining metal.

The closer he advanced it toward the cloud door, the more its own light brightened. Then he thrust it straight into the center of the darkness as a warrior would strike with a spear. There answered a glare of light so brilliant

Merlin's eyes were blinded, and a sound as if a thunderclap had burst just above his head.

He smeared his hand across his eyes, willing sight back to them.

The doorway before him was now clear. And, if the sun did not reach beyond it, there was light of another kind in the windowless interior, no light of lamp or torch, but brighter.

Merlin, holding the wand before him, crossed the threshold.

As the cave had been when he first sighted it, so this vast inner room, which must include all of the lower story of the tower, was crowded with a huge number of installations. He recognized some as resembling those which fostered the mirror, having the same flickering of light across their surfaces. Others were strange. And there was no mirror. In whatever way Nimue received *her* instructions it was not in the same manner as Merlin had his.

There was no life there but for himself, none he could detect. Against the far wall was a stairway which wound up, cut into the stone itself, leading to the floor above.

Merlin strode down an aisle between the flashing boxes. The very familiarity of some of this equipment reassured him. Now he began to climb up to the second story where there were windows. The bold light of the interior came from long rods set into the walls, but those were only below. As he came up through an opening in the floor he was greeted by not only the light of day entering much more dimly and wanly through the slits of the windows, but by scents he himself knew. Here were the odors of herbs and cordials. Sniffing, he could detect that and this which he had harvested and stored in his own chamber.

A long curtain divided the round room into two. On one side were stools, a table, garlands of dried herbs against the wall, a chest with shelves set above it on which stood lidded pots and beakers. Studying this array, Merlin felt entirely at home.

Yet there was something else to be sniffed in this half room—sniffed or discovered by that other sense of his. For the wholesome scent of the herbs did not entirely disguise another odor, and that was far from pleasant. Someone had dealt in illusions here, but such dealing had been reinforced with drugs such as Merlin knew better than to employ. That was the stink of evil, insidious, half hidden, but there.

He passed the edge of the curtain to the other side. Here was a carved bed covered with linen which had been steeped in saffron for a golden tinge. Over that was drawn a coverlet of deeper gold on which was worked a complicated design in sea-green thread, looped here and there to draw a pearl into line. On the walls were hangings worked with gold thread on green. But there were none of the fanciful beasts, hunters, other patterns such as the ladies of the court were wont to use. Rather the lines were sharp and stiff, consisting of angles and squares, drawn in a manner not altogether strange to Merlin.

In his dreams of the tower cities he had glimpsed paintings which were not unlike these. And it was the trick of such work that the longer you stared at it, the more an uneasy feeling grew in you that something lurked within those lines, watching and skulking for no good purpose. Yet he could glimpse nothing he was sure of but the lines themselves.

There was a chest also, carved like the bed and, standing on it, one end propped against the wall, was a mirror. A mirror! Merlin made a careful way across the room, taking every precaution to keep his reflection from its burnished surface. It could well be that this was set as a trap and that on her return Nimue might summon up on the surface the likeness of any intruder. When he came close enough, however, he was certain that this was not the same as the mirror of his cave, merely an article aiding to adornment.

This side of the upper chamber was not tainted with that trouble he had found in the other. He decided that it was no more than Nimue's own quarters. As there was no further way up, the tower must contain only the two rooms.

He had seen no sign of any servants. Nimue must live alone—except for such as needed no quarters and perhaps no food nor drink, unless what he picked up in the herb chamber might be termed that.

Back in the other section, fronted once more by all the raw materials of a healer's training, Merlin again swung the wand widely, pointing the metal-covered gem at the wall, turning very slowly so that any movement of his indicator would be noted.

But the wand lay quiet in his hand. What was here had no affinity for the star things. All that must lie below. He returned to the crowded lower section.

What he wanted most was complete destruction of everything that stood here. But there might be more than he could hope to control if he attempted that. Slowly he paced among the machines, noting those which were in any way different from the ones he had come to know—if not wholly understand—in the cave.

There were three of the latter. One stood upright, a little taller than Merlin himself. Its front panel was unlike the rest, which were of smooth metal, while the one he faced was pebbled and rather akin in substance to an opaque glass. The wand in his hand came to life. Before he could tighten his grip on it, the gem-and-metal tip thudded against that panel at the height of Merlin's breast.

Though the panel was not broken there came a change in it. It was as if an inner skin was sloughing away as he watched, to show what stood behind. What stood. . .

Merlin caught his breath. He was looking now on a woman, propped upright in the cabinet or else standing there. But, though her eyes were open, there was no sign of life about her. She might have been some statue, except she was far too lifelike.

Red hair lay in long, ribbon-entwisted braids down her shoulders, shining brightly against the clear light blue of her robe. She had a torque around her throat, a bracelet of bronze curiously worked around one wrist. To Merlin's eyes she was young, yet in another way she carried about her a kind of ripeness, as if she knew well the pleasures of the body.

At first he believed that he faced the dead, cunningly preserved after no fashion this world knew. Then he stared more closely, even venturing to tap with one fingertip against the now transparent panel. There was a swirl of small particles across the face of the girl in answer. She stood there fully engulfed in liquid, just as he had lain under the protection of the mirror so that he might live, not die as Nimue willed.

Nimue was once rumored to have brought someone here—Morgause, Uther's daughter! But this was only a girl. She could not be the mother of Modred, a fully grown youth . . . unless she had been so imprisoned shortly after her son's birth! When Merlin studied her longer he was sure he could indeed trace a faint likeness to Uther, but certainly none to the dark-browed Modred!

Why did Nimue hold her prisoner so? The Lady of the Lake must foresee some future use for Uther's daughter, not as she would have been if time had dealt commonly with her, but as she was when Uther had sent her forth from his court. And, knowing Nimue, Merlin did not believe that that purpose could be any good one.

He inspected the box carefully for any fastening or latch. It seemed sealed on all four corners as well as the top. Perhaps it was the sort of coffer which could only be released by the right word, spoken in just the proper tone. Though he pitied the girl who slept, he could see no way of freeing her.

Oddly enough, that opaque backing which had been dislodged by his wand was beginning to gather again, spreading over the inner surface as frost covered a stone. It was thickening and for that he was glad, since the fewer signs left of his visit here the better.

Now he went past Morgause's strange prison to an object made of fine wires spun with ribbons of metal. This was woven into a crown-like head covering, though some of the wire rose up from the top of that crown into a tall pillar standing behind it, where they were swallowed into the substance of the pillar itself.

Before that pillar on Merlin's side was a bench, on which the crown waited. He considered the whole thing carefully. Then suddenly he was excited. He had the mirror and the voice; this crown might be a device for communication just as the mirror was for him! If that were so. . .

Merlin edged around to the back of the pillar. It was entirely smooth and rose nearly to the ceiling overhead. There was a space about half the length of Merlin's wand between its top and the overhead beams. Some glistening rods about the thickness of his little finger jutted into that space from the crest of the pillar at irregular lengths, no two the same.

Not even in his dreams of the lost cities had Merlin ever seen its like, but if this was Nimue's link with those who had set her tasks here on this earth, and if it could be destroyed. . .

He had a hearty respect for anything fashioned by the Star People and so little knowledge—simply because he had none of their devices in common use—of what they might be, that he was loath to interfere with any of this. Yet he also knew that he finally had before him the chance to deal his enemy the greatest defeat.

The wand warned him of force inside the pillar, such a flow of force that he dared not test it. However, the reaction was far less when he pointed the off-world gem in the direction of the crown on the bench. And those wires that wedded crown to pillar looked very fragile.

Merlin drew a deep breath. Even if he awoke here such a force as would sweep him into death, defeating Nimue and those behind her would be worth such an ending. He had obeyed the orders laid on him—the beacon was set to bring in those of his kin; Arthur knew what they would have of *him*—so what matter if he died now, as long as he took with him Nimue's greatest tool?

Slowly, with caution and all the skill he could bring to the task, Merlin slid the tip of the wand along the surface of the bench until it lay directly under, but not touching, the wires that led up to the pillar. Then, just as he had used the knife blade to compel the King Stone to his will, now he began tapping with the metal-encased gem. And in a low voice he chanted. Tap—chant—tap—

He made no move to touch the crown, but bent his will on its anchorage. Slowly the crown itself lifted from the surface of the bench. It rose by jerks, as if it were a sentient thing fighting against his control. But still it rose. Now it was higher than Merlin's head as he stood there, and the wires to the pillar were pulled taut as harp strings.

Merlin did not hesitate. Tap—chant—tap—

He sensed that beyond the reach of his own mind there were things gathering, prowling unseen, moving on a level not open to the eyes of man. But he would not give heed to those things, concentrating his whole will on what he would do.

The crown tugged fiercely at the wires that held it, bobbing down to strain upward again with a quick snap. Still those thread-like filaments held. But Merlin persevered.

There was a sharp ringing sound. One of the wires had at last broken, trailing back against the pillar limply. The crown, freer now on one side than the other, made desperate swoops and soars to win loose in answer to Merlin's command.

Another snap. It was held now by a single thread only.

Merlin did not allow any feeling of triumph to slow his invocation. The crown dipped low like a tethered bird, nearly flying into Merlin's face as if it resented what he would make it do and was now minded to attack. He did not flinch but his tapping grew stronger and he raised his voice a fraction, uttering a single loud ringing word of command.

The crown flew from him as if to escape whatever fate he laid upon it, rising in a whirl of motion overhead, and the last wire parted. Now all virtue went out of the crown; it fell to lie at Merlin's feet and he deliberately set his boot on it, crushing its fragile weaving into a mass of broken wire. Raising the tangle by the tip of his wand, being careful not to touch it with his bare hand, he carried it before him as he went.

The last of the installations he did not understand was another pillar, but this had no crown, no wires, no surface break, not even any flashing lights along its front. He could make nothing of it . . . And those presences he sensed when he had attacked the crown were growing more restive.

He did not know them, could only feel that in some way they were akin to the watchers in the forest. His own inner force had been badly eroded by his destruction of the crown so it seemed better to meet out in the open any attack which might be aimed at him now—not facing it in Nimue's own fortress where the unseen attackers might be able to draw upon energies he could not locate. In spite of Nimue's usurpation of this section of the forest, Merlin had some strengths which the earth itself would feed and nurture.

He ran through the doorway, out of that well-lighted room. When he reached the break in the causeway he turned and hurled the wreckage of the crown far out into the lake, where the glittering water swallowed it. It would have been better to bury it in the earth—for this water had been englamoured by his enemy—but Merlin now needed his hands free for what might come.

What did happen surprised him so much that he nearly lost control for a startled moment. He had been dreading the return across those slippery stones. Not only did he know that he was already under a silent attack which sucked at his control and his inner powers, but he feared that Nimue's forest servants had been alerted. Caught on those slimed rocks he would be easy meat.

However, when he turned to look in the direction of the land, he glimpsed something that was not the false sheen of the water, but was suspended above it like a nearly invisible link between the two broken portions of the causeway. If water itself could form a bridge, Merlin believed, it would look so.

Dare he trust it? This might be a subtle trap. He thought he had the way of testing that. Leaning forward a little, Merlin stretched out his wand to touch what he could hardly see at all. The stone-metal point thudded down against a surface which was very real indeed.

Thus, tapping gingerly before him with the tip of the rod as he went, Merlin stepped onto the invisible bridge, forcing himself not to see with his eyes but with his mind, to *know* that he had footing even if it appeared to be only empty air.

16.

He gained no confidence during that crossing, even though his wand continued to report that steady footing formed the bridge. Only when he was down again on that other length of stone he could see as well as feel did Merlin give a great sigh of relief. Yet this was no time to relax his guard.

Facing the trees in the dark wood through which the trace of that very ancient road ran, he stiffened. They were alert at last, those eerie guardians Nimue had set to patrol her boundaries, and they were closing the path before him. There remained the way he had taken in, the stream. With the memory of the serpent still paramount in his mind, though, descending again into any water fed by this lake was a task which needed firm willing.

Merlin dropped down into the deeper runnel, his wand in hand, feeling the slight swing of that which, added to his extra sense, would be his warning of any imminent attack. The water here was not as clear as it had been farther down the stream and, as he walked, slipping and sliding across a very uneven footing, clouds of silt rose to make it more murky.

He was well down that water road, near the turn where it became a more honest and natural stream, when his wand turned sharply in his hand. At the same moment a strong warning of his sense of Power brought him half around.

He expected to see a monster, perhaps the same monster he had beguiled in the lake. Not—not a woman standing as if her sandals were set on the surface of the water, which had now become a firm flooring at her command.

She smiled lingeringly. As he had first seen her on that night he held the barrow sword, so did Merlin see Nimue now. She made no attempt to conceal her slim white

172

body, which was all woman's curves; she even shook back her cloak of hair to display herself more wantonly. She was bare save for a girdle of stones as milky white as her skin, two wide armlets of the same and a neck chain which held a single stone carved into the sickle of a new moon, hanging between the proud upsurge of her breasts.

She shook her head in the mock playfulness one might use toward a child who had done ill but did not understand.

"Merlin—" His name came like the sighing of the wind, yet he noted sharply that her lips had not shaped it. And with that small hint of what she might be, he lifted the wand and struck—even as if he handled a spear in battle.

That point fashioned of metal and gem pierced between her breasts just below the moon pendant. There was a flurry in the air, then nothingness. Illusion!

But the fact that the illusion had called his name was highly disturbing. Nimue must have suspected that he would come or else she would not have fashioned such an apparition. Or did she know from afar of his invasion, from Camelot itself?

Either way he was disturbed. Though he might deal with certainty and wisdom with everything else in this world, yet this woman could stir his emotions and make him as awkward as any untried youth. It was not the strength she might summon and control, as he summoned and controlled forces, which made him uneasy. No, it was that subtler, other influence which reached the man in him no matter how he tried to control such longings. He knew they endangered all he could command, and that he would be far less than he now was if he were to yield to them.

For a long moment after the disappearance of the illusion Merlin stood waiting where he was, half expecting it to form again, but it did not. Now, feeling like a hunted fugitive, he splashed on, setting the best pace he could out of that evil wood.

Did Nimue know from a distance what damage he had wrought in her tower? He was willing to attribute all kinds of knowledge to her. And had his destruction of the crown defeated her future plans in any way? He knew so little and needed to know so much!

Breathing faster but turning his head from side to side, gripping the wand so he would feel the first stirring it might give, he pushed on steadily. It seemed to him that gloom gathered under the trees on either side of the stream, folding in thicker, almost like the curtain he had dispensed at the tower. And behind that—what prowled behind? He closed the door of his imagination, refused to allow such speculation. To look for that kind of attack was often to open a way for it.

No birds twittered in this woods now. Merlin could no longer pick up the smallest hint of any animal life-force. When no other manifestation rose to confront or threaten him, he began to believe that Nimue's image had been random only, set up in simple expectation that some day he might venture here, and was not keyed to this one exploit of his.

The moon necklace she had worn—that he knew. Not from any teaching of the mirror, rather from the legends of his mother's people. It was the sign of one of the three who were chosen in the old days to serve the Earth Mother: Maid there always was, with the new moon for her ranking, Mother, with the full moon, Old woman with her waning orb. Why had Nimue chosen such an archaic symbol? This countryside was sparsely settled and he knew that the people here might well cling to the old ways. It could be that many, perhaps the women chiefly, secretly worshiped the Old Goddess. At that thought a small unexplainable shiver ran down his spine. This matched that faint scent of evil he had detected in the herb chamber, a hint of something that was a warning, but so veiled a one he could not understand it.

Merlin breathed deeply with relief as he came at last out from under the daunting canopy of the trees, but the sun would not be with him much longer. This time he got well away from the fringe of the woods before he sat down, his damp breeches and boots clammy on his body, to eat and drink.

Tonight there would be a full moon, ripe and yellow-white in the sky. Merlin licked crumbs from his lips. He was very tired; the outflow of energy which had obeyed his will to destroy Nimue's crown had closed down on him. To go on when he felt so weak and tired was folly. Still, even in this open, he was not easy of mind. He sat cross-legged, his wand lying on his knees, and realized he was listening, listening with a fervor he could not understand. Listening for what? Who?

Twilight faded and still he sat there, every sense alert.

He often stared at the black blot of the woods, but it was not from there that this feeling of dark awareness came. He also watched the slopes of open land around him. He was sure they had once been cleared by the hands of men and then abandoned to the wilds, so that shrubs and bushes had begun to reclaim the forest's territory.

Merlin heard the bark of a fox, the rustle of some flying thing swooping low near him, perhaps to make a hunting kill. The night was alive again, but that life was normal to it. Why then did he sit waiting?

Now and then he glanced down at the wand. Its white length was barely discernible, and the gem and metal on its point did not gleam. He began to believe that whatever threatened was not a weapon of Nimue's armory, at least no off-world one. There were times when he tried to compose himself to sleep, the light drowse he had known the night before, but that inner sentinel his mind had set refused to be ignored.

The moon rose, as whole as a piece of Roman gold tossed into the sky to overawe the stars with its light. Then, very far away, there began a disturbance which Merlin could not hear; he could only feel it like a vibration through earth and air picked up by his inner sense, not any outer one. It grew stronger until at last he heard as well as felt it.

There was a chanting which raised the hairs along his neck, made him breathe more quickly, his heart beat faster. Though he dealt with words of Power and knew what could channel through them, still this was wholly alien to his own forces. There was something utterly strange and wild in that wail in which he could not yet distinguish any words. Old, old, said his own knowledge, back, far back. This was nothing of the Star People, but entirely of a young earth before the coming of their ships.

The chanting broke into a series of shrill yelps. At last Merlin knew.

There was a hunt up under the moon, and he was the quarry. The goddess whose symbol Nimue's illusion had worn also had her dark side. To that portion of her character men had shed blood—the blood of their own kind. She had two faces, that goddess, as well as three ages, and the second face was turned to the outer Darkness, which men had always feared and tried to propitiate.

The Great Mother—and the Great Destroyer—of mankind!

Yet yielding to atavistic fear meant utter defeat. Merlin swallowed twice, working to calm the beating of his heart, to marshal what he knew, the forces he himself controlled. There must be an answer—and that was not to run. For if he gave way to that . . .

He shook his head. There *was* an answer! It lingered in the far part of his mind, overlaid by all the mirror had taught him. This was not of the mirror, however, it was of his own world alone.

The Great Mother and her priestesses who watered the earth with the blood of men—

The Great Mother and—

From that far-hidden place in his memory Merlin dragged what Lugaid had once told him very long ago. The Mother had her rival. In latter years that rival became her mate: the Horned God, to whom hunters paid tribute that they might ever find the herds they preyed on. The Horned God . . . and how greatly did these priestesses hold *him* in awe?

There was little time for self-questioning. He could either run, which his nature forbade and which he knew would condemn him anyway, or he could stand. In his standing, he would have to hold the strongest illusion he had tried for years. It had to be strong, for the power of the Mother was not like any force he had faced before.

Merlin rose to his feet. He deliberately shut out as best he could the screams of the huntresses. He steadied his mind, concentrating, hoping with every breath he drew that his command over his own powers had not been too devastated by what he had wrought at the keep in the lake. There was no mirror fronting him now in which he could check the illusion. He could only hold the picture in his mind.

They were close enough now so he could see their white bodies darting in and out among the scrub bushes, the tossing of their hair. Like Nimue, they wore no clothing, but had necklaces of acorns. And the pack was of all ages, girls scarcely into puberty, matrons with sagging breasts which had nursed children, hags so old their skin was seamed leather under the moon.

As they drew in on him, now, their faces showing only the frenzy which was the dark aspect of their goddess, their clamor stilled. There was an avid blood lust in their eyes, just so had they once gathered to slay the Winter King. Merlin must not allow himself to think of anything but the protection he had woven for himself.

The first of the pack came within leaping distance, but now they faltered, their stares fixed, then wondering. If his own powers worked they saw no man, rather a dark figure bearing stag horns on his raised head—a figure which displayed no fear of their goddess-frenzy because the Horned Hunter was himself of the earth, the sky, the land about them.

The leader of the pack snarled, a tall woman with pendulous breasts who wore about her loins a thong supporting the disk of the full moon. Twice she started to reach for him with her long-nailed fingers, crooked to claw the flesh from his bones, but she still did not strike. Her following hung farther back, glancing uneasily from their priestess to Merlin.

He raised his wand, though the star things had no power against such as these. Yet with that in his hand his confidence was greater. Now he spoke:

"You do not hunt *me*, women of the Goddess." He did not make that a question but a statement. "You may call the earth to answer you, to take the seed into it, to conceive, to bear the fruits of full harvest. But *I* command that which roams about the earth. Behold—"

With the wand he pointed to his left. There stood snarling the great Dire Wolf, a hound such as no living man had ever seen. And to the right he pointed, so that there crouched a giant cat with long fangs, and it hissed even as the wolf growled.

The women behind the priestess started back. But she stood her ground, and her teeth showed in a snarl as open as that of the cat's.

"Hunter," she spat, "do not try to oppose the Mother!"

"I am not a hunter," Merlin replied, "I am *the* Hunter. The Mother knows me for I, too, am of her breed. I am no Spring King to share her bed for but a season. Look upon me, Priestess! I am of the wild kind and, as in the wild kind, so does my wrath rise! You serve your Mother—I do not bow knee at any shrine of hers. Thus between us lies a balance of power, each equal with the other. Is this thing not so?"

Very reluctantly the priestess inclined her head. But she did not surrender her fury.

"We hunt when the Mother is threatened," she stated.

"Do I threaten her then, Priestess?"

For the first time she looked uncertain. "Perhaps—perhaps you are not the one we seek."

"Yet it is to me you have brought your pack," he countered. "I mean your lady no wrong, for both she and I serve the powers of earth life. Seek your man elsewhere, Priestess."

She stared straight at him, puzzlement on her broad face. Then she backed away, her women scattering behind her. Merlin watched them go. He had no doubt that Nimue had somehow been at the bottom of this abortive attack. Had the Lady of the Lake brought back one of the oldest beliefs of all to cement new numbers of devoted followers to her?

The women were gone and once more he could hear their bare feet thudding against the earth around the bushes. Plainly they were indeed casting about for another trail. He hoped no wayfarer was abroad in this wasteland tonight for he was sure that, once balked of what they thought was their prey, they would take an added vengeance on any they found.

Was this how the Star Lords of his half kin first presented themselves to men, taking on some illusion of an earth god? He could almost believe that he had only followed a pattern of contact devised very long ago. Simple men needed symbols to tie themselves to their belief in the great Power which was beyond any man's description. And there had been many forms of gods walking this earth. An ancient Sky Lord might have assumed the form of one—that would be the easiest way to make men listen, to direct them into new ways of living and thought.

Merlin had already relinquished the illusion with which he had clothed himself this night. Now he set out through the moon-and-shadow-checkered land to follow the old road, to be away from this place as soon as possible, drawing on the dregs of his strength to keep walking.

It was three days before Merlin saw the high rise of Camelot's hill before him. He was very tired and hungry, though he had broken his fast at a shepherd's hut that morning. The man had little news, except a rumor that the High King ailed and kept to his chamber. So Arthur still played his role. But when Merlin came nearer to Camelot he saw a party of horsemen spurring down the slope at a pace that suggested some need for haste. When they had gone, Merlin made what speed he could up to the outer wall of half earth, half stone.

There were twice as many guards at the entrance, and within a bustle of men were preparing to march. The first sentry swung his spear up crosswise, barring Merlin's passage.

"Stand!" the man commanded.

"You know me," Merlin countered. "Why do you this, fellow?"

"By Lord Cei's orders, none is to enter—"

"Then send a message to Lord Cei," Merlin returned. "I am not one to be kept waiting thus."

The man seemed undecided and there was a shadow of hostility on his face. However, one of his fellows did go off, and Merlin settled his shoulders against the firm wall to wait with what patience he could summon. He was eager to know what had happened. That Cei gave the orders here—that either meant Arthur still played his role or— Merlin tried to list the factors which might have gone wrong with their plan.

The messenger was already returning. "You are to come to Lord Cei," he told Merlin shortly, using no courtesy in that command. Nor did Merlin ask anything of the fellow who stalked by his side through the enclosure.

All the signs were of war. Saxons? Had there been some unlooked-for invasion during his absence? He kept his ears open but he could gather little from the shouted orders and general talk of the men.

Then he mounted the inner stairs of the palace to a balcony room where Cei stood by the outer window frowning out at the ramparts. He turned quickly at Merlin's coming and his scowl did not lighten.

"Arthur?" Merlin made a question of that name.

Cei's scowl deepened. "How near you are to traitor, bard," he said menacingly, "I do not yet know. When I learn . . ." He held out a hand between them and slowly curled his fingers into a hard fist. "If I find it to be as I suspect, so shall I take your throat and crush the life out of you—slowly!"

"It would save time," Merlin pointed out, "if you would

tell me what has happened. When I left the King was playing ill for purposes of his own—"

Cei showed his teeth wolfishly in what was far from any smile.

"So he told me. But look upon him now, healer. And if you can indeed heal, then do so speedily!"

Nimue! Merlin nearly said the name out loud. Perhaps he and Arthur had been defeated in trying to keep her from her stronghold. Poison was a handy weapon and Nimue knew her herbs well—those which were baneful, too—as he had sniffed in the tower room.

He had already turned again to the door. "I will see him now."

If Cei had tried to stop him he would have struck the younger man down, for Merlin carried an icy fear which armed him doubly. If Arthur died . . . !

So once more he came into the King's chamber. Bleheris rose from where he had crouched by the bed. He, too, turned a bleak face in Merlin's direction. But all Merlin had eyes for was the man on the bed.

Arthur's face was not flushed by any pseudo-fever this time. Rather it wore a sunken look and the skin seemed gray; it might almost have been a dead man lying there. Merlin went to work instantly, all his healer instincts aroused.

The King's body was chill, too chill. Merlin called for stones to be heated and wrapped, put about him as he lay. Next he used his sixth sense, and that recoiled immediately. Though the fell symptoms he saw might well come from some ailment of the body, it was surely the evil of some possessive hold which kept the King prisoner.

Cei watched and now he demanded: "What is it? Yesterday when the Lady Nimue departed he was well and able once again. This morning—" He flung out his hands, his face twisted with pain. Though Cei seldom showed his feelings outwardly Merlin knew that the tie between him and his foster brother ran deep and clear. "Then that nithling, that stinking traitor—"

"He is under ensorcellment," Merlin answered the first question. "And he must be swiftly awakened thereit."

"You can do that?"

"With certain remedies, aye. Let me go to my chamber, but you stay here. Allow no one but the two of you near him." He nodded to the Pict now. "I shall be as quick as I can!"

Alive and well when Nimue departed, he thought as he strode along the hall. Then perhaps she had placed on the King one of those delayed mind-orders which would strike when she was gone. What else Cei had said did not hold Merlin's attention now. He must save Arthur!

In his own chamber he chose hurriedly from his supplies, gathering small jars into a rush basket. And he also carried his wand with him as he returned to the King's chamber. Once there he sent Bleheris for a pot of boiling water, then had the Pict set up a brazier into which, on a bed of live coals, Merlin tossed leaves of various sorts he hurriedly culled from his selections. An aromatic smoke arose while Merlin brewed a tankard of liquid with the water.

"His sword—" He turned to Cei. "Where is his sword?"

It was Bleheris who answered, not with words but by scuttling across the room to fetch the sheathed blade from behind a chest.

"That one came hunting," he said as he put the sword into Merlin's hands. "But he did not find it."

As Merlin drew the sword and the firelight caught the blade, turning it into a shimmering bar of light, he asked of Cei: "Modred—is this nithling you speak of Modred?"

"Aye." Cei's voice was hot with fury. "He tried to put his will on the lords because the King ailed. They would not swear to him. Then—then he wooed the Queen. And she listened to him! In the night she rode off with Modred, and men who saw her go said she went willingly. Faugh! She is near twice his years and yet she colored like a maid when he looked at her. She deems Arthur as good as dead and she would still be Queen! What will you do now?"

"I summon our lord's presence back. A part of him strays in a strange place and it is a place which is death to man. Now be silent!"

Merlin raised the sword until the point rested lightly, tip only, on Arthur's forehead above and between his eyes. Though both Cei and Bleheris listened and this was not meant for the ears of common men, he began to chant. His eyes were closed as he tried not to believe that he stood in the familiar chamber of the King, but rather ranged in another place to which someone, doubtless Nimue, had banished Arthur.

There was a kind of nothingness, though odd crooked dazzles of light still ran through it. Each of those flashes was a personality which had either chosen to enter this limbo or had been banished here. Merlin's chant rang, not as words, but rather as muted sounds. With that a path of light also spread out and out from Merlin's own stand here. The sword was a pointer he could use in his search to locate Arthur.

Merlin began to move along that path of light while the dazzles drew back or fled away. But one red-gold flash was touched and held in spite of frenzied contortions. Seeing that, Merlin changed the flow of words. Earlier the words had been of far-seeking, now they formed an imperative summons.

Down the path of sword light came that wriggling figure, fighting because the compulsion to remain here had been set upon it. Merlin's will must defeat that compulsion. He commanded, as one who had full right to do so. Into that command Merlin poured all his concern for Arthur, his belief in the other and the mission which they both shared.

Back drew that fighting fragment of twisted light. It was fairly caught and held by the power of the sword. Merlin released his own hold on that strange far country to open his eyes.

He was never sure if he actually saw that last flicker of light slide down the sword blade to the King's head, but he heard Arthur's groan and saw his head move a fraction on the pillow. He had won.

17.

~~~~~~

The breeze at the top of the windswept wall did not carry away the words of the man who stood below. Arthur, his face drawn and set in lines of haggard strain, stood firm-footed gazing down at that bard. Behind him was ranged a ragged showing of his once-proud court. Cei's voice was a thick growl, monotonously cursing the bard, who by the ancient custom of the tribes must be free from any retaliation in physical form.

Merlin studied the man. This was so ingenious a move that he did not believe the idea had been Modred's at all. He could see Nimue in this—or was he too ready to see Nimue in *all* which moved against Arthur or him? The plan could even have been partly Guenevere's, for the bard below was from her father's court, well noted there for the sharpness of his tongue and the evil twists of his mind which profaned bardic uses to his own purposes.

This was a threat which had brought proud lords and kings to dire disaster in the past: for the bard was engaged in singing aloud the tale of Arthur who lay with his own sister to beget a son whom now he hunted from him, of Arthur who was demon-possessed and no true king at all.

Since his recovery the King had refused to listen to Cei and the others who had pressed him for the instant pursuit of Modred and Guenevere. He had patiently pointed out over and over again that to pursure with a sword was to break apart the Fellowship of Britain. And that, if the Fellowship failed. Britain would also break asunder while the sea wolves would be quick to pick her bones.

Merlin had thought Modred more farseeing than to move thus openly with the old scandal. He could not expect the lords to rally to him after revealing his mother's shame to pull Arthur down. Even though he was of the

Pendragon blood, no lord hearing this would raise his voice for Modred to wear the crown. By tainting Arthur he tainted himself. So why?

Guenevere, too, had much to lose. If she had chosen Modred as the coming ruler, thinking Arthur on his death bed, then why would she wish to dash his chances? Too many questions and they all led, he was sure, to Nimue.

If she had discovered his attack on her stronghold then her fury might have erupted, pushing her to act without the careful intrigue he associated with her, to throw aside all cover and make such a deadly attack. Nimue—he was positive of that!

On and on rang that chant, derisive, penetrating, tearing at the innermost feelings of a man who had no way of taking counteraction. Maybe Arthur could not, but . . . Merlin moved. There was an answer, abrupt, perhaps dangerous in a way. Yet he could not allow this reviling to continue. In the past, mighty men of good life had been led to commit kin-murder by just such goading.

Merlin raised his wand, pointing it at the head of the bard. This was no real weapon; he was not putting an end to the law of bardic freedom of speech by physical means.

No, it was thought command which he hurled, knowing full well that the man below would never have ventured to the very walls of Camelot with his obscene attack were he not defended by shields no man could see. Merlin concentrated. The words sing-songed on.

Then suddenly the bard was silent. His head shook from side to side. He raised frenzied hands to claw at his own mouth.

Merlin's own voice rang out: "The one who has spat forth poison now must chew on it! Speak, man of little power, speak now the truth!"

It took all the power of his will to hold the bard. He had been very right in his belief that the fellow had come well armed. He had strong defenses of the old lore to counteract, yet he did so.

The bard had fallen to his knees. He looked straight up at Merlin now, his face working hideously as if he indeed held some fell poison in his mouth and could not spew it forth, so that it ate into his tongue and jaws. Again Merlin pointed with the wand.

"Speak out, with the truth. Give us no more lies of your

foul imagining. Who sent you to so bemire the High King?"

As if against his will the bard's lips parted.

"She—" he said. That single word might have been wrenched from him by a torturer's instrument.

"Give this woman a name," ordered Merlin "Or as you have spouted forth lies, so shall it be that the truth will be ever closed to you. Henceforth all men will know you to be a liar, and none will listen to you again. For there comes a time of judging when one answers to his own Power. And if you were true bard you would also know—"

There was red hate burning in the man's eyes as he stared back up at Merlin. But accompanying that hate was fear, and the fear was growing stronger.

"It is the Lady Morgause who has told this thing," he said thickly, "and how better would anyone know the truth than she?"

Morgause—the girl Merlin had seen imprisoned in Nimue's keep? Was this the reason Nimue had kept her on hand and ready for all these years? Merlin could hear a shocked murmur of those behind him on the wall.

"You saw the Lady Morgause." Merlin forced his calm to hold. "And you say how better could anyone know than she. How—"

Arthur's voice cut across his own. "Let it be, Merlin. The High King does not fight with women."

Now the grimace of the bard below turned into a snarling grin. "Speak fair, Lord King. Cling to that shadow of honor you have never wholly had since even before the day of your crowning. Let this demon's son strike me speechless. There have been ears enough for the hearing. Men remember evil quicker than good; it is the way of the world. Even if you could by some miracle prove yourself innocent of this act, more will listen to the accusation than to any words which absolve you. Listen well! Lord Modred sets dishonor upon you. He marches now to bring justice into this land. If you would meet him, then let the Power itself decide what is right and what is wrong."

"Good enough!" Merlin heard Cei's instant answer to that. "Lord King, each lord who listens seriously to this foul lie is a traitor. And with traitors there is only one way of dealing. Let them speedily face the sword edges of honest men!"

A small cheer followed his speech, but Arthur's frown came swiftly. However it was to the bard he spoke, not Cei.

"Bard, you have delivered your message. Now go."

"And what return do you make to Lord Modred, High King?" The man accented the title tauntingly.

"That I do not propose to wrench Britain apart to suit his will," Arthur replied somberly.

"You have no choice," the bard returned, "unless you creep away in full dishonor before the faces of all men. Remember that!"

Then he rose from his knees, favored Merlin with a last glare and strode away, his back turned without courtesy upon the King. Cei grunted.

"A spear between that one's shoulders now," he said wistfully, "that should be his full payment. But he is right, foster brother. You fight or else you leave full power open to Modred. And how do you think he will use that right to rule? He is a nithling. The great lords will break apart, for he will find few to do him homage. Lord will quarrel with lord, each reaching a hand for the crown. What comes of that? A riven land will open as easy meat for the Saxons. So it was at the death of Uther. Lord King, you have no choice. You ram these foul lies back down the throat of that nithling, using your sword hilt to do so, or else you stand without honor before all who have followed you through these years."

Arthur's set expression did not change, but his eyes turned from the retreating bard to Cei and then to Merlin. "Attend me," he curtly bade them both, and strode along the rampart, men falling back to give him passage.

But too many faces in that company were sober, too many eyes rested on the High King questioningly. Cei's summing up of the situation was very apt. Arthur would be damned before all men if he did not fight and a war between lord and lord in Britain would come either way. Everything he had wrought would break apart like a fruit rotted at the core.

And Merlin, as he obeyed the King's summons, thought of the beacon How long, how far? To those questions he had no answers. Perhaps what he had set in motion would draw their off-world kin into utter chaos. Yet he could not see what he might have done differently at the time.

With Cei he entered the King's chamber close on Arthur's heels. The King strode back and forth across the room, his hands clasped behind his back, his chin sunk upon his chest. There was pain in his face, such pain as no physical wound would have raised.

"Brothers," he said, "you alone know the truth which lies behind my heritage. Aye," he spoke now to Merlin, "I have shared the truth with Cei for he is also of the Old Blood in part. But there is this: will any man, either those out there who heard that down-chant, or those who have apparently flocked to Modred, believe it?"

Cei spoke first. "If they did, brother, they would find it an evil truth and look upon you with even greater hatred. Few men will accept that there may be a race somewhere, either on this earth or off it, which is greater in gifts and talents than themselves. The priests teach that there was a Christus who was so, but he is dead. And so, being dead, men can now accept him. Yet in his time men hated and reviled him for that difference, and conspired to send him to the most shameful punishment they knew, one reserved for slaves and traitors. Men bow to gods, but if those gods appeared they would fear and hate them.

"It is the nature of man to wish to drag down to his own level all who have climbed above. You are the greatest king Britain has seen, even greater than Maximus, for you have not deserted your duty in pursuit of ambition. Had you not been given the crown, still you would have struggled to serve. Men know this and it does not make them revere you the more. Do you think that Lot, who was in position to claim the throne, loves you now? Nor may the Duke of Cornwall, nor any of those others who might aspire to your crown.

"Aye, they shall use this old scandal against you. But this was an act of a lusty youth and it can be made plain that the Lady Morgause was unknown to you as being close kin. Besides, she was one who had warmed other beds and it can be hinted that Modred was none of your true get—"

"No!" Arthur interrupted. "We do not befoul a woman's name to answer this threat. She perhaps was—is—all that you say. But I will not hold her up meanly before all and cry 'The woman deceived and tempted me!' Such action is not for any king."

Cei nodded. "So would you decide, brother. But such fairness will not work for you either. Men will accept forbearance as an open admission of guilt. However, to tell the truth is even worse. We shall have 'demon-born' hurled in our ears until that cry will deafen and turn from us even the most strong-hearted of those who would otherwise support you."

"He is right," Merlin said quietly. "This is a time when either choice will make strong enemies. The web has been well woven; the snare is around us."

"You are sure this is of Nimue's doing?"

Merlin answered the King forthrightly: "As sure as if I had heard her order Morgause to teach the bard his lines. She is taking her revenge now. But there is this, Arthur, I am also certain that she can no longer speak with her guiding voice, therefore what she may do is of her own thinking. And the beacon cannot now be overset—"

"This beacon—" Cei rounded on him. "You promise it will bring the Sky Lords. In what numbers will they come, and when? Will they raise weapons to aid our King, or stand aside and let man struggle against man, perhaps then making some treaty with the victor?"

"I have answers to none of those questions," Merlin returned. "Time to the Sky Lords does not pass as our days or years. They live much longer than we do. It may be that years will pass before their ships drop from our sky."

Cei shook his head. "Then it is best to forget them in any plans we make. But Modred must be handled, and speedily. As yet his force will be small, but men will ride to him. And do not forget, he also has the Queen. Her very presence in his camp will argue that she believes this shameful tale and so has withdrawn from you, Arthur."

"That I know," the King returned. His voice sounded tired, as worn and ravaged as his face. "Men will also say that I ride out against my own son."

"You ride against a traitor!" returned Cei forcefully. "You," he said, turning his attention to Merlin, "this was of your doing! If your knowledge was so great and all-powerful why—"

But Arthur replied with more strengh in Merlin's behalf than he had for himself. "Waste no time, brother, on the counting of many 'ifs' which lie in all our pasts. Merlin did only what was given him to do. And it is on him that all our success will lie in the end."

Merlin, startled, regarded the King narrowly. There had been a note in Arthur's voice when he said that, as if suddenly the talent of farseeing had been given to him.

"What do you mean?" he asked.

"When the hour comes," the King continued in that same assured voice, "then it shall be known to you, kinsman. We each have a part to play, ill-fated though such may be. It is, as you have pointed out, Cei, well that we move to the playing of them now."

They rode out of Camelot, not ablaze with colors waving and high confidence in their might, but soberly, yet not in any degree showing that they believed their mission any the less rightful than when they marched against the invaders.

News was brought to Arthur. The forces had indeed split, and it was true that many of the great lords, perhaps through jealousy as Cei had foreseen, were either holding aloof from taking sides or had openly joined Modred. He had dared to raise the Dragon standard and proclaim himself High King, Arthur being no fit ruler.

Cei laughed harshly when that was reported at their second night's camp.

"He is a fool," he said bluntly. "Does he believe that Lot, who waits now to see how fortune favors us, would allow him more days on that unsteady throne than it would take him to offer Modred open challenge?"

If Lot was one who waited, Constans of Cornwall was not. With his Boar banner waving proudly, he brought his train of fighters into Arthur's camp. There before all gathered he reaffirmed his sworn allegiance to the King. So an old ill was forgotten and Arthur gained heart thereby, for Constans was the son of Goloris' son, and the only other true-born lord of Arthur's kin.

On the fourth day, when their army had been augmented again by two troops of the Black Horse fresh from duty along the Marches, Arthur called council, meeting with those lords and commanders who had remained true to their allegiance.

"We march now," the King said with a harsh note in his voice, "against those who have been sword brothers and shield comrades. A hundred times or more have we faced a common foe and braved the threat of death together. It is not meet that we now turn steel against one another in anger. I will not put aside my crown, not because I choose to be king against the will of all men, but because I will

not step aside from my duty to this land. Yet it is a very
grievous thing to slay old friends."

He paused but no man of that company spoke up.
Merlin thought that Arthur had not really expected any
answer. Then he continued slowly:

"Let no man be able to say in days to come that I do
not wish well those who have been seduced from me by
lies. Therefore, I would send a messenger to Modred and
say to him that we should meet in open company, all
weapons sheathed, and speak together, that he break not a
peace so hardly built."

Constans, who was the greatest of the lords now in that
company, though almost the youngest also, then answered
him.

"Lord King, this is the act of one who has indeed
thought of others first. Few men who have had a bard
sing against them would hold out a hand in peace to those
who sent that bard. If you go meet this traitor, then I
shall stand at your side!"

"And I—I—I—" They had caught fire, Merlin saw.
No one there, having looked on Arthur's face as he spoke
of that offer, would ever say that it was one made out of
fear; rather it came from his love for Britain, which he
had served nearly all his life long.

So one of the oldest of the lords, a certain Owien, who
had in his youth ridden in Ambrosius' own bodyguard,
offered himself as messenger. And Arthur, knowing the
high respect in which all men held Owien, was well
pleased. Having the King's words given to him, Owien
went forth from the camp. And they rested, waiting
through a day and a night. On the second day Owien returned.

He came directly to Arthur, "Lord King, I have spoken
your words to Modred. There was some talk among his
people, urging this and that, but at last he agreed that it
shall be as you wish. He has said to meet with him at the
Lesser Stones of Langwellyn, bringing with you ten of
your lords, as he shall come with ten of his. The priest
Gildas spoke up saying that Merlin must not be one of the
ten, for he would lend the Devil's own strength to you. But
Modred laughed at that and said he had something which
would defeat any Devil's work. Lord King, with their
forces rides the Lady Morgause, yet she is not aged, but is
even as she left the court at Uther's sending. And with her

is the Lady of the Lake. Men look sidewise at them, even in Modred's company, for it is not natural that age has not touched the Lady Morgause."

"If she be the Lady Morgause at all!" snapped Cei. "Uther had bastards in plenty and this one may even be a daughter of one of them, if she looks so young. It is but another trick for the undoing of our lord!"

Arthur gestured as if brushing aside this addition to Owien's report.

"All that matters now is that Modred has agreed to this meeting. Let us take heart in that."

But later, when night had closed in, he came to Merlin. "You have powers," he began. "Can you use them over Modred, making him repeat before his lords words which will commit him to peace? I do not believe that one man should command another so against his will, but this is a man who would plunge our world into blood. If there is anything I can do to stay his hand without a killing, that I shall attempt."

"It depends," Merlin answered as frankly, "on how well Nimue has armed him. Mark his reply to Gildas made before Owien. I have done what I can to weaken her power. But I shall not know how well I have succeeded until we have a trial of strength. Be sure, however, that all I can raise in the way of force is at your disposal, kinsman.

"More than that I do not ask," Arthur returned. "I wish that it had been given me to learn as you learned. For at this moment I feel that I need more than human strength and will to aid me." He rose slowly, "Well, let us sleep, if any sleep will come to us. Tomorrow brings either peace or blood, and which choice we cannot now foresee."

"There is this," Merlin told him. "They have appointed a meeting place in the middle of ancient stones. If this is part of some forgotten temple, even as the Place of the Sun, then I can command more of the Power to our service. For much lies sleeping in such places."

"Providing they are not places hostile to us."

"Lord King, I have found many such places in this land. Only once has any had the stench of the Dark about it, and that was the hold of Nimue. I hope that none was built elsewhere."

If the King slept that night, Merlin did not. He lay on his cloak, his eyes closed, to be sure, but his mind awake; he sought through his memory for anything which might prove either armor or weapon. Piece by piece, word by word, he assembled all he knew, all he had learned from the mirror that might at this time add to his inner forces. He understood that this was a trial of strength with Nimue, perhaps the final battle between them.

Though he had not slept, yet the morning found him alert and eager for that confrontation. And as they moved on, he fingered his wand as a boy might finger his sword hilt before his first battle.

They came to a place which was like a finger of firm earth poked into marshy land. There were ponds here and there, some scummed over with green, others clear but dark, with water reeds and the strange growths of such country standing tall. On the finger of firm earth were the stones Modred had named, while on the slope of the hill on the other side were drawn up the rebel forces, making a parade of banners.

Arthur's men did the same on this slope, while the King dismounted and with him Merlin, Cei, Owien and others. He had refused to take Constans, rather giving into the Duke's hands the command of the force behind. Constans would have argued but Arthur pressed on him that this was his true duty, for after Arthur now no other man had clear right to the crown.

Then with Arthur to the fore, Merlin and Cei shoulder-to-shoulder behind him, they moved on down to the stones. The rhythm of chanting from the rebel forces sounded, and Merlin saw robed monks in a tight group under the unlawful standard of the Dragon.

Though he searched carefully with alert eyes he could make out no sign of any women. If the Queen, Morgause and Nimue were there, they were somehow hidden by the warriors.

He next studied the stones as they slowly drew closer to them, their pace being carefully matched by Modred's group coming down to meet them here. To Merlin's eyes there was little outward difference between these rough rocks and those he had seen at the Place of the Sun. But he still wondered at Modred's selection of such a site. Such places were abodes of the Devil, to the monks who had given their good will to Modred. Why then . . . ? Mistrust strengthened in Merlin, for he felt that Nimue would never have allowed her puppet prince to select a place where the old forces slept and could be awakened.

Unless she was finding Modred—her own creation perhaps—a weapon which turned in the hand, and that he,
not she, now gave the orders of their company.

The stones were set in a single small circle. Two lay
prone. Merlin swung his wand a little. He felt no pull, detected no spark of energy. These stones were as dead in
that respect as any ordinary rock. Well, he had not really
expected that they would be otherwise.

He watched Modred now, that narrow dark face which
bore so much the stamp of the Old Blood, yet had something within it which subtly repelled. Modred was smiling;
he gave the appearance of one whom fortune had favored.
And Merlin, thoroughly alert for trickery, began a subtle
probing, only to meet a barrier as strong to his mind's
thrust as steel might stand to the prod of a single fingertip.
Modred was well armed indeed.

18.

~~~~~~

Merlin did not relinquish his struggle to touch the younger man somehow. He caught Modred's slanting gaze once and was answered with a sly smile, as if Modred knew what he would do and had no fears. Then Modred spoke directly to Arthur with open insolence.

"You have asked that we meet. What plea would you make to me?"

Merlin sensed the stiffening of Cei, knew that it was only with difficulty that the other must be restraining his growing rage at such an insult to the King. But Arthur's answer came calm and clear.

"I make no plea, Modred. I only tell you the truth now; if we war, Britain fails. Then all we have won will be lost forever."

"Your throne will be lost," Modred returned, flaunting his insolence without any shading of prudence. "Have you come then to beg for your crown, Arthur?"

Merlin saw the flush rise on the King's face. That Arthur kept his self-control was a measure of the man, and Merlin's pride in him was great. He himself strove to pierce Modred's barrier, to reach the man. And so intent was he on the task he had promised Arthur he would try that he nearly lost the warning of a more subtle attack.

He turned his head swiftly. Something moved by the nearest stone, rustling in the grass. Before Arthur could answer, one of Modred's men uttered a cry of surprise and fear, drawing his sword and striking downward. For a moment they saw the upraised head of a serpent. But it was no true serpent. Illusion, cried Merlin's own senses, too late.

"Treachery!" Cei's blade was also out, slashing at the man who had driven his sword into a serpent which vanished even as he tried to impale it.

Modred sprang at the King, his sword out and ready, but Cei's charge shouldered him aside. Then battle swirled openly around the stones. From behind, Merlin heard the sounding of the trumpets where Constans was ordering a charge. Inches of steel reached for his own throat. He brought up the wand and hurled a mental blast at his attacker.

The man howled madly, his sword wavered, his eyes became fixed in his head. He plunged on, hurling Merlin back against one of the stones. The force of that crushing against the rock drove the breath from Merlin's body in a mighty wheeze.

The fighting swirled around him. The man he had mind-struck staggered on, to be cut down by one of Arthur's men. Down the slope thundered those of Arthur's guard, the man in advance leading the King's own charger, cutting his way in so that Arthur might swing into the saddle. Modred was gone. Merlin, clinging to his stone lest he go down and be trampled under hooves, saw him leaping from tussock to tussock across a band of marsh to join with those milling there, striving to find a dried path to come at the King's forces.

There were four bodies among the stones. One was Owien, his aged face turned up, his sightless eyes staring straight into the sun hanging over them. There was a look of vast surprise frozen on his features, as if death had come so swiftly that he had not even had time to realize it before the stroke fell.

The fighting had already whirled away from the stones. Merlin got back his breath, went from one body to the next. Healing craft was his and by the looks he would be well needed this day. But these were all dead.

He made his way back to the wagons which carried the supplies for the wounded. There he shrugged off his robe of office, leaving his body freer in his under-tunic as he went to work. But in him was the stricken knowledge that he had failed Arthur. Had he not been so intent on mastering Modred, he might have seen that illusion, dispersed it before it incited this slaying. Whether he had seen Nimue or not, the serpent was hers, he had no doubt of that.

Now he labored to staunch grievous wounds, perhaps saving lives while in the valley below others were as intent on ending it. Whoever won this day, Britain might well be lost.

Time ceased to be counted as passing hours. Merlin wrought with his hands and with his mind among those brought to him. Many he could only ease into a painless parting, others he could grant a chance. And of those who still had their senses alert enough to give coherent answers he asked about the progress of the fight. But the men he tended had seen only portions, those which had centered about them. Sometimes they reported retreats, at other times small victories, with a beating back of the rebels.

At mid-afternoon they brought him Cei's young shield bearer. And the boy wept as Merlin set splints around a broken arm. His lord, he said dazedly, had been cut down, though he had taken with him at least four of the enemy who had surrounded him.

So Cei was gone, even as Ector had gone before him, Merlin thought wearily. He had indeed ever been Arthur's right hand, and now that was cut off. Owien and Cei, and how many more who would have and did follow Arthur no matter what tattling lies could be told?

He felt as if he moved now through some dreadful dream, perhaps that hell the followers of the Christus were wont to say lay ready to engulf all unbelievers. There was blood everywhere, and dead men asprawl, their bodies dragged hurriedly aside when no more might be done to aid them.

The stench of blood filled his nostrils, clung about him, just as it splashed and clotted on his under-tunic, bespattered his arms and legs, even his cheeks. And with it hung the smell of death from which there was no escape. The sun that had been overhead at the beginning of this slaughter was now far down in the west.

"Merlin—" Someone pulled at his arm, tugging in spite of his efforts to shake off that touch. He moved on toward a man who lay groaning, his hands clasped across a great gash in his belly, the touch of death already on him.

"Merlin!"

Dazed, he looked down into a small dark face across which was a cut which had dribbled blood now clotting in a smear. There was a name for this man. Merlin searched his memory . . . .

"Bleheris," he said.

"Merlin!" The other jerked at his arm. "Bring your healing things and come!"

Merlin shook off the stupor which had grown out of

suffering and his attempts to relieve it. There could only be one reason why Bleheris sought him out. And he discovered at that moment that all the fear which he had ever known in his life was nothing compared to the terror which gripped him now.

Arthur!

Though they had known that death ever waited in battle, still Merlin had not really foreseen in his heart that this might come to Arthur. It could not! All he had, all he was, would rise to fight for the last of the Star-born.

Savage anger followed that thrust of agonizing fear. In that moment he wanted two throats between his hands—Modred's and the slender one of Nimue! Catching up a bag of linen strips, grasping at two pots of salve, he rounded on Bleheris.

"Where?" he demanded.

The Pict was fairly hopping from one foot to another in impatience.

"Come." He started on a run and Merlin easily matched his pace.

They threaded a way through the human wreckage of the battle The fight had swirled away. Only distantly now could they hear the shouting, the cries, groans, screams of wounded horses and men. Bleheris bore to the right, pounding along the bank of the river whose overflow fed the swamplands. There were more dead here, even wounded who cried out faintly. But Merlin's ears were still closed. Arthur was all that mattered, for Arthur was Britain—Arthur was the shining future of the world!

"It was Modred," the Pict babbled between gasps as he ran. "The King, he had cut straight through all the others to get at the traitor. He speared him, but Modred would not die. He held to the King's lance and cut up. He would not die!"

There were tears washing away the clots of blood on Bleheris' cheek. "Dead he was, that foul traitor, but he would not die until he left his mark on the King."

There was a hut ahead, a rough thing probably used during the hunting season by a fowler. And outside it stood two of those Merlin knew as Arthur's guard. He pushed by them, and then was on his knees where a body rested on a heap of stained and tattered war cloaks.

Arthur's eyes were closed. There were beads of sweat on his forehead and cheeks. His breath came in the ragged gasps of a man in torment. They had stripped off his ring armor, bared his body, and there was a mass of cloth plugging a wound in his lower belly.

Swiftly, but with care, Merlin drew that away, sodden as it was with blood. What he saw there—

Men did not live with such wounds. Not in this day. But Arthur was not just a man; he was more. Merlin worked deftly, cleansing, binding up that wound.

"He—he will live ... ?" Bleheris hunkered to watch, and beyond him was Gawain of Arthur's guard.

"I do not know." Merlin sat back on his heels. His mind had at last broken free of that deadly stupor which had gripped it since the battle began. Clear as if he saw it actually before him, he was remembering that coffin box in the cave. It preserved life—could it heal Arthur or at least keep him asleep and living until the Sky Lords came? For their knowledge was greater than Merlin or any in his world would have.

But that cave was distant. Could he keep Arthur living until they reached it? What did he have? Only the small knowledge of this day, a little aided by what the mirror could share with him, though he was unable even to comprehend the learning long since lost. But he also had his will! And if will and purpose could keep Arthur living, then he would set all of his to that task alone from this moment forward.

"How goes the battle?"

He could not transport Arthur through a land where they might be hunted as they went. Now he saw the young guard near Arthur's head look at him angrily, as if nothing mattered except saving the life of his wounded lord. But Bleheris guessed the reason for his question instantly.

"If you would take the Lord King hence, Lord Merlin," he answered, "Modred's men are broke. They flee before the vengeance of the Black Riders."

"Where would you take the High King?" demanded the guard then.

"He is sore hurt," Merlin answered. "He must be taken where those well versed in heal-craft can tend him."

"Merlin—"

Their heads all swung around. Arthur's eyes were open, his voice so thin, a thread of sound, that they tried to still even their breathing that they might not drown out his words.

"I killed him . . ."

That was not quite a statement, not quite a question, but Merlin treated it as the latter.

"He is dead," he replied flatly.

"He forced me to it. He was so greatly my enemy that he threw away his life to make sure of my death. Why?"

Merlin shook his head. "I do not know, save that he was only a weapon in another's hands. This hate is old, old beyond our understanding. Once it turned this world into ashes—"

"So does it again." Arthur's voice had grown a little stronger as if he must get out the words he would say. "The Fellowship is broken, Merlin." His hand moved a little by his side as if seeking something which should rest there. "Where is the sword?"

"Here, Lord King," Bleheris burrowed beneath the edge of the massed war cloaks on which the King lay. He found the weight of the ancient blade heavy but he held it up so Arthur could look at it without turning his head.

"I shall not . . . put hand to its hilt again . . ." the King said.

"Not until your wound is healed," Merlin corrected quickly.

"Brother-kin." Arthur's lips curved in the faintest of smiles. "Do not deceive yourself. Great may be your powers, but on all powers there is a limit."

"There was also a promise!" Merlin's eyes caught and held Arthur's, setting his will on the King. "You are he who was, is and shall be!"

"Shall be . . ." repeated Arthur drowsily, his eyes closed.

Bleheris regarded him fearfully. "Is he—has he gone from us?"

"Not so," Merlin assured the Pict. "He sleeps and will continue to sleep free from pain. So shall he rest until we get him to where he may be cared for."

"Lord Merlin, what of—? Who will lead us, then?" asked the guard.

"The Lord King has given Constans the leadership. But when you speak to the Duke tell him also that Arthur lives, he only goes hence that he may be cured of his wound. Also" —he was thinking clearly and logically now—"do you tell the Duke that he is to search in Modred's camp and there he will find the Queen and two

others—the Lady Morgause and the Lady of the Lake.
And these he will say nothing to concerning the King, save
that he is wounded a little and rests. But he shall also
make sure that those three do no more mischief."

"Lord Merlin, as you have said it, so will it be told to
Duke Constans. But how bear you the King hence and
where—"

"As to how, he shall go by horse litter, well wrapped in.
And where, to the mountains where there is a place well
known to healers."

He began to give orders and they were obeyed. It was
as if those who had served Arthur so faithfully were
willing to do anything to maintain their fragile hope that
the King would survive. By morning Merlin was ready to
lead forth a small party.

The King, as well protected as they could make him,
was secured in a horse litter, with Bleheris, mounted on
his own small pony, leading the horses. Merlin brought up
the rear. He had spoken to Constans, who had sought him
out with the news that Modred's forces had suffered such
a defeat as would make the kingdom safe.

"Duke," Merlin had answered him. "I do not hide from
you, though I ask you for the sake of the men's spirits not
to set it generally about, that the King is sore hurt. He has
only one chance for life and that is to reach a place of
healing. I shall fight, as you have, to keep breath in his
body until we are there. Into your hands did he give command, and to you he would leave his rule. Britain has
been torn sorely here; you must heal the country's wounds
as I will strive to heal the King's."

Constans listened and then said, "Healer, I have heard
many strange things of you, but never has it been said
that you were unfriend to the King. Rather it is known
that to you he turned when he was in sore trouble. Therefore I believe in what you say. I shall hold Britain, not
as her king, but as one who rules for another. Unless word
comes that your hopes have come to nothing. Then will I
reign as Pendragon."

"So be it. Now what of the women?"

"The Queen has been found, much distraught and
nearly out of her wits. She begs to be sent to the house of
the holy women who call themselves sisters and live at
Avalon. The Lady Morgause—she has also been found—
dead. Though the manner of her death we do not know,

for on her body was no wound, nor were her features distorted as if she had drunk poison. Rather she lies as one asleep. But of the third you bade me seek there is no sign."

Merlin sighed. Guenevere and Morgause were neither of any great matter, but Nimue was different. Having wrought this great tragedy, would she now seek to make it greater by bringing death to Arthur? His rage awoke. Not so! Arthur must live in spite of all the spells and illusions of that dark one.

"Seek her diligently," he said now, though he was sure Nimue would not be found unless she willed it, "for of all the enemies of the King she is the greatest, being who and what she is—a mistress of great magic."

Constans nodded. "Will you take an escort?"

Now it was Merlin's turn to ponder for a moment before answering.

"No. Where we go a large party would be noted. You have broken Modred's forces, but there will some scattered few, with the name of traitor rightfully laid on them now, who will be willing to risk all to kill Arthur. A small group may go by hidden ways; a large one can be quickly seen or tracked. I shall take only Bleheris the Pict. He has all the trail skill of his people and so he can cover and conceal our path that few can follow."

Thus it came about that they traveled with what speed they could along wilderness ways. And Merlin's will kept the King asleep and perhaps even life in his body as they went. Nor did they see any others in the wilderness Bleheris chose for their passage save twice at a distance, when they were in hiding, small bands of men Merlin believed fugitives from the rout.

Up into the mountains they came until Merlin could see ahead the peak which marked the ground of the cave. Then he turned to Bleheris.

"Good comrade, ahead lies where we must go. But I know not what we shall find there. If the King can reach a certain cave still living, I nurse hopes of his survival. However, though he may so live, it may not be granted to us—"

"Healer," returned the Pict, "I have already lived longer than a warrior of any clan can rightfully expect to do. The King gave me life once, shall I now deny it to him? I am a clanless man, but the Lord King sat me beside his home hearth and named me liege. What is to be done, tell me, and that I shall do."

It was difficult to get the horse litter up the final grade and at length they had to loosen it and draw it up by their own strength of arm. But at last they reached the cave entrance.

Nor was Merlin greatly surprised to find one there before them. She sat on a rock, her face turned toward them, a certain patience about her as if she had waited for some time.

Merlin placed the litter gently on the ground before he turned to her.

"Look upon your work," he said. "Take pride in it, Nimue!"

To his faint surprise there was no triumph in her face.

"There is no pride to be taken in the death of any man," she said. And there was about her now none of those enticing graces, none of that appeal to his senses. "What was done was enacted because it had to be."

"Why?" he asked baldly.

"Because once before men became playthings of Star Lords who used them carelessly, taught them what they were not yet ready to know, drew them into their own disputes one with the other. Finally this world itself was riven and nearly destroyed. There was a war among the stars afterward and an oath taken, that never again should those of another species come under our command—"

"Yet it seems that oath was not honored." Merlin pointed out. "You are the servant of the Dark Ones and you have wrought such a bloodletting in Britain as will not be forgotten for a thousand of man's years, maybe more."

"I did what had to be done," she said tonelessly. "You would have called down knowledge which men of this age cannot learn, or in their half-learning would use to greater evil. It is you, Merlin, who brought in your High King to change the world, and it is you whose acts killed him."

"He is not dead," Merlin retorted. "Nor shall he die, sorceress. On the day appointed he shall stand before the beacon and welcome those of his fathering."

She glanced at Arthur almost indifferently. "Your beacon, Merlin, is a useless thing. The Sky Lords do not measure time as we do. It will be perhaps a hundred centuries more before that beacon will have an answer, if it ever does. And by that time perhaps man will be better readied to know how ill the Sky Lord's gifts will be for them. You have set your beacon, Merlin, but I have defeated your king."

Merlin shook his head. "Not yet. I have the promise: he was, he is, he shall be!"

Now she looked at him pityingly. "Merlin, you could have been so much, yet you have chosen to be so little: a spokesman for only half-told knowledge, guardian of a barbarian kinglet soon forgotten." Now she rose and stretched wide her arms, so that the loose sleeves of her robe fell away from her white arms.

"Merlin," and the old teasing note crept back into her voice, "you and I are akin, you know. I can look on no man of full earth blood with any lighting of heart, nor can you lay hand on any maid of the tribes. My tower and lake can fade from the sight of the common kind, and yet we can live there undisturbed. Our lives are long, past the years of the true human kind. Are you never lonely, Merlin? We have done our tasks, now we are free. . . ."

He faced her and in him there was a mighty surge of all he had pushed away from the fore of his mind. Nimue laughed.

"Ah, Merlin, I see you remember! Aye, I can be many women if I choose, all lovesome and willing. Much can I teach you, much!"

Merlin stepped back a pace. "I do not doubt that," he said dryly. "But I serve the King."

"A dying man!" She looked at him now not mockingly, nor with any dark laughter, rather with a droop to her lips. "Lonely Merlin, would you be ever lonely then?"

Her words opened a door to a chill which shook him inside, for now she played on another part of his nature, and one he also knew as a weakness.

"If that be my portion"—he was glad his voice sounded so steady—"aye, I shall be lonely."

Nimue turned from him then, her shoulders sagging a little. And he realized that she at last played no games but was letting him see her as she was. He was torn within, for he knew that never again would he see what he might have had, what would bring the warmth of full life into him. He almost took a step after her. But there was Arthur. . . .

He watched her go away slowly, knowing that there was still a chance to call her back, that in a fashion they had both been cheated by the Sky Lords who had made them, perhaps coldly and without any feeling, to be what they were. Then she was gone. And it was too late.

He went to the hidden cave entrance and began to pull aside the stones. Bleheris came to help him after a moment. The small man's face was full of distress.

"Lord Merlin, what is this place? I have a pain in my head which grows ever the worse—"

"Forgive me." Merlin remembered the safeguards which had been set there. "There is that here which is set as a guardian, Bleheris, so get you hence. No," he added as the Pict sat down on a nearby stone, "I can enter here and so can the King. But we shall not come forth yet awhile, perhaps for a long time, Bleheris."

The Pict shook his head. "Lord Merlin, it will not matter if it be days or a year before you come forth. If fortune wills, you shall find me waiting. This is good land," he said, looking about him, "somewhat like my northern mountains. I shall wait."

And against all Merlin's protests he swore that was what he would do. Finally Merlin freed the King from the litter and, taking Arthur in his arms, he somehow won through the passage. He carried the King to the box and there brought it open. Stripping Arthur of all but the bandage which bound up his wound, he lowered the King to rest. Arthur was still breathing—that was all Merlin knew as the lid slowly settled again on the box.

But Merlin, having watched the sealing of that coffin, went for the last time to the mirror. In his hands he held the sword which Bleheris had passed to him before he ordered the Pict to reclose the entrance.

Now he stood facing the polished surface of the mirror seeing a gaunt, dark-faced man, his clothing stained with dried blood, his hands enfolded on the hilt of a tall sword. Around him the installations hummed.

He had done all this by instinct alone. What would follow now?

It was the mirror that answered him:

"Go to the box at your right, Merlin, and press there the four small buttons. These shall master time for you. When you awake, you will find that men are again looking to the stars. Then your hour will strike. This time was flawed—we must wait for a better day."

"Arthur?" he asked.

"He was, is, will be. . . . You will find another such resting place prepared for you. Enter therein and sleep."

For a moment Merlin hesitated, and then he asked a last question:

"And Nimue?"

"Her fate is not within our knowledge, Merlin."

He laid the sword on that bench before the mirror where he had sat so often. The blade still shone with all its glory undimmed. Only men's hopes had failed. Merlin sighed.

Slowly he turned and found the buttons. He pressed as he had been ordered. Lights flashed back and forth. He stood dully watching them until once more they were still. Then he went to the box. Taking off his clothing, he settled within, felt the liquid rise about his body. Time— time—how long would be the time?

A white body beneath the moon, laughter bidding him come, bare feet running fleet as any deer could go across shadow-dappled ground. . . . Merlin began to dream.

DAW

THE SPECIAL MAGIC OF
ANDRE NORTON

Andre Norton is one of the foremost names in the world of
fantasy and science fiction. Here is high adventure on other
worlds and in other dimensions, from the hands of a master
storyteller.

DAW

Savor the magic, the special wonder
of the worlds of
Jennifer Roberson

☐ **SWORD-DANCER**
Here's the fast-paced, action-filled tale of the incredible adventures of master Northern swordswoman Del, and her quest to save her young brother who had been kidnapped and enslaved in the South. But the treacherous Southron desert was a deadly obstacle that even she could not traverse alone. Then she met Tiger, a mercenary and master swordsman. Together, they challenged cannibalistic tribes, sandstorms, sand tigers, and sand sickness to rescue Del's long-lost brother in a riveting story of fantasy and daring.   (UE2152—$3.50)

CHRONICLES OF THE CHEYSULI

This superb new fantasy series about a race of warriors gifted with the ability to assume animal shapes at will presents the Cheysuli, once treasured allies to the King of Homana, now exiles, fated to answer the call of magic in their blood, fulfilling an ancient prophecy which could spell salvation or doom for Cheysuli and Homanan alike.

☐ **SHAPECHANGERS: BOOK 1**   (UE2140—$2.95)
☐ **THE SONG OF HOMANA: BOOK 2**   (UE2195—$3.50)
☐ **LEGACY OF THE SWORD: BOOK 3**   (UE2124—$3.50)
☐ **TRACK OF THE WHITE WOLF: BOOK 4** (UE2193—$3.50)

DAW

MAGIC TALES FROM THE MASTERS OF FANTASY

- ☐ **MARION ZIMMER BRADLEY, Lythande** (UE2154—$3.50)
- ☐ **LIN CARTER, Mandricardo** (UE2180—$2.95)
- ☐ **C.J. CHERRYH, The Dreamstone** (UE2013—$2.95)
  The Tree of Swords and
  Jewels (UE1850—$2.95)
- ☐ **JO CLAYTON, Drinker of Souls** (UE2123—$3.50)
- ☐ **B.W. CLOUGH, The Dragon of Mishbil** (UE2078—$2.95)
- ☐ **SHARON GREEN, The Far Side of Forever**
  (UE2212—$3.50)
- ☐ **MERCEDES LACKEY, Arrows of the**
  Queen (UE2189—$2.95)
  Arrow's Flight (UE2222—$3.50)
- ☐ **MICHAEL MOORCOCK, Elric at the End of Time**
  (UE2228—$3.50)
- ☐ **PETER MORWOOD, The Horse Lord** (UE2178—$3.50)
  The Demon Lord (UE2204—$3.50)
- ☐ **ANDRE NORTON, Spell of the Witch World**
  (UE2242—$3.50)
- ☐ **JENNIFER ROBERSON, Sword-Dancer** (UE2152—$3.50)
- ☐ **MICHAEL SHEA, Nifft the Lean** (UE1783—$2.95)
- ☐ **TAD WILLIAMS, Tailchaser's Song** (UE2162—$3.95)

Write for free DAW catalog of hundreds of other titles!
(Prices slightly higher in Canada.)
